Waiting for August

JESSICA SHOOK

WAITING FOR AUGUST
Copyright © 2019 Jessica Shook

ISBN: 978-0-9980706-3-6 (paperback), 978-0-9980706-4-3 (ebook)

For more information
www.jessicashook.com

Have you ever had a day on the calendar that clings to the back of your mind, hanging on by a tiny memory thread? Not a birthday or anniversary, but a date that, in decades to come, you see on the calendar and your stomach lurches to the ground.

For me, it's August 26th. It's been ten years and that date still haunts me. It's been ten years and I still wonder what could have been. Who could the five of us have become if we'd made one or two different choices? Could we have saved ourselves? Could we have saved each other?

Then something inexplicable happened to me.

This is that inexplicable story. My story. You may not believe it. And that's okay. Because I'll always remember what happened, even if I can't explain it, or tell a single person about it...except you.

Part One

AUGUST 1999

One

There are some secrets you don't tell anyone, even your best friend. I never used to have secrets from Juju James. She's my kindred spirit. But we haven't seen each other since I visited last summer. And I have held this secret inside me, locked away like a princess in a tower. If she found out, it would change everything.

The grit under my fingernails distracts me as I turn pages of the book in my lap. I tried to scrub them clean earlier, but my fingertips were sore and my palms red with the making of callouses, so I gave up before the dirt did. My blue nail polish was massacred in the process.

The back door swings open and Drew's sweaty profile streaks by in the hallway. "I swear Grandpa saves his big projects just for us," he grumbles as he passes.

Summers in Michigan with my grandparents can be as much work as a mission trip to a third world country. Not that I've ever been on one of those. But I prefer my summers curled up on the couch, with the sun streaking through the windows, a cup of sweet tea in hand, and a good book in my lap.

Instead, I spent the day shoveling grass and dirt in the expanse of my grandparent's backyard digging a new septic line. Or part of it anyway.

Grandpa enters after Drew and grumbles a few of his own undecipherable words.

For the last eight years since we moved away, my parents trek our minivan family across the country to Michigan. My parents stay for a week then drive back with my little brother, Robbie, because Mom doesn't think he's old enough to stay. But Drew and I get stuck—I mean, are left—for the rest of August until just before school starts. Mom says it's because, if we stay home, we are bored out of our minds by the end of the summer. Dad wants to keep us—mainly Drew—out of trouble.

Drew acts like it's a modern form of torture, but we both secretly treasure our time here.

The shower down the hall turns on. Drew can't stand to be dirty, that's why he plays basketball, because it's not on a field with dirt and grass. Also, because he's tall. Unlike me.

I'm basically Drew's opposite. And not in a Yin and Yang kind of way, where we complement each other. He is tall, lean, and athletic. I am short and top-heavy, which nixes any athletic ability. His skin is perfectly golden from the sun, while mine is white with red splotches like someone splattered me with a watercolor sunburn. His hair is dark and rich with the perfect amount of wave to make it look effortless. Mine is frizzy and the brown of Drew's dirty socks. It's like the DNA gods graced Drew with all our parents' amazing qualities and tossed me the rest. I'm the DNA version of soggy cereal leftovers.

I guess that's what happens when your parents have two kids 12 months and 19 days apart. (And 17 years later, Dad is still joking about how Mom couldn't keep her hands off him. Gross.) How could that poor body of my mother's know that when it gave all the best nutrients to her first born there wouldn't be much left over for me a few months later?

I'm not bitter. Really, I'm not. I wouldn't want to deal with all that popularity. Drew's life exhausts me—girls giggling every time he talks to them; phone calls at all hours; people bothering him every time he walks down the hall, high-fiving and shoving; pep rallies and award ceremonies and parties each weekend.

I'd rather be reading.

Grandpa's staring at me from the kitchen, with his hands in his pockets like he's waiting for me to answer a question. (Two Augusts ago, Drew and I laid the wood floors that are under his feet.)

"Hm?" I ask.

"D'you get the line dug?" He wags his white eyebrows toward the yard behind me. He doesn't sound annoyed—Grandpa's rarely annoyed—so I think he's trying to make conversation.

"It's not done, but I did a lot of it." I smile through the throbbing of my raw fingertips as they revolt at the thought of more work tomorrow. Gloves or not, hours of shoveling have done my hands in. "Took me all day."

I'm not complaining, exactly. I just want him to know how hard I worked. On my *summer vacation*.

"That's it?" Drew walks through the kitchen, bare-chested, with jeans hanging off his *Simpson's* boxers. "C'mon Mincemeat. You gotta do better than that. I shoveled out an entire sandpit. You dug out, like, two feet." His wet hair drips on his shoulders.

"Be nice," Grandpa mutters with a wink at me from under his John Deere cap.

I just want to get back to reading before Grandma comes home from Meijer's with groceries and makes me help her with dinner.

Drew plops down on the couch next to me and lays his head on the tan suede. A wet spot spreads behind him, and I don't even care that Grandma's going to be livid. *I just want to read.* At home, I would lock myself in my room, but I don't have my own room here. Grandma's stuck in the year where I was afraid of the dark and the basement, so she makes Drew and I share the guest bedroom. She told us to trade-off between the air mattress and the bed, but I don't want to use the same sheets as Drew's sweaty size 14 feet—they smell worse the bigger they get—so I gave him the bed.

His body goes limp, with lanky arms at his side, palms up, like he's melting into the couch, and he lets out a long, open-mouth sigh.

"I don't think Grandma's getting the hint about the creepy dolls in the bedroom," he says, without moving anything other than his mouth. "She cleaned the dirty shirts that I had covering their faces."

Pursing my lips, I refuse to look at him, even though we've complained about the creepy dolls lined up on a shelf in the bedroom all month.

"Don't worry. I replaced them with today's dirty laundry."

I hide my smile from him. If I give him one ounce of attention, he'll keep talking. He's like a puppy dog.

Don't get me wrong, my brother doesn't want to spend time with me. When he is chatty, he wants something, and it only happens while we're here. If we were home, I wouldn't see him except down the long halls of school or at our mandatory family dinners.

He sighs again, drawing it out like a fishing line, and I know he's about to lay the bait.

"Graham came to the club today," he begins. "Uncle Frank had him bring us lunch."

Uncle Frank, my dad's brother, works with Grandpa at the golf course. He and my dad started off, like Drew, doing the grunt jobs, but Uncle Frank worked his way from maintenance into managing the whole golf course. He is technically Grandpa's boss, although anyone who knows my grandpa would say nobody but Grandma is his boss. I'm pretty sure my dad left the golf course and moved because he couldn't stand being bossed around by Uncle Frank.

"He brought us sub sandwiches, but not Subway because you know how they are up here about chain stores. Anyway, the sandwich was all soggy, but I ate it anyway."

Get to the point Drew, I think as I roll my eyes.

Graham used to help around the golf course and our grandparent's house too, but he always screwed up because he wouldn't listen to directions. Maybe he did it to get out of working.

"He's into motorcycles now. Graham is." For all of Drew's gabbing, he hasn't moved any other muscles, like he's paralyzed below the jaw. I turn the page of my book even though I haven't read the last paragraph, in hopes that he'll get to the point if he thinks he's lost my interest. And it works.

"He invited us over tonight." Drew knows I hate parties or get togethers or anything where I have to talk to people I don't know or don't like, so he rushes through his sentences to get them out before I say no. "Nothing flashy, just some food, maybe a movie. I mean, it's a weeknight in Stone River, so how crazy could it get?"

I open my mouth with a snarky answer, but he cuts me off.

"Levi and Juju are back in town, so it'll be all five of us."

My heart stutters, and the air freezes around me. Breathing is impossible. But for Drew's sake and my own sanity, I act like it's no big deal. The fact that he's holding their attendance as bait suggests he knows, but I can't let him know that I know that he knows. All these years I've held up this paper-thin shield from Drew, not letting him know the truth. I mean, everybody knows. But nobody *knows*.

"Juju's home from soccer camp and Levi's back from whatever it is he does." Drew sticks to the subject of Levi and Juju James because he knows he has me now.

I stall, but we both know I'll go. "My bed is already calling me—"

"You mean your air mattress." Drew threads his eyebrows together. Finally, muscle movement.

"No. After my day of hard labor, I'll be taking the bed, thank you."

His argument can easily be that he did more hard labor than me, but before he can open his mouth, Grandma walks through the door with white Meijer grocery bags in her hands. I elbow Drew in his muscular yet scrawny ribs and mutter, "More hard labor."

We bound off the couch before Grandma can ask for help. My fingers groan as I close them around the plastic handles, the weight pressing like wire into my skin. "What's in here?" I ask no one, but Grandma answers anyway.

"Sweet potatoes and spaghetti squash. Drew's favorite." She winks at me.

Drew has this ongoing competition with himself as to how many grocery bags he can carry at one time. His record is eleven, and he's rivaling that right now. He can barely eek through the doorway with so many bags in hand. "Got 'em all," he says, lifting them to the counter and unloading them without Grandma having to ask.

"Mmm, my favorite spaghetti sauce," he says.

I roll my eyes. Grandma *must* see through him, even if his skin isn't translucent like mine.

"I sure hope you're not making this tonight," he continues, juggling the glass container between his hands, making me and Grandma nervous, "because Graham invited me and Maggie over, and I don't want to miss your famous spaghetti."

Grandpa lets out a grumble. "Drew, now, you see how Grandma went shopping for all this teenager food."

Drew and I sneak a glance at each other. *Teenager food.* Grandpa uses that term for basically everything Grandma doesn't normally buy. Doritos. Frosted Flakes cereal. Coke (except they call it *Pop*).

"Oh, it's alright. You kids go have fun tonight." Grandma puts the plastic bags inside of a lidded container, then slides it back under the sink. She reuses everything. The plastic containers that lunch meat comes in, the glass jars for pickles, even wrapping paper. Everything is cleaned or folded up and neatly organized as though she may never have enough money to buy them new. I suppose it has something to do with living through the Depression. Or Grandma's a closet hoarder. At least with Grandma, everything is organized. Everything has its place. Even reusable plastic bags.

Drew puts his hand on her shoulder and bends down to kiss her on the forehead. "Thanks Grandma. You're the best."

Her eyes sparkle at him the way they always do. "Now go put a shirt on," she says as she pats him on the chest.

I continue putting the groceries in their rightful place in the refrigerator, freezer, and cabinets. I can feel their eyes on me as I move, but I don't acknowledge them. I simply continue on with this chore as though no one is staring holes into the back of my head until I feel like my skull is smoking.

Grandma puts her hands on my forearm. Her arthritic fingers are covered in gaudy gold rings, with thin bands and tiny jewels, and I stare at them instead of her. She has hypnotic eyes. Eyes that make you want to do whatever she tells you to do because you desperately don't want to disappoint those sweet, grandmother eyes.

"You don't have to put the groceries away, dear. Go see your friends." Her hand rubs my forearm gently the way I imagine she did when I was a sleepy baby.

"Are you sure you don't want me to have dinner with y'all?" I ask. My stomach bubbles like it's filled with carbonation, hoping she doesn't call my bluff and ask me to stay.

She clucks her tongue and looks up at me with those eyes that I am trying to avoid. "Oh Maggie, you've seen us every day. Go to Graham's. Say hello to Levi and Juju James for us."

All my plans to spend the evening reading evaporate at Levi's name.

"Thanks, Grandma. I guess I'll go change, too."

Grandma pats my arm as she says, "Good," and the gold bands of her rings bang against my wrist bones. "You're only young once. Have some fun." Grandma is full of grandparenty clichés.

A *hrmph* sounds from Grandpa in the sunroom. "Not too much fun, young lady." Grandma and I both smile.

When I open the door to the bedroom, Drew is still shirtless, but he has on different pants. "Gah, Maggie, can't you knock?" he says.

"Can't you put a shirt on?" I pop back.

Dread encroaches on my excitement about tonight. Our cousin Graham isn't the best influence over Drew, and frankly, he's an ass. He hasn't always been. Graham used to be the free-wheeling guy who had the best pranks and dares that made you pee your pants a little from laughter and panic.

I don't know what changed, but now he's a typical rich, only child. There's really no other way to say it. He's flipped and/or totaled all three cars he's owned, which were all brand new and fully-loaded, by the way. And he's into motorcycles now, so I might have to be a little concerned for his life.

Besides Graham is family. He's Drew and Levi's best friend. He was Juju's first crush. And vice versa. It's always been the five of us, for better or worse. But he isn't the person I dread seeing.

It's Levi. It's always been Levi.

I dread seeing him and desperately long to see him within the same fraction of a second.

***

When you're a child, things always seem bigger, then you grow up and they shrink. At least they seem to. But not this house. Graham's house is and always has been enormous. The gray siding with white trim contrasts against the greenery it stands upon. I would bet money that Uncle Frank hired a landscaper from the golf course for this house.

Red Hot Chili Peppers croon from the radio as we pull Grandpa's old Ford truck into the driveway, and my shoulders relax. Sort of.

Graham opens the front door and lifts his hand in a wave that's strange even for Graham. I've seen him several times this month, but I'm still weirded out that his once shoulder-length, snow-boarder hair is now cut short and crisp. Almost like he's grown up. Then his wave smoothly turns into flipping us off, and I chide myself. Nope, not grown up at all.

"Drew. Mincemeat. Welcome." He sounds high. But he always sounds that way—like a teenage Keanu Reeves.

They call me Mincemeat. For all of my childhood, the boys called me Magpie. Then when I was 12 and all awkward, we visited for Christmas. Our family had a big dinner before heading back to Texas, and mincemeat pie was served. It was my first time eating it, and it looked okay until I saw it up-close. My mother is adamant about us eating all the food on our plate when we are at someone's house. She gave me her stank-eye, and reluctantly I took a bite, then another until it was all gone.

My mother looked satisfied until I grimaced. I think I knew from the first bite that it wasn't going to stay down. I mean, its beef and fruit. In a pie. It tastes the way body odor smells. Whose stomach would want to keep it down? And there it went, all over my aunt's fine china. Little half-chewed chunks of beef and apple and whatever else.

Graham and Drew laughed until they cried. And that day Magpie became Mincemeat.

This house holds a plethora of memories like that. As I step over the threshold, Graham puts his hand on Drew's shoulder and says something that makes them both laugh. He looks back at me and winks. But I'm used to them.

Just inside the entrance are stairs down to the basement where Graham's bedroom is plus a large living space. It's practically his own apartment down there.

I hesitate to join them until Juju arrives, so I move into the kitchen where Aunt Tammy is laying out "teenager food" on the countertops.

"Hello sweet girl. You want anything?" Aunt Tammy asks as she gives me a hug. She looks just like Graham before he cut his hair.

I take a Verner's ginger ale. We can never find it in stores back home.

Behind me, the door opens and I hear footsteps. I know without even looking that it's them.

"Come in," Aunt Tammy says in a sing-song voice. "The boys went downstairs. If you want anything, make yourself at home as usual."

"Maggie!" Juju squeals behind me. Before I can turn to see her, she twirls me around into a tight hug. She giggles, and I can't help but laugh back.

Her brother stands behind her, and I'm face-to-face with him now. His hands are stuffed into his pockets making his shoulders hunch. He looks as uncomfortable as I feel.

"Finally. I've missed you," I say to Juju. Then, "You too, Levi."

And even his name on my lips tastes like licorice. But I can't decide if it's the black, bitter kind or the sweet red. I wish I could say it over and over again to decide. Levi James.

He looks the same as I remember. Older, obviously. Taller even. But still the same. He has his garage-band t-shirt on, "The Toilet Bowlers." Last year they played at the LaGrange County Fair. Punk rock isn't my cup-o-tea, but it's Levi so whatever. He got us in free.

His copper-red hair has grown long enough to fall in front of his eyes. He reaches past me for a bag of chips, coming so close that even the hairs on my arms stretch to reach him. Leaned in, he looks at me and says low, "Hey Maggie." And he winks. Or at least I think he winks, it's so quick maybe I imagine it along with the slight smirk he makes after my name crosses his lips.

I wonder if my name has a taste in his mouth. If it's sweet.

He jerks his head to the side to move his hair out of his face before he says, "Thank Ms. T," to Aunt Tammy, but his eyes are still on me. His voice is warm and smooth. My skin tingles like the sun is shining through the roof into the house.

Juju grabs two bottles of water, a bag of white cheddar popcorn, and my arm in hers. Giggling, she drags me out the front door. Her silky strawberry hair that girls would kill to have sways back and forth with every step. I don't know if she is oblivious to the invisible overly taut guitar string between her brother and me or if she is so excited to see me that she simply doesn't care.

There is a park around the block that we have come to for years. Soaked into its gravel are the tears of teenage girls, and hanging in the air beneath the swing sets are the secrets that Juju and I have told while swinging at all hours of August nights. We have learned not to trust the space our brothers share with us. They listen through walls. They read journals. They laugh at our dramatics.

But there is only one secret I have kept from Juju. Ever. The secret of Levi.

Two

In a small town in Michigan, where even the nicest houses were built in the '70s, pretty much nothing changes. The park we walk to is no different.

Back home in Texas, everywhere you look there's construction. The Metroplex is in a constant state of upgrade. In one direction, they're adding lanes to the highway; the other direction, they are building a 500-home development, where the houses will be so close, kids will open their windows and hold hands with their neighbor. By the time I'm in college, I'll be that old lady saying, "I remember when that whole area used to be a corn field."

Not here. Here, the air is open and free. And I don't feel like I'm sharing it with hundreds of neighbors. I am breathing in my own oxygen, organic and farm fresh. Because that's how everything is here.

Walking through the streets to the park, I don't hear cars honking their horns and traffic whizzing by. I hear bird's wings fluttering as they land on thick tree branches overhead. I smell familiar pine trees like its Christmas year-round, and oak trees stand as tall statues of serenity on either side of the road. I feel freer here.

Juju complains about the heat as we walk. She cracks open a water bottle and guzzles like she's on the soccer field.

"You don't know heat. At home, I would have back sweat just walking down the street." I tell her. She scrunches her nose and the perfect dusting of freckles that appear painted on.

She pulls open the white cheddar popcorn bag and starts to eat it. Even as thin as she is, she could finish that whole bag herself.

"So what have you been up to?" Juju asks between bites. "I can't believe I've been gone the whole time you've been here."

To be fair, Juju was at some intense soccer camp until yesterday. "Just family stuff mostly."

Grandma always makes plans for us while the whole family is here. She likes showing us off to her friends and distant family members. Our first night here, Grandma insisted we attend a potluck with her Sunday school class.

My favorite tradition is when Mom takes us to Shipshewana so Robbie can see Amish horse-drawn buggies and the cheese factory, where we load up on weird flavored cheeses that we'll eat before we make it home. And the antique stores where Mom and I always find a ton of stuff we want to take home but never buy anything, because really, how we would get a refurbished refrigerator from the 50s home and where would we put it anyway.

Of course, Drew somehow got out of all the family stuff. Unless you considering drinking and cruising with Graham as family stuff.

"And I've read six books." I add like a punctuation to my trip.

Juju smiles her glossy lips. "Well I've only read one book this summer." I raise my eyebrows, impressed. "It was required reading." She shrugs. "But we did go visit Sam and Em." Her oldest brother, Sam, lives in Seattle with his wife. "Oh," Juju bounces off the ground, "And I went to an N'SYNC concert!" She squeals. "We had to drive to Illinois, but it was so worth it."

Her summers are always more exciting than mine. No one in the James family can be still for too long, while my family has a long-line of homebodies—except Drew, but I don't always claim him.

She fills me in on her friends from school, a verbal yearbook of her sophomore class. Some of her higher-classmen friends are talking about college. But Juju has already picked out her dorm room décor and has every summer since junior high. She plans for college the way some girls plan their weddings.

While Juju carries on, telling me about the fight Amber Chasting and Casey Rhodes got in at the movie theater on Main Street over a boy, we get to the park and sit on the merry-go-round. I crisscross my legs under me while she tells me how Mr. Cannon, the principle she's convinced is a distant relative of Harrison Ford, had to break up the fight while on an alleged date.

She opens the popcorn bag wide and offers me some. The white cheddar powder clings to my fingers instantly, and Juju pauses in her story to lick her own.

Listening to Juju talk, I feel more at home here than I do in my own hometown. I probably know more people here too. We moved away when I was nine, but like I said, not a lot changes. Juju has, at some point or other, introduced me to nearly every person in the surrounding towns. She knows everyone. Soccer has practically made her a local celebrity—that and she has the looks of a runway model with the personality of the nicest cheerleader.

But to me, Juju is just my best friend. Only 1,000 miles away. Email and Instant Messenger makes that easier, but it's still hard.

At home, there is one girl I'm close to, Ally. The two of us spend more time talking about characters in the books we are reading than we do the people in our own classes. I mean, I don't really need to talk about them considering Drew spends every moment at the dinner table that he isn't stuffing his mouth with food telling us about every person in the school and their latest embarrassing moments.

I suddenly miss my mom's meatloaf and garlic green beans. Instead I grab another handful of white cheddar popcorn and crack open the can of coke. The fizzy sound echoes across the park, and a bird skitters from a tree. Juju hangs one of her mile-long legs off of the merry-go-round, the curve of her calf muscle props against the edge while she scuffs the toe of her bright white tennis shoe into the dirt to start the merry-go-round moving.

"Hey, what ever happened to that dickhead at your school?" With her delivery, I can tell she's been intentionally holding the question behind her silly stories and small talk.

It may sound ambiguous, "that dickhead at your school," yet I know exactly who and what she's talking about.

What's more popular at school than me? Other than everything? My boobs. They grew faster than the rest of me, and though I try my best to hide them behind big sweaters, flannel shirts, or overalls, nothing helps. The male species, in general, seems to notice body parts even when they are covered up.

Juju doesn't have to worry about that. She is all confidence and strength. Every curve is there for a reason.

Anyway, the dickhead is Roman Sewell. He's a grade ahead of me. Not a jock or a football player or star of any team. Just a guy who blended in with the walls of every classroom until two weeks before the end of school, when he "fell" into me walking down the hallway. And his hands "fell" onto my boobs. Cupped and all. But he didn't pull away. He just stared at his hands on my boobs and snickered.

I dropped my books and push him away. I pushed so hard, his backpack rammed into the lockers on the other side of the hallway. Our episode created quite the whirlpool around us. Girls who witnessed it cussed at the boys who were laughing and fist-bumping Roman. He went from peripheral vision in the school to the hottest topic among everyone.

It didn't seem like it was something that should have plunged him into fame. Wrong as it is, I'm sure it happens around the school every year, every month, hopefully not every day but I'm not naïve. So, what threw Roman Sewell into instant popularity for something that guys all the way from chess club to the football team would have tried to pull? I am Drew Thayer's little sister.

While Roman was feeling up Drew Thayer's sister in the hallway, Drew was coming down the stairs adjacent to the whole scene. There was a pause among the crowd as each classmate noticed Drew. Breath hung in the air waiting to see how he would react, how hard he would punch Roman, how loud he would condemn him.

I fantasize about it sometimes and all the things he could have done. Throw his Nike backpack on the floor and wind up for a punch. Or grab the collar of Roman's sweater vest and spit in his face while telling him to leave his sister alone. Hell, I'd settle for a simple, "Not cool, man."

But Drew didn't do anything. His eyes bounced from me to Roman to a couple of the guys around who couldn't quite keep their tawdry snickers to themselves. Then back to Roman, and with a jut of his chin, the same way he says, "What's up" to his boys, he turned the corner trudging down the hallways to his next class.

Then everyone started breathing again, whooping even. The girls who were upset for me were now deflated. One girl, Ginny Arnold, whispered to me, "That's not right," but that was all. Even she walked away.

At first, I thought Drew didn't see what happened. I hoped. But I caught his eyes as he was turning down the hall, and they were drawn, knowledgeable of how fragile his popularity was, embarrassed that its fragility was more important than his own sister.

Maybe he regretted it. I don't know. I never had the guts to bring it up to him. At dinner that night, our typically chatty Drew was silent. He shoveled his food as usual, but didn't stop for a word between bites, then wiped his mouth clean and excused himself to do "homework" while Mom and I watched the latest episode of *Dawson's Creek.*

I remember Mom asking, "Do you know what's wrong with him?" And I shrugged.

If I said anything, my parents would have a made a way bigger deal of it. With Drew. With the school. With Roman. It would have gone on forever, and I would have had to think about it. I would have had to remember the light squeeze he'd given. Or Roman's overlapping, white teeth as they peeked out from the lips of his leer.

Just like I blew it off to Mom, I shrug to Juju, keeping my eyes focused on the quilted metal of the merry-go-round. There are flecks of mustard paint on the metal that haven't quite been scraped off by the weather and the bottoms of kid's shoes. "Nothing really," I finally answer Juju.

"Did you talk to Drew?" she asks, trying to keep the conversation light by tossing another piece of popcorn in her mouth.

Is it really a big deal? I ask myself that over and over, at night when I toss my sheets off my bed because I wake up in a sweat. Why has it bothered me so much? I am fully aware I developed faster than most girls in my class. I've been called names for it. Even teachers talk to my boobs instead of my face.

I shake my head. "There wasn't anything to say."

Just thinking about it, I cross my arms over my chest, pulling the bib to my overall shorts a little higher.

Juju scoffs. "As if. You say, 'Hey ass of a brother, why'd you diss me in front of the whole school? Why didn't you punch that guy in the face?'"

Again I shrug. At first I was more upset at Drew than Roman. But the more I thought about it, I understood. Drew's whole life was his popularity. Between basketball, flailing grades, snarky comments, and rad parties, he held it up like a house of cards. If one gust of wind blew his way, even if it was his sister, then it could all come tumbling down right before his senior year. So I let him off the hook.

"If it had been Levi, he would have ruined the jerk," Juju casually adds.

"You didn't tell Levi, did you?"

Juju laughs, and it sounds like tinkling glass. "If I did, Levi would have driven all the way from Michigan on his motorcycle to open up a can of whoop-ass."

The image pops into my mind. Levi driving cross-country *for me.*

"As if. He might do that for you, but not for me." I pull my knees up to my chest, resting my hands on my Doc Marten boots.

"What*ever.*" She flicks my hands with her long fingers. "He would. Definitely for you."

Our eyes meet, and I know she believes it. But I don't know if I do.

We are quiet for a bit. The rusted metal underneath us creaks in our silence. I pull back a piece of unruly hair that blows into my face, and my hand has the coppery smell of metal, so I rub my hands against my legs.

Juju stares into the sky. There is no awkwardness between us. Silence, I have learned, often speaks more than words.

"I bet the boys are wondering where we are." She winks at me. We both know it isn't true, but we get up anyway. The wood chips on the ground shift under our weight. Juju bounces with each step. I smile when she laughs a little, grateful to her for knowing exactly when to ask the hard questions and when to be silly.

***

At the house, Aunt Tammy has put out a whole new round of "teenager food." Although Juju and I are still licking the white cheddar from our fingers. Juju tips the bag over her mouth, pouring the last few crumbs in, before she crumples the bag into the trash bin.

"The boys are downstairs playing video games, but don't feel like you have to join them. You're welcome to stay up here," Aunt Tammy says, wiping the countertops down. The kitchen smells like lemon, even among the junk food.

I have spent more time in the basement than I have in the rest of the house. Now that I think about it, I don't ever remember seeing Uncle Frank and Aunt Tammy's bedroom. As kids we barely even came upstairs to eat.

As though summoned by our presence, Levi saunters upstairs. He moves with more grace than any other male I have ever seen. It doesn't look like his feet leave the ground.

"Hey, where'd you go?" Levi says, pulling on a strand of Juju's red ponytail.

Juju winks at me as though to say, "Told you so."

Being in this house, I can't help but remember all the years gone by. The laughter, the arguments. The five of us have grown up together. In elementary school, we were glued to each other. There were no girls or boys; it was just *us*. Then Drew and I moved to Texas. Through middle school, when we visited, the rivalry of girls vs. boys began. We could do everything they did but had to do it even better. With high school came the awareness that we were girls and they were boys. Suddenly, my brother and cousin noticed that Juju was pretty.

But I had always been aware that Levi was, well, Levi. Handsome isn't the right word. Hot doesn't fit either, although I've heard many girls use that word when they didn't realize I knew him. I'd say I have a good vocabulary, but I still can't find a word that suits Levi.

He deserves a new word altogether. A word that describes him and him alone. A word whose definition is simply Levi James.

He stands there in the kitchen, inches from me, talking to Juju and Aunt Tammy while I'm staring, looking a fool. Is my mouth gaping open? I touch my hand to my mouth to make sure, and it isn't. But I still feel like I've been gaping.

Not because he is so beautiful. I mean, he is. He is handsome. He is hot. He is all of those words. But they aren't enough. I know him too well, inside and out. I've known him in every stage, before he had freckles speckling his face and arms, when his teeth were too big for his face, when his head was too big for his body. I've seen his awkward lankiness turn to building muscle in all the ways of becoming a man. I've known him so long that I can already picture him as he will be in adulthood.

The voices stop, grabbing my attention, and they are all looking at me. Are they waiting for a response? Did they ask me a question? This happens too often to me.

"Huh?" I say. So eloquent. So much for a good vocabulary.

"Are you going to the Homegrown Festival this weekend?" Aunt Tammy repeats, leaning on the spotless countertop. It's easy to forget that Aunt Tammy is my mom's age. Nothing against my mom, but she looks like a mother. How criminals in movies can spot a cop, that's how I feel about her. She wears mom clothes and mom jeans.

Not Aunt Tammy. She wears the newest trends, with her long, flowing J-Lo hair that's never out of place. Her skin is smooth, and her tan looks fake, but nothing on her is fake except the thin highlights in her hair. And she talks to us.

My mom talks to us, but in an I'm-here-for-you, lecturey way. She wants to turn everything into a teachable moment. Everything. Aunt Tammy talks *with* us. Her gossip train is bigger than ours. The way Uncle Frank reads *USA Today* and gets home from work asking, "Did you hear what so-and-so did?" about big wig celebrities or business owners, Aunt Tammy does with high school and local gossip. We've joked that she gets by-the-hour phone calls from a school monitor.

"I'm not sure," I answer her, distracted by Levi who is leaning back against the granite countertops across from me with the muscles in his forearm flexed.

Drew bounds up the stairs. "Hey, we're about to put in the new Tony Hawk skateboard game. Y'all wanna play?" he asks, reaching an arm through me and Juju—not coincidentally—to grab a can of coke.

"Yeah, yyyyy'aaaaaaalll, wanna play?" Graham asks as he follows, drawing out the y'all to make fun, but instead he sounds like his tongue can't figure out how to make the sounds.

They gather enough snacks for the night, but knowing the boys, they'll finish them off before the round of games is over. I follow them downstairs. A gust of memories rushes through me like the spirit of Patrick Swayze inhabiting Whoopi Goldberg in my mom's favorite movie, *Ghost*.

Video game cases are splayed across the floor. I step over them carefully like a minefield. Final Fantasy, WWF, some others I haven't seen before.

Everyone cozies up on the suede couch. The same couch that was my hiding place the August before fourth grade, when I was mad at Levi and Graham for making fun of my favorite gray Babysitter's Club sweat suit. So mad that I grabbed my diary from my suitcase and wrote in all caps, "I HATE LEVI JAMES!!!!!" I hadn't gotten much further when Graham popped out from behind the couch, grabbed the Lisa Frank diary covered in teddy bears and hearts, and started reading my words aloud as though they were Shakespeare for all to hear. Of course, I tried to get it back from him, but he was taller so he held it where I couldn't reach. I might have cried as I ran up the stairs to tattle on him.

Sitting on the couch, I am engulfed in the cushions, so soft and plush that I wonder how it has kept its youth after all the years of us bounding all over it. This poor couch has been put through the ringer.

Juju grabs the Nintendo 64 controller, taking the first turn against Graham. Her whole body moves with every twist of the game controller, each skateboard jump in the game mirroring how much her body moves.

"Shut up," she says, intently watching the screen.

We laugh at her, but she can't play unless she's moving.

I am suddenly aware of how close we are sitting. Levi is next to me and Juju plops down on my other side, giving up the controller to Drew. When I lean in to her, she puts her head on my shoulder. But I can still smell Levi. He smells like leather (even though he isn't wearing any), gasoline, sunshine, grass. He smells like summer.

After a couple rounds, I've lost interest. I sneak to the back of the room and down the hallway. I assume they think I'm going to the bathroom, but I head out the back door. The cobblestone path from here leads to the dock and the private pond. Yeah, this house is a dream.

I sit on the dock, my shorts riding up and exposing my legs to sunbeams. Magic hour, as they call it, when the sun hangs low and the light is filtered for a glowy picture. I lean back on my elbows with my knees jutting up to the cloudless sky. Wishing to put my feet in the water but ever since the summer this pond was infested with water snakes, I just can't. But I take my shoes and socks off nonetheless.

I close my eyes and soak in the sun. Being that I'm solar-powered, I need to do this a little each day or I turn to stone. Okay, not really.

Behind me a wooden board of the dock creaks, and I know it's him. Anyone else would have spoken already. He sits down next to me, throwing his legs over the edge, unafraid of snakes—or anything else. He rests back on his hands to match me.

"What, they weren't exciting enough with all their skateboarding talk?" I break the silence but instantly wish for it back.

"No. Just more exciting out here." His reply is followed by his pinky finger brushing up against mine, the slightest movement from a boy who is always in motion.

An electric thrill flows through my nerves. His other hand brushes at my hair running wild by the breeze. I can't help but notice the black motor oil stains living at the edges his fingernails. A sure sign of his hobby of working on cars and motorcycles.

"Have you been to our bookstore without me?" The way he says *our bookstore* is unexpected. And breathtaking.

Before I can answer I hear a banshee cry behind me. I turn to see a blur of skin and legs and then Graham is jumping over us into the pond. Drew quickly follows. I shriek as the water splashes on me. I don't realize until he's coming up out of the pond water that he's shirtless, but not naked, thank God. Juju joins us. In a movie, the girls would take off all their clothes except their underthings then jump in, but not Juju. She doesn't take the time to do that. She jumps in fully dressed.

The water they splash at me is sun-warmed.

"C'mon on in, Mincemeat," Graham hollers from halfway across the pond, which isn't a tiny pond. Uncle Frank does nothing small. It's bigger than any pond at the golf course.

"I'm fine here," I say loud enough for everyone to hear.

The sun is warmer on my face because Levi turns to me. When I meet his eyes, he winks, then lifts his shirt over his head with one hand. I peek at his lean muscles as they each move as independently as their owner. He stands, tosses the shirt at me like a rock star tossing it to a fan in the crowd, and does a front flip off the dock. The barrage of water splashes against me. I have to wipe my face off on his shirt.

"Get her in, Levi," Drew calls when Levi's head comes back above water.

Levi whips his head in a crescent to move his hair out of his eyes. That one movement knots my stomach.

The guys all laugh when Levi starts swimming toward me in strong strokes. My stomach knots even more.

When he breaches the water a foot from the dock, his eyes glisten with mischief. Around him the sun glitters off the water, and I have to squint to look at him.

"Don't," I say.

He reaches out of the water and grabs my bare legs from their safety of the dock.

"No!" I squeal. "I have a book. It can't get wet." I lift up the paperback book that I have stowed away next to me.

All four of them groan. Graham swats at the water, far enough away from me that there's no chance of it hitting me.

"Of course you do," Drew says, losing interest.

Levi's hands grip my ankles for longer than necessary. "I'm

not afraid," he says. And I catch his hint of a double meaning. Our secret.

His hands pull down on my legs, scooting the rest of me closer to the edge.

"Don't!" I say, but my nerves giggle out of me.

He stops, just as I ask. His moss-colored eyes reach me, teasing and promising in the same stare. "I won't." He slowly releases my legs, but not before his palms trace their way down to my toes. "Not until you're ready too."

Air catches in my throat. Levi pushes off of the dock support under the water, on his back, never releasing my eyes from his hold. He laughs aloud. Then dunks under the water.

But I'm already sunk.

Three

Here's the secret. The one thing I've kept from Juju. Last August, everything changed. It was a typical visit to the bookstore, winding my way through the aisles, paying little attention to genres or sections, losing track of time. Against the back wall, between Grafton and Grisham, my eyes roamed over the colorful spines shoved every which way. Then someone was behind me.

I could *feel* him, like sound waves bouncing off his skin. I heard his footsteps trying to sneak up on me, and I chose not to say anything, let him think he was as ninja as he wanted to be.

An arm reached over my shoulder for a book on the shelf. A random book that I'd never heard of. His hand was tanned against the blue spine. "Ach hmmm," he cleared his throat.

"Oh, excuse me," I said, turning to him. My breath stuttered at how close he was standing. I righted myself and looked up at him with a smirk. "Am I in your way?"

"You knew it was me," he said, without question.

"Yes."

I couldn't remember the last time Levi and I had been alone. Had we ever? But I had gotten my driver's license and Grandpa was brave enough to let me take his old work truck, so I didn't need to tag along with Drew. (That August we helped Grandpa re-carpet the basement.)

The bookstore phone rang, but the shrillness was muffled as though it was a world away. There were mumbled voices into the phone, but all I could hear was my heart thudding as Levi and I shared the same air.

"Maggie,"

I knew I was in trouble when he used my real name.

There was a difference in Levi's green eyes, a hunger. The only thing between us was the book he had pulled off the shelf. He held it with both hands like a shield, the only thing keeping him from touching me.

"Is this a good book?" he whispered, toying with the frayed edges.

"I haven't read it," I breathed. He towered over me.

"Maggie," he paused. "Have you ever thought about—?" He gestured the book back and forth, pointing it at me then at him.

I nodded. He had no idea how often I daydreamed this. But the simpler answer was, "Yes."

He tilted his head, surprised that he wasn't alone or maybe surprised that I admitted it.

"Can I—?"

Even though I didn't know what he was asking, I nodded. This moment may have taken him by surprise, but I had wanted it, maybe even imagined it, dreamed of it, for years. So many years. Whatever he was asking, the answer would always be yes.

Then the book was gone from between us, I don't even know where, and there was no space separating us. His hands touched my face at the same moment his lips pressed against mine. I felt his warm breath, tasted it. A flame bloomed under his hand against my cheek. Every cell in my body stood magnetized, reaching out for him. I could hear nothing, feel nothing but Levi. Everything was Levi.

One of his hands moved down my neck, from my shoulders to my waist. The other caught in my hair. He was everywhere at once. His touch was air to me; his breath was my oxygen.

Until a loud bell rang at the front of the room broke through my fog, and he pulled away from me. All the places he had been touching, the cells that were reaching out for him, went cold. My lungs fought to breathe again. Goosebumps caressed my arm instead of the fabric of his shirt, already missing his touch.

"What the—" Graham's voice reached across the store. "Man, what you doin' in a bookstore? You going soft?"

That's when Graham and Drew saw me. In my natural habitat, they didn't think anything of it, or not that I could tell. They barely acknowledged me.

"Come on, man, let's go."

I assumed Levi would disappear with them. I assumed he would act like it never happened. But he didn't.

"Yeah, give me a sec," he said, holding the blue-spined book, reappearing as if from thin air. Where had it been if his hands had been all over me? He waved the book for them to see.

"A'ight," Graham hollered, too loud for a bookstore, then they were gone.

Levi's eyes were on me before the front door closed. They felt like sun shining on me after a long winter. He smiled at me and replaced the book on the shelf over my shoulder. His arm brushed mine and the flame on my skin followed. He nuzzled his nose against my hair, wild and tangled, and then whispered,

"I've wanted to do that for forever."

Heat flooded my stomach and my neck at the same time.

"Better late than never." I smiled.

He smiled.

I felt like I'd woken up in the pages of a book. Did real people even talk that way?

That August, we stole away moments when we could. A kiss behind a pantry door, hands touching when no one was looking, a sunflower picked out of a field and left for me to find. It wasn't much, but it was everything.

This was the one thing I had kept from Juju. To most, it wouldn't seem like a big deal. But she was my best friend. My sister of sorts. I didn't know how she would take it. I tried to imagine how I would feel if she had kissed Drew, but the picture was too bizarre for me to even know.

So we kept quiet. Not only because of Juju. Neither of us knew what would happen when I returned home. What was the point in complicating everything if I was only in town for one month out of the year? What would happen the other eleven months? It was only a few kisses.

Magical, life-altering kisses.

That was Levi's way. To me, Levi was always magical and life-altering.

In a state with millions of people, one shone like a neon light. If I looked at a map of Michigan, all roads led to Levi. He was greater than Lake Superior. He was larger than life.

When I got home from Michigan that August, my first stop was the mailbox. It was overflowing with junk mail and bills for my parents. But there was no letter from Levi. As disappointed as I was, I figured I'd give him time. I'd only been home one day.

Here's the thing, he and I had written letters back and forth since the summer before. I had read a book about a girl who had pen pals all over the country, and I thought I could get to know Levi better without Drew and Graham over my shoulder. I'd sent the first letter in a birthday card, feeling like I would throw up when I placed it in the mailbox. But the delight of receiving a letter back from him rivaled the release of a favorite author's new book. I remember the beginning of his first letter by heart:

"It is a windy Tuesday night. I can't seem to see the moon anywhere. I am done eating my peach Jell-O. Scrumptious. I am lying on my bed all warm and snug. I decided to write you and tell you that, ah, receiving your letter <u>shocked</u> me. I was intrigued. My mom was the only one who saw it and wanted me to pay her $5 bucks to claim it. Even though you said I don't have to write back, I still am."

The letter was seven pages long, and I kept it under my pillow, reading it every night, until the pages were no longer crisp but soft as fabric against my fingers.

I like my books well-loved. They don't have to be new. The pages don't have to be bright white. I like to know that the words have been read many times. I like to wonder who held them before me.

Levi's letters were the same way.

But after our kiss, a new letter never came.

By November, while Juju and I instant messaged, she let it slip, "Levi and his girlfriend came to my soccer game..."

The screen went out of focus for a few seconds. My fingers were paralyzed over the keyboard. When did that happen? How did he move on so fast? Oh god, did he already have a girlfriend when he kissed me?

Finally, my questions motivated my fingers to type. "When did Levi get a girlfriend?" Enter.

I could only hope that Juju didn't read into my question.

"They were into each other last year, but he didn't bring her over all summer, so I guess they started going out after school started."

The hurt tasted like bile.

"Her name is Danielle. You should meet her. She's—"

But I stopped reading. "Gotta go." I typed, and clicked the X on the AOL messenger screen.

The next week an envelope appeared in the mailbox. My name, Ms. Magdalene Thayer, in box letters above my address. I brought it upstairs, sat in it my lap and stared at it, my finger resting on the flap until I had the courage to see what he wrote.

A smaller envelope was inside the first one, and another inside it. Each one covered in drawings that looked alike, like Russian nesting dolls. Each one stacking the bricks of dread on my chest.

Dear Mag, Sorry for the wait. I know Juju told you about Danielle. I didn't want to write at first. It just didn't feel right, but I knew I needed to.

If you lived closer, a lot of things would be different.

Have you gotten a car yet? Sometime when I visit, you'll have to drive me around. (If you even want me to visit still.)

Although, I think you should get a sport bike. Maybe then you'll meet some biker hunk and run off with him. I know there's someone for you. Somewhere out there. Like the Fifel song. You know that cartoon mouse who moves to America. Anyway, I have to say that I am very sorry if me going out with Danielle has, you know, hurt you or however you felt. She was jealous when you were up here. Dating isn't as glamorous as it seems. You have to be ready for the responsibility of hurting someone or being hurt. But I've already done that. I'm sorry.

I miss you. I had fun when you were here. You know what I mean. My mind is racing for the right things to say. I wish I had more to write. A song or a poem that I had written for you. But I hope this letter will suffice. Although, I did get you a sunflower. I knew it would die in the mail, so it's fake. I would send you real flowers if I could.

Come visit me again. You'll always have a place in my heart. (The left ventricle to be exact.)

~The funny looking red-head up north

That was the last letter he sent me.

Four

My current book is tucked under my pillow when I wake up. Its hardback corner pokes my cheek when I roll over to check the clock. It's 10 a.m. Late for me. I dreamed that Roman Sewell made a speech at graduation and dedicated his senior year to me and my boobs.

If I stay in bed late enough, will Grandpa give all the work to Drew and have nothing left for me? No wait, it's Sunday. Grandma and Grandpa will be going to church. It's also our last day here—our flight is early tomorrow morning—so the manual labor has come to an end, which makes me happy, but that also means our visit is ending, which makes my stomach roll.

Our last few days passed too quickly, the way summers do. From helping Grandpa during the day, to pool parties at the homes of people I barely knew, hanging at Graham's, or cruising the main street that's not called Main Street to catch up with everyone. The five of us managed to fit a month's worth of hanging out into three days.

I pad into the kitchen with bare feet. Breakfast is way over. Grandma doesn't leave anything out if you miss it. Maybe I should go to Shipshewana and find an antique "Kitchen is Closed" sign for her. Grandma comes out of the laundry room with a mound of folded clothes. She is dressed for church: fancy sweater (even in August), pencil skirt, pantyhose, red lips, gold necklace.

"Good morning, Sleeping Beauty." She smiles. "You slept longer than Drew today."

"I don't think that's ever happened," I say, groggily, reaching for the sugary cereal that Mom never buys at home.

"Juju James called," Grandma says as she places the folded kitchen towels in the drawer by the sink. She always uses Juju's full name as though there are a hundred Juju's in Stone River. "I think she choked on her drink when I told her you were still asleep."

I smile.

When I don't jump out of my seat to grab the phone and call Juju back like Drew would, Grandma comes to sit by me at the kitchen island, leaving the rest of the laundry on the counter. My feet wrap around the iron barstool legs bracing for a lecture.

Grandma's approach catches me by surprise. "How about you stay home from church so you can go out with your friends this afternoon?"

My spoon clangs against the cereal bowl, and I stop crunching. She doesn't make us go to church, but she's certainly never let us off the hook without a heavy dose of guilt. "Really?"

"Grandpa's only been trying to keep you busy, but summer's almost over and you should have fun." She pats my hand and her braided gold wedding ring hits against my knuckle. "This afternoon is the Homegrown Festival. I'll invite Juju James to drive with us."

As she gathers the folded piles of Grandpa's plaid shirts and a pink pair of her own pajamas, she turns back toward me. "We want you both home by dinner. Grandpa wants to do something special on your last night."

"Okay," I say, taking another bite of cereal. A droplet of milk dribbles down my chin, and I leave it there, feeling like a kid.

***

Close to one in the afternoon, Juju pulls into the driveway in her cyber green Volkswagen Beetle, blaring Ricky Martin's "Livin' La Vida Loca." When most teenage girls I know dress in their most comfortable summer wear with their hair pulled into a messy ponytail, Juju is the exact opposite. She doesn't know the meaning of dressing down. She wears a white tee with an American flag on it that she has tied in a knot in the middle of her waist, showing less than an inch of her stomach. Her long legs are clad in whitewashed jeans and rooted in white Keds; her strawberry hair is up in a half ponytail. Very Tommy Hilfiger. I couldn't pull any of it off, but she looks perfect.

"Hello." Grandma holds the front door open for her. "Don't you look lovely as always."

"Hello, Grandma." Juju hugs her and kisses her wafer thin cheek. She's always taken ownership of my grandparents, which I love. That way I can imagine we really are family.

I, on the other hand, don denim overall shorts with a white tank and my typical plaid shirt wrapped around my waist. And of course my Doc Martens, but Grandma never comments on my style.

I still haven't seen Grandpa today. He's been out back in the barn doing something to his tractor since he and Grandma got home from the early bird service. We know better than to venture into the barn when he's working.

My grandparents arrive everywhere promptly, never late but often early. So, when Drew trudges to the bathroom, stinking from his run, five minutes before we are supposed to be leaving, Grandma tsks to herself. "That boy," she says.

After the showers turns off, she waits outside the door of the bathroom to say goodbye.

"Shi—" he starts, then catches himself when he realizes he's looking into the piercing eyes of his grandmother. "God, Grandma, you scared me."

"Will we see you at the festival?"

"Oh, the festival, oh man—" Drew stammers.

I roll my eyes so big that my head rolls with them.

"That's alright. Enjoy your day." She hugs him around the waist, even though he's still bare-chested. "But we want to see you tonight."

At least Drew won't be at the festival complaining all day.

Outside, Grandma hollers toward the barn. "Leaving."

Grandpa emerges with his Navy Vet hat on his head and a rag in his hands. He swipes the rag around both hands as he walks, his boots crunching the pebble driveway underfoot. He throws the rag into a dirty bin in the garage and slides into the driver's seat of their truck. It's an old Ford that he's been fixing up for years, one piece at a time. Juju's dad, Greg, is a mechanic, so Grandpa's been able to get the parts he needs at an especially good price. Or so he told Dad when we first arrived and took a look in the barn.

"Good afternoon, Grandpa," I say through the window, cheery.

"You smell fabulous," my grandmother chimes in.

"Afternoon," he says to me then grumbles at his wife while he buckles his seat belt.

Juju says, "They're so cute." One of her grandfathers died a few years back of liver disease, and the other isn't close to their family. So I gladly share mine. They have enough love to spread around.

The Homegrown Festival is like everything else here in Stone River. Quaint, cute, and fun if you let it be.

Local musicians, artists, and businesses come from across the county and sometimes further, so I always expect the vendors to be subpar and the music to be average. But I'm always wrong.

Vendor tents line the park in the middle of town selling all sorts crafty items: handmade soaps and bath salts, painted signs, hand-dipped candles, old drawers and window shutters stained and repurposed.

Children dance barefoot in the velvet grass by the stage while a folk band, complete with a harmonica, plays.

My grandparents set up lawn chairs near some of their friends. Juju and I wander toward the booths. My Juju never ceases to amaze me. She is a year younger than me, but far and away more mature. She is immediately at home, picking things up, talking to the vendors, complimenting their items. I watch her, while I am unable to think of anything to say to them, and yet she comes by her conversations organically.

After we look at every single booth, we return to the sitting area. The folk band's set ends, and they make way for the next group. We return to Grandma and Grandpa, who are talking with a family in Grandma's Sunday school class. On the stage, a guitar is being tuned and a drum cymbal clangs. Juju's expression shows no recognition, but I turn to toward the noise.

Levi grins from behind his drums, staring at me as though he had willed me to turn. I shake my head and laugh aloud.

"Isn't that your brother?" Grandma says to Juju, pointing her crooked finger.

Juju answers like it's no big deal. "It is."

"Isn't that something?" Grandma says, gazing at the stage like Frank Sinatra is about to croon.

This seems like the wrong setting for The Toilet Bowler's punk rock sound, but I am pleasantly surprised to hear them begin with a Beatles' cover song of "I Wanna Hold Your Hand" mixed with a little punk rock.

A girl of four or five tiptoes to where we sit. Shy as she is, she looks for Juju's attention.

"Alice!" Juju says, hugging her. She turns to me, "This is my friend, Maggie. Maggie, this is Alice. I teach her Sunday school class at church."

"Nice to meet you, Alice," I say. But the little girl hides behind Juju's denim-clad leg.

Juju swings the little girl's arms to and fro to the song's chorus. Alice's ivory hair blows in her face, sticky with pink cotton candy, as she giggles along with Juju. They both reach out their hands to me, "Dance with us," Juju says between laughs.

The thought of people watching me the way everyone watches Juju and Alice does not appeal. "That's okay. You two are doing great."

A mosquito buzzes around me until it finds a landing pad on my neck. I swat him away, but he is more persistent than I am, returning to my ankle before I catch him. The midday sun is out in full force now, and I wish for the shade of a tree, but there are none in the middle of the park. Nothing to obstruct the view of the stage.

My eyes fall to the group of girls who have clustered near the stage, roadies or groupies or whatever they would call themselves. And I spot her. Without ever having met her before, I know which one is Danielle. Her bleach blonde hair is parted down the middle, dusting her shoulders. Of course she's blonde. She isn't jumping or cheering for the band as the other girls around her. Good thing, since her rubber-soled, platform shoes would break her ankle if she jumped in them. When the surrounding girls lift their arms to grab for attention, she stands confident, her eyes fixed on one thing—Levi. When he glances her way, she sways and sings the lyrics to the song.

I watch the scene unfold like I'm watching *California Dreams* reruns on Saturday morning TV. This is how peripheral I am to him. States away. I had wondered if they were still together. Not brave enough to ask, but curious nonetheless. Now, I have no doubt. Because the way he's looking at her is the way I look at him.

Bolstered to my feet by this, I step toward Juju. "Hey," I say to her. "Wanna grab some coffee?" I don't wait for Levi's set to be over, or even the song for that matter. I've held on to Levi for long enough.

"Okay," Juju is out of breath from twirling with Alice.

The little girl drops on her back on the ground like she is making a grass angel instead of a snow angel, "Bye Juju!"

Juju waves goodbye, her fingers delicate like a Disney princess.

We stroll to the main street and stop at the coffee shop that just so happens to be a couple doors down from the bookstore.

"You can't pass a bookstore without going inside, can you?" Juju says, after we grab coffees. She bites the straw of her iced coffee through a smile.

I shake my head and laugh. "I'm always a bit more at home inside a bookstore."

Together, we take our iced lattes to the bookstore and drift in different directions. The building is old and narrow, with a second floor for the less popular books. I head upstairs, while Juju stays in the magazine aisle. I don't stop by the familiar back wall between Grafton and Grisham. After seeing Levi and Danielle, I don't want to be reminded of what I can't have.

Juju finds me upstairs, smelling books the way most people smell lotions in Bath and Body Works. She jumps on my back so that I'm giving her a piggy back ride. I laugh off the ache of being in this building; Juju makes it easy to do. Her arms are around my neck when she leans forward and takes a drink out of my iced caramel coffee. "You gonna buy anything?"

"Nope," I drink out of her straw and grimace at the vanilla flavor. "Just looking."

"Then you gotta come with me." She hops off my back. "I confess. I wasn't really looking at magazines. I found something next door."

Everything is a mystery with Juju, even when the suspense falls flat. But this time it doesn't. She drags me to the thrift shop next door, and while it looks like any other thrift store, Juju James is a master at finding treasures in odd places. And she has found another one.

All her excitement evaporates as we step into the store, transforming into her best poker face. "Can I take a look at that one?" she asks the sales guy, pointing behind him to the case of special items that are too valuable to place among the random shoppers. Her tone is as sugary as the whipped cream on top of her iced coffee.

The sales guy jumps to action when Juju turns her attention toward him, straightening his shirt as he smiles at her. He's a young guy, but his hairline has the ameba shape of early balding. "This one?" He points to the case.

"No, over one." She leans onto the counter and sips from her straw. To the untrained eye, she seems flirtatious, which negates her attempted poker face. But in reality, this is just Juju. She acted this way before she was gorgeous, back when she still wore glasses too big for her face and thought it was cute to wear her hair in uneven pigtails. She isn't flirting. She isn't pandering for special treatment. She's just being herself.

I can tell, because I have seen her flirt, and it is excruciating.

The sales guy unlocks the case and pulls out the treasure she seeks.

Her eyes glow as she looks at it, like Rachel Green's looking at the latest Bloomingdale's sale.

"It's a Polaroid 600. In excellent condition. Comes with some film." He hands her an old Polaroid camera that Juju would call *vintage*.

The two talk gibberish back and forth about the camera. I don't bother to feign interest. I pick up a nearby book and flip through it.

"I've been looking for a SX-70," she says, but I know those eyes of hers have found exactly what she's looking for.

"They are pretty similar. This 600 is more sensitive to light than the SX-70, and the 600's don't get damaged as easily."

She nods her head along with each of his points. He talks to her about the cameras not running on batteries, something about them being powered by their film cartridges, which doesn't make sense to me at all.

Juju shifts her body and stands up from the counter. The sales guy must think he's losing the sale, because he adds, "We don't get these often, and when we do they don't last long. So, if you're interested, you don't want to leave this one behind."

He does a couple things, his hands moving adeptly over the camera. It looks like a camera I would pick out for Juju. Cream-colored, that originally could have been white but I can't quite tell, with a rainbow line directly down from the lens to the opening where the photograph shoots out. And two buttons on either side like rosy cheeks, one red and one black. Like a cute, alien clown.

Proficiently, Juju grabs the camera from him, flips it around so the lens faces us, presses her cheek into mine, smiles, and takes a photo. I have no idea what my face is doing, but I guess I'll find out soon.

"It works!" she says with elation. "I'll take it!" She doesn't even wait to see how the film looks, which I think should be a pretty important part of buying an older camera, but what do I know.

I look around while they finish up their business, drinking deeply of my iced coffee. I know Juju has her own job, but I also know that I could not have spared the money to buy a book at the bookshop nevertheless a camera.

No, I'm not jealous. Okay, maybe a little. But in a happy-for-her-too way.

By the time Juju shoves the developed photo in my face, I've passed over the swell of envy. Our photographed faces are overexposed and slightly blurry, but quintessential of our friendship. We have photo albums full of photos just like this. Her glossy, wide, open-mouth grin outshines my close-lipped smile. Our smiles, like our personalities, are opposites, but they go together like a ton of cream goes with iced coffee.

***

Out of the shop, the revving of engines growl behind us. We turn to see two motorcycles stopped in the middle of the road. Levi's black and silver one idles next to Graham's cherry red that boasts the Harley Davidson logo on the side. Drew clings to Graham's back, resulting in shrieks of laughter from Juju and I. My brother has never looked so much like a child. If only his friends back home could see him.

"What?" Drew hollers over the roar of the engines. He lifts his hands palms-up indicating a shrug that makes me laugh harder. "Dude. Stop," he yells at me. But I'm now in tears, and like a contagion, the laughter jumps on Graham too.

"You guys missed the Toilet Bowler's set!" Juju yells over the engines.

"We caught the last song." Graham matches her volume. "Levi had plenty of fans," he says with a dirty chuckle in his voice.

Before the guys drive off, Juju unboxes her camera and snaps a photo of the three of them—Graham snickering, Levi looking over his shoulder for traffic they could be blocking, and Drew clutching Graham's waist.

"Meet us at the Industrial," Graham shouts above his engine, between residual chuckles.

"Drew," I bellow, but I can't tell if he hears me or not.

"Grandpa wants us home tonight. We should get back for dinner."

Obnoxious as usual, Graham revs the engine over my voice. I repeat myself, but Graham wails the motorcycle equivalent of a cowboy's "Yeehaw" and drives off.

The photograph is still white with predevelopment, but Juju waves it in the air like it's bounty.

"It's okay. We won't stay too long," she says.

"Where are we going? Is the Industrial like a club?" I ask.

"It's just an abandoned building. But a club in Stone River? Yeah, right."

***

A book hides at the bottom of my canvas bag, stowed away in case the festival wasn't all that. But it could come in handy at this abandoned building situation. (Some girls carry lipstick with them at all times. I have books.)

Juju's VW Bug pulls around the back of the concrete warehouse that looks as vacant as promised. Though, a mysterious, abandoned building implies that we will be cloaked in shadows as we trespass. Instead, the Industrial stands in the middle of a main road with bustling stores and shops. The railroad depot that my brother Robbie obsesses over is a couple doors down, and a neighborhood sits behind the lot where we park.

My stomach flips when I think about getting caught breaking in and entering. I imagine Grandma and Grandpa driving home from the festival to see Drew and me in handcuffs being hauled away to Stone River's tiny jail.

"Is this really a good idea with so many people around?" I ask quietly, hoping no one but Juju hears.

The building looms above us, tall and foreboding. The exterior walls are stained with water damage, and some of the large windows at the top are broken. I picture a drunk Graham throwing rocks at them, higher and higher, until they break.

"What are you, chicken shit?" Graham quips.

"It's okay. We do it all the time," Juju says with such nonchalance that my stomach almost relaxes. "Graham sort of has an *understanding* with the local cops. As long as we keep it small, clean up, and don't break anything, they don't really care."

I didn't realize my cousin could keep something quiet or small. I clutch my bag for safety, even though we are the criminal trespassers.

We pass four open loading docks, and I wonder why we can't hang out there so we don't have to break in. But I suppose that takes the excitement out of it.

Graham is already at one of the many doors, shimmying something around the locks and handles. I can't see from here, but it seems to be something he has practiced a lot.

The door opens with a creak, and Drew cheers too loud. "This place is tight," he says, as he walks through the doors behind Graham. They each haul a six-pack. I hate when Drew drinks. He's a sloppy drinker and even worse with Graham.

I step inside the door, wincing with each step, waiting for an alarm or police siren. When I look up, I see it's just one big empty warehouse, with exposed beams and open scaffolding rising to the ceiling. All sorts of wires are exposed where the ceiling should be. The interior wall panels are half missing, ripped even. By appearance, I expect it to smell like urine from homeless people taking cover at night; instead it smells wet. The floors look damp at first, but they're just stained. Juju lays out a quilt to sit on.

There are stairs across the way that lead to a similar section with exposed metal pillars.

"This place is huge," I say standing on the top stair, looking into the next room. My voice carries even though I didn't speak loudly. "Have y'all explored the whole place?"

"'Course, we have. It all looks the same. This is the easiest part to get in," Graham answers, pulling a beer can from its plastic holder.

"Somebody talked about making it into condos, but nothing's happened yet," Levi interjects.

"Yeah, condos in Stone River would go for a high price," Graham says, brimming with sarcasm. He pops the top of a beer, then holds one up for Levi who shakes his head. Levi and Juju don't drink. Their grandfather and uncles were raging alcoholics and died from liver disease. Plus, they both drove…as did Graham, who clearly doesn't care.

"Don't waste one on Maggie," Drew says before Graham can offer me a can. "She hates beer." He's right, and I would rather be snickered at for not drinking than laughed at for spitting it out.

Graham doesn't ask before tossing Drew a can.

My cross-body bag is still around my shoulder, and I pull it over my head as I sit on the quilt next to Juju. "This is it? We just sit here?" I ask Juju, missing the cool factor.

She laughs. "Better than sitting at home."

I could make a case for the opposite. I count down the minutes before it has been the acceptable amount of time to pull out my book. The quilt is not plush enough, and the concrete is hard under my tailbone. I long for the softness of Graham's gray couch. But I would even settle for the squeaky springs of Grandma's guest bed.

Just when I'm about to grab my book, Levi climbs atop the stairs and positions his left foot long ways on the scaffolding rail. He finds a spot in the wall to place his right foot that gives him the boost he needs to reach the higher beams.

"What is he doing? He's crazy," I say to everyone on the ground. Then to Levi as he steps to a higher level on the scaffolding, I say louder, "That's not going to hold you."

He reaches a thick beam closer to the ceiling, wraps both hands around it, then lifts his legs and wraps them around the beam like a monkey. "Why don't you come up here and join me?" I hear the smile in his voice even if I can't see his face.

My mind automatically goes to the scene in *Anne of Green Gables* when she walks the ridgepole of the Barry's roof. Knowing me, joining Levi in the rafters would result in much worse than Anne's sprained ankle. Watching him is painful enough.

Juju leans her elbows back on her quilt. Her legs stretch out for miles in front of her. "He's obsessed with rock climbing and these extreme obstacle courses. Really anything dangerous." Her voice hints at mockery.

"Ah," I look up at Levi who has pulled himself atop the beam and squats on it with one stabilizing hand.

His molecules must move at a higher frequency than mine, since he can never be still. He's always in motion, always looking to the next adventure. Rock climbing only makes sense.

I think of him falling to the concrete and wince. "So you wanna climb mountains, huh?"

"Maybe." He's already looking for the next beam to hold him.

"He's spent every day he wasn't at work driving across Michigan to go to these indoor rock climbing places. We are honored you chose to spend the day with us." Juju flips her hair off her shoulder, but I detect admiration in her voice.

"The best place was out in Grand Rapids." He grunts the words, as he shifts his weight toward his next move. He looks down at me. "We should go."

Graham starts on his next beer. "He hasn't climbed any *real* rocks, though."

Levi doesn't bother to respond.

I keep my voice low and ask Juju the question that pulls at me. "Is Danielle into rock climbing too?"

Juju runs her fingers through the ends of her hair, checking for nonexistent split ends. "I don't think so."

My fingers run over the edge of the book still hiding in my bag. The familiar act comforts me. "They're still together though, aren't they? She was at the festival." My voice stays loose, and I have never been so proud of an achievement.

At the question, her lips smack. "I don't even know. He may talk to me about everything else, but he does *not* talk to me about girls."

In a minute or two, Levi has vaulted himself to a different section of scaffolding. When he stands up on the new beam, Juju pulls out her camera. "I'm going to document it when you fall." Her voice echoes. "Smile for the camera." She clicks the photo, and with a mechanical sound, a blank picture emerges.

He swings down from one beam to the next, and then lands both feet on the ground with a loud stomp. "Lemme see that." His fingers snap together as he tries to grab the square from her.

Juju gets up and runs from him. "It's not ready!" She squeals. Then Graham and Drew are chasing her too. Graham gets her by the waist, and Juju kicks her feet up in the air. She waves the photo above her, holding the thick white corner, while the other boys try to snatch it away.

We're all laughing amid Juju's squeals to "Put me down." But Graham doesn't put her down. Her hand pulls at his fingers while she holds the photo with the other. He holds tighter, his arms moving upward on her torso, causing her shirt to ride up, as she wriggles to get away. She lets out a giggle, but it sounds off.

And it's funny. Until it isn't.

Her eyes turn panicked. I'm not sure if she can't breathe or if she's just over it, but Graham won't let her go. Her t-shirt has ridden up so high that the underwire of her lacy bra is visible. Graham's forearm presses against it, digging the wire into her skin.

"C'mon, Shortcake, you wanna show it to me," he says, nuzzling his nose into the crook of her neck. His words are slurred.

She flails.

The photograph flutters to the ground like an autumn leaf.

"Seriously, let her go," I try, but Drew and Graham still heckle her. One of their shoes trample the photograph underneath.

"Stop," she says.

With that one word, Levi moves as quickly as I've ever seen him. He yanks Graham's arm away, releasing Juju. Graham spins around while Juju falls to the concrete on her ass. He swings at Levi, who sidesteps it easily but returns with a hand that goes straight to Graham's throat.

Their eyes lock. Every one of us is silent.

Until Drew breaks it. "Dude."

Graham's smugness drops, like Levi squeezed it out, and he says, "My bad." And Levi let's go.

"What the hell?" Juju says, standing and wiping the concrete's filth from her pants. She picks up the dirty photograph of Levi on the beam, but there is a smudge over his face. "Why do you ruin everything?" I assume she's talking to Graham, although I'm not sure. She grabs her keys, drapes her quilt over one arm, and stomps to the door. The gait of her walk isn't right. She must be hurt from her fall.

"I was just screwing around," Graham stammers.

"Well screw yourself. You're disgusting like that," she gibes. As she slams through the door, she lifts her free hand in the air and flips him off.

All is quiet when the door closes behind her. Nobody moves, but my eyes fall to the corner with Graham's empty beer cans.

"You're drunk," I spit out. To Drew, I whisper, "We should go."

He makes a face. It looks a lot like the face he made after the Roman Sewell thing. I shake my head at him, more disappointed with each motion. Then I follow after Juju.

Levi opens the door for me. Daylight is nearly gone. The sun has descended beneath the surrounding buildings.

"You shouldn't leave them alone. Who knows what they'll do," I tell him.

He lets the clunky, warehouse door shut behind him. "They'll be fine. I want to check on Juju." His hand touches my forearm. "And you."

His touch is an electric shock that I pull away from. Our posture is eerily similar to the day at the bookstore last summer.

A whole year ago. His eyebrows draw together suggesting he remembers the same thing.

"I'm fine. I'll take care of Juju." I gesture my head back to the building. "Stay with Drew." *Because I can't be anywhere near him right now.*

"I'd rather stay with you," he says.

I inhale courage. Maybe I want to hurt him, or maybe I want to push him away enough to keep him here. "I saw Danielle at the festival."

His eyes drops to the pavement beneath our feet, then they drag their way back to mine.

"You're still with her, aren't you?"

A crunch of gravel sounds under his feet. "It's complicated."

I roll my eyes at the cliché.

He starts to say more, but I cut him off, "Don't."

"Maggie."

"It's like you said in your letter, right? 'If I lived closer things would be different.' But I don't." I shrug. It sounds simple when I say it out loud.

His eyes blink before they focus on me again.

"She wasn't—she just—" he whispers it, like he doesn't want to say the words.

"What?" I have to know.

"She's what everyone else wanted for me. Everyone told me I should be with her. I put her off for a long time, but I caved. Okay? You were across the country, and I caved."

Oh, it hurts. Even more than I expected. Like my insides being ripped away from me.

"It wasn't fair. It was just easier than fighting."

I flinch and step away from him. *Easier to hurt me than fight for me. Easier to choose someone over me.*

I have nothing left to say. "Stay with Drew."

He draws back and nods. A floodlight from an adjacent parking lot gives off just enough light for us to see each other's faces. His sage green eyes hide in the shadow, but still they pierce through me as I move toward Juju.

I feel like I'm choosing between them. Like I always have been. Juju, my best friend, or the possibility of Levi.

Right now, I let it be about her. I don't want to feel all the things sneaking up on me, so I choose Juju.

Expecting her to peel out of the parking lot any second, I rush to the passenger door and climb in next to her, only to see that the car is still in park and she stares into the night.

I don't look at her; I don't get out of the car; I don't say anything. I just sit with her. The way I wanted someone to after Roman Sewell felt me up. Just sitting, in silent understanding.

After a couple of breaths, she speaks. "I don't know why Levi stepped in. I can take care of myself." And she can. She's always shown up for herself, spoken up when something needed to be said. She's the youngest of us all and the least afraid. Her confidence is as attention-grabbing as her red hair.

Levi stepped in for the same reason she thought Drew should step up for me. But that's not for me to say. I let her feel what she's feeling. She has a right to.

"I forget, you know, that I'm not just one of the guys," she says as she runs her hands through the edges of her ponytail. "Sometimes I still feel like the awkward girl who only got along with her brother's friends." Then she reaches for my hand and squeezes. "And you. We always got along."

Her low voice reminds me of little Juju with uneven pigtails falling down around her face. Sometimes I miss that Juju, but I have her in this moment.

"Thanks for coming with me."

I squeeze her hand in return.

The smeared photograph of Levi is in the console between us, and I'm grateful I can't see Levi's eyes staring at me.

A knock at Juju's window startles us both. He points down and says a muffled, "Roll down the window."

With a heavy sigh, Juju complies. "What, Levi?"

"Please don't go."

"I'm not—"

"You don't have to come back inside. The bonfire's tonight. It's—" he pauses, shifting his gaze from Juju to me, then back again, "It's Drew and Maggie's last night. Screw Graham. We'll go."

Juju glances at me, and I give a one-shoulder shrug. "It's up to you." Because I don't want that to be our last memory of tonight.

***

Cars scatter the field at Prairie Grove Farm, the way Robbie's Legos usually scatter his bedroom floor. Juju parks on the outside where we can see the thin crest of flames, even before the sun has fully set. We weave our way through the car maze to reach the bonfire. Music blares from a few different directions. A guy sits with his guitar near the fire strumming along to the radio.

Barefoot and braless girls cluster together, dancing to J-Lo's "If You Had My Love," while a few handsy guys join in but most others sit back to watch. We are drawn into the pulse of the party, near the bonfire, close to the music.

I hold my canvas bag in front of my chest as a shield from the stares I've already caught. Juju tugs at my hand, "Stop that. You look crazy uncomfortable."

"I am."

"C'mon, just have fun."

Juju moves naturally among the dancing girls. She's just another wheat stock swaying in the field, and I watch her, always feeling on the outside when it's more than the five of us.

I start to step back—maybe even leave because this isn't my scene—when some girl I don't know hands me a wine cooler. She says something but the music makes her words indecipherable. I take the bottle from her and twist off the top. Holding the cold glass in my hand, I gulp it down.

I'm an impostor. Just because I showed up with Juju James, everyone thinks I'm like her, that I come to parties and dance with friends, that I'm cool and popular. They have no idea.

Another sip of the strawberry alcohol passes over my tongue when I feel breath in my hair. It could have been the breeze, but I know it's not.

"Will you dance with me?" Levi's words tickle my neck.

I'm about to ask where Drew is or even Graham, but he touches me. His hands rest on my hips in a casual way that is entirely new. He's never touched me like that. No boy has.

Bryan McKnight sings "Back to One," but I hardly hear it with Levi so close. I look over my shoulder to speak to him, and our noses almost touch.

"Where are the guys?" I ask, pretending I'm not breathless. My eyes scan the crowd until I see them across the way talking to a gaggle of girls, more beer bottles in their hands.

"They didn't want to miss the party."

"Somebody needs to make sure they behave themselves."

"You're avoiding my question."

He spins me around or I turn toward him; I don't even know because our movements are one in the same.

"Dance with me." He answers my objections before I even voice them. "Nobody will think anything of it. You're not going to dance with your brother, and after how Graham acted—it's the perfect scenario."

"I don't dance."

"Everyone dances. You just sway back and forth. Like this." His hands find the bare spot on my waist between the edge of my tank-top and shorts. When I give in to it, he moves me right and left like the pendulum clock in my grandparent's dining room.

Oh, my grandparents. They wanted us home tonight.

But Levi's nose touches my jawline as we sway to Bryan McKnight's vocal runs. And I forget everything—my grandparents, Juju, my flight tomorrow—hypnotized by the motion and flickering fire that is reflected in Levi's eyes.

I study his face, the shadows hidden from the firelight, the glow that makes his hair redder like it's afire.

"Look at you two." I hear Juju's flirty voice bubble through the air, and she pinches my butt. "Way to go, Levi. I haven't seen Maggie dance outside of the raves the two of us have between pillow fights at our slumber parties," Juju says too loudly, winking at some boys nearby. She raises her own wine cooler in the air, her arm outstretched, and she shakes her hips like Beyoncé. "Don't go getting all nasty," she says with another exaggerated wink in our direction.

Then she's gone in the crowd, and we are alone again. Or as

alone as you can be at a bonfire with half the student body surrounding you.

When the music switches to Sixpence None the Richer's breathy vocals singing "Kiss Me," I think it's going to happen. I think he's going to kiss me. Even with all of these people around. Even with Juju and Danielle.

I am only focused on the intensity of his eyes, the flame of his hair, the parting of his lips, the feel of his breath. He's going to kiss me, and I want to be present for every millisecond of it.

A commotion sounds around us. I can't push people away the way I can my thoughts, so when a party goer bumps into us, I hear Graham's voice. He's so drunk that every word he says touches the next one. My ears attune to him quickly, though, when I realize he's talking to Juju.

"Oh, now you'll drink. Not such a high and mighty princess after all." He smiles like it's a joke, but the reflection of the fire on his face turns it to a sneer. I've never seen Graham like this—not the drunk part, I've seen that plenty, but the frightening part.

"I never said I was a princess. I just don't like drinking around *you*," Juju responds, unfazed.

Graham's voice is heard over the music, "I guess the princess Juju likes her boys poor and easy to take by the balls."

"You're embarrassing yourself, Graham," Levi says before I even notice that he's walked further from me and closer to their feud.

"Not as embarrassed as you when I finally bone your sister."

Levi hurls himself at Graham. Even sober, Graham couldn't have moved fast enough to dodge him. I see Graham's head bounce against the dark earth as he lands on his back. Graham's eyes have turned from devilish to horrified as Levi straddles him, his fist already in the air. There is no stopping him. He punches, a right hook to Graham's jaw, flinging his head to the side, right into Levi's other fist.

It isn't their first fistfight, but this one is different. One punch is so furious that the sound of skin hitting skin makes me queasy. I don't want to take my eyes off them, but I do to gauge Juju. Surely she will stop this. But she stands appraising the brawl with her arms crossed, the half-drunk wine cooler in her hand.

No sound escapes when I try to holler Levi's name. I panic. I'm not sure if I want to stop him Levi either. Isn't this what I had wanted to happen to Roman? Isn't this a sort of justice for something we couldn't tell anyone about?

My ears buzz with the crowd's cheering and taunting. I scan the sea of faces but can't find Drew. Which shouldn't surprise me, I guess. He's likely hiding as always.

All at once, Levi's posture changes, his arms fall to his side, spent. He raises himself up while pushing Graham down once more. Ragged breaths heave out of Levi. Both of his hands are red and swollen. Splotches on his cheek and jaw show that Graham hit back even though I never saw it.

Graham's legs move. He bends his knees like a football player lying on the field after a hard hit, and the crowd around us is as quiet as a crowd in the stands.

The music still spins from the speakers, but nobody moves to it.

Levi stalks over to Juju, mumbles to her. She nods. She doesn't look happy with him, but she doesn't say anything either. He jerks around, and a few kids flinch at his abrupt movement. I want to yell at them. To tell them who he is, how kind and gentle. How Graham pushed the limits. That Levi was serving justice, brave enough to stand up for Juju. And when I look into his eyes—and Juju's eyes—I feel like he stood up for me. Like Roman Sewell is the one lying in the gravel, with grit in his hair and dirt smudged on his shirt. Roman and Graham meld together. They've become one.

"Drew?" Levi hollers above the beat of Smash Mouth. "Come out, Drew."

Kids glance around, looking for a face to match the name they don't recognize. Drew's head appears sheepishly above someone's shoulder.

"Take him home," Levi hollers at him.

I step toward Levi, my throat sore from holding back panicked screams. "He's had too many drinks. You can't let him drive."

Levi rakes his beaten hands through his hair and sighs. He stalks back toward Graham, who still hasn't moved, and wrangles Graham's wallet out of his back pocket. The only opposition Graham gives is a groan. Levi fishes a wad of cash out and holds it up above his head.

"Anybody wanna earn some coin?" A few wary takers step forward. Invading their personal space, Levi smells for alcohol on their breath, then chooses a lucky schmuck. "Get them home," he says, as he thrusts the wad of bills into the guy's chest.

Then he turns to me, his eyes a lake of pain and hurt and want—a lake I would dive into not caring what lay under the surface. But not tonight. Even though I go home tomorrow, tonight isn't going to turn out the way Levi or I want it to.

Dancing resumes around us. The kids finally decide "the show" is over. I don't watch Drew leave. I don't speak to him before he goes. I don't say goodbye to Graham. Tonight is broken, and I wonder if the five of us are broken now too. I'm not sure how we go back after this.

"Come," Levi says, low so that only I can hear, "with me." The breath of each word flutters through my hair, heats my blood.

When I don't respond right away, his fingers reach out, hidden from all other eyes, and touch my fingertips just enough. A current runs from his skin to mine.

Every cell of my body wants to move toward him, to go with him, wherever he leads me. But something holds me in place. Not fear. Fear is too common a word. Down to my bones I know that my heart is his to crush all over again.

"I can't." My eyes flicker to Juju who is oblivious to us, yet always between us.

His fingers drop from my touch, the current broken. "Why?"

The crackle of the party is louder than my thoughts.

His fingers lift to my shoulder and curl around the strap of my canvas bag, slowly inching it off my shoulder and down my arm. He opens my bag and pulls out my book.

"Aren't you tired of letting everyone else write your story?" His voice aches with sadness. "Cause I sure as hell am."

He grips the strap of my bag like it's an extension of my body. My lungs stutter. "Let's make our own way, our own ending."

The words slice me open. I want to go with him. I want to leave all of this behind, all of my pretending to be like Juju, all of the hiding my feelings for Levi, all of my indecision. It could all be gone with just a few steps.

But he chose someone else.

He might be choosing me tonight, but tomorrow I'll be home.

I take a deep breath and jerk my bag away from him, my weapon and my shield.

Pity looks out from his eyes, like something is wrong with me and tonight he can fix me, make me what he wants me to be. I guess I'm not enough as I am. Maybe then I'd be worth waiting for.

He knows he's losing me. "Maggie."

But it's too late. He wrote his story. He chose his heroine. And it wasn't me.

I shake my head. Every character in every book I have read would know what to say. Something narky but poignant. Words strung together to explain how I want a boy to want *me* just as I am. How I had thought he was that boy until now.

Yet I can't think of a single word. Not one.

My throat is dry and scratchy, protesting my own silence.

"Maggie," he says again. He reaches for me, but the mountain between us has grown and not even a rock climber can scale it.

"No," finally slips through my lips. My hands shoot up in front of me, holding the chasm between us in place. "No," I repeat louder, drawing Juju's attention.

She comes to my side and shoves her brother away from me. Levi's expression is pained and confused. "Ugh," she rolls her eyes at him. "Not you too."

I am pulled away by Juju, and Levi is consumed in the sea of guys high-fiving him or offering him beers and girls who think they have finally scored the chance to woo him.

Suddenly, I am in Juju's car defending him. "It was nothing. He just said something stupid." I pivot the conversation around to her, because I know she'll let me. "Are you okay?"

"Ugh." Juju's legs bounce against her key chain hanging from the ignition. "Boys are idiots. I could have handled it, you know. I was fine."

Even as she speaks, I catch myself wondering if Levi is right. Maybe I do need to write my own story and think more for myself. Even in my response to him I was trying to think of what some feminist character would say, instead of what *I* would say.

All of those pages and pages of books I have read taught me nothing. I thought they molded me into the person I am, but maybe they have been my excuse for never having to be me when I could be Jo March or Anne Shirley or Francie Nolan. But I wasn't bold like those girls. I was just Maggie Thayer.

"You wanna grab some ice cream?" Juju's core belief is that ice cream solves every problem.

"Yeah," I admit, most of the time she's right.

***

Stepping to the front door fills me with instant dread. I tell Juju to wait outside until the coast is clear. Grandpa will be disappointed; Grandma will be angry. And I'm sad that I missed time with them both.

The door opens quietly, and I am surprised to see my grandmother seated on the brown couch in the living room staring at me when I walk through the door. No lights are on, only the moonlight streaking through the front window, lighting up her drawn face. She's in her nightdress and robe with fuzzy slippers even though its August. Neither she nor Grandpa have ever waited up for us, and I feel the dread Drew must feel when he steps into the principal's office.

"Close the door," she says. Her voice is a whisper, but it pierces the air like a needle in her sewing kit.

I obey.

"Sit down."

I sit.

. I haven't been in trouble with my grandmother since I refused to drink milk with my canned green beans at dinner the summer before fifth grade. Drew is always the one who incurs her wrath. I'm a little frightened right now.

"You missed our plans," her voice says, but I haven't seen a centimeter of her move. If I didn't know any better, looking at her in the low light, I'd think she was asleep.

"I know. I tried—"

"Don't," she interrupts, and I notice her head move slightly. "Right now, I want you to listen. Your grandfather was looking forward to tonight for weeks. He planned it himself. Now, he won't say anything to you about it, but I saw how disappointed he was when you stood him up."

Even in the dark, I can't look at her face. Instead, I watch her fuzzy slippers and the shadow of the tree branches outside the window dancing across them.

"I would expect this from Drew. But you, Magdalene? I did not except this from you."

My heart puddles in shame when she uses my full name.

"I'm so sorry."

"Don't be sorry to me. Tell him yourself."

I nod and stand, not quite sure if she means right now or in the morning.

"And I forgive you," she says as she rises from the couch. I smile a heartbroken smile. "Now tell Juju James she can come inside."

Five

Grandma is happy to let Juju help me pack up. Juju hauls her Polaroid camera in and takes about ten pictures of us laughing and dancing and making faces, all too close-up and over-exposed, and perfect.

She is supposed to help me pack tonight, but mostly we talk, the brokenness of the evening buried under my freshly-laundered-by-Grandma clothes. Juju and I fall backward on the bed laughing about something or other; at some point I lost track of the subject. We are giddy on sugar and denial.

"What if I move to Texas after graduation?" Juju blurts, after the giggles die down but our stomachs are still sore from them.

"Seriously?" I ask, rolling my head to the side to look at her. "You have a few years to decide."

Juju's hair fans out like a strawberry waterfall over my flannel shirts and jean shorts. "Well, it was Levi's idea first. But I can't imagine living in Michigan without Levi. And I can't imagine him being in Texas without me," she fiddles with her camera strap, her feet propped on the edge of the bed, knees jutting in the air.

"Why Texas?" An anchor settles in my stomach. Just when I'm about to leave, finally getting over that feeling whenever I hear Levi's name.

"Because of you," she says with an implied *duh* in her voice.

"Me." The word is supposed to be a question, but it's delivered with a period.

"Well, and Drew, but I wouldn't think he would stay close to home for college. He doesn't seem the type with basketball and everything."

But I do seem that type. Everyone just expects that I'll stay home and not move away to college or spend time traveling or be spontaneous. I'll follow the safe path. Whatever local college accepts me and maybe even gives me a small scholarship on the merits of my exceptional entrance essay. Four, maybe five years of classes until I graduate with an English Lit degree and a minor in journalism so I have the option to teach or maybe write, but probably teach. Because that's safe. And everyone else has me figured out.

Aren't you tired of letting everyone else write your story?

I don't want to be all figured out.

The truth is, I want to escape Texas. I've never felt at home there.

"What would you do in Texas? What about soccer?" Because I think I have her figured out too.

"I don't want to play soccer forever."

Turns out, I don't.

She continues, "I'm a big fish in a small pond here. I know that. But the whole world is out there, Maggie, and I don't know if I want to kick a ball around it."

I guffaw at that.

She raises an eyebrow like I'm mocking her so she defends herself. "It's not that I don't love soccer. I do. I just don't think I love it enough."

"Hm," I say. Because I don't know what I love *enough*, either. Enough to live the rest of my life doing one thing. Why do we have to decide that one thing we want to do forever when we haven't even experienced everything…or nearly anything?

I close my eyes, because my inner thoughts have started to sound like Levi.

"Well, I think you can do whatever you want," I say, attempting to break the tension in my own head.

Before I realize what she's doing, Juju turns the camera around and takes another too-close picture of us.

She grabs a couple of my shirts and tosses them in the open suitcase on the floor. "I hate that this is the way you're leaving."

I sigh. "I hate that I'm leaving."

"We're supposed to send you off with a bang."

I look around the quiet room, remembering the bang of the field party. "This is more my style."

***

It's almost midnight when Juju leaves, hugging me so tight that she almost squeezes tears out of my eyes. Who am I kidding? Tears flow as soon as she closes her car door.

A car stops in front of the house not much later. There isn't a digital clock in the room where I am, so I don't know what time it is. Is Grandma waiting on the couch for Drew to sneak in? I wonder if she gives him a similar speech to mine, or if the humiliation and guilt was only spent on me because my disappointment was a surprise and Drew's was expected.

I avoid going out to the living room where he is. I don't want to see his face, his eyes, his apologies. Or lack thereof.

Grandma's never awake this late, but it's our last night here, so she'll be up as long as we are. My packing isn't finished. I'm not sure if Drew has even started yet. He's out in the kitchen, sounding like a raccoon in the refrigerator. I refold the clothes Juju and I rumpled and place the last of my shirts on top of the others. Grandma's shuffled steps come down the hall and stop in my doorway.

"You finishing up?" she asks, peeking her head inside.

"Almost." I pick up my pair of Sketchers tennis shoes reserved for the days Grandpa put me to work and tuck them in the corners of the suitcase. "You can come in."

She takes ginger steps inside the doorway, relishing the privilege to be allowed in a teenager's room, I suppose. I lay out my clothes for the next day since the flight leaves early. A rare pair of jeans instead of shorts for the cold airplane, but the rest is my usual.

Grandma takes the clothes from me. Her hands are cold when they pass over mine even though she is swaddled in her pink robe over a nightdress in August. When I notice their temperature, I also notice their fragility. She is so thin. My clothes look heavy in her arms.

"It always goes by so fast when you kids are here." She lays my wardrobe over the quilt rack and smooths it out.

I sit on the bed that creaks under my weight, and the bed springs poke my thighs. "I bet you'll get a lot more rest when we're gone though," I say, trying to keep it light.

"Oh, I don't care about that."

I move my makeup bag—it's small because there isn't much in there—so that she can sit next to me. In front of us, against the wall, stands the antique vanity with its tall, rounded mirror. I watch her in the reflection.

"It's always too quiet when you all leave."

I lay my head on her shoulder, which is kind of difficult because she is smaller than me, but in this moment I think it will mean something to her. "Would you and Grandpa ever move to Texas with us?"

"No, no. I don't think we could handle the Texas summers." She laughs and pats my leg. "But we do wish we were closer to you and your brothers and your mom and dad."

Grandma always does that. She always includes everyone. She can't leave anyone out.

"But you'll visit soon?" I ask. "When it's not too hot."

"Of course." She rests her hand on my pajama clad leg. "Before too long, we won't be able to travel that far, so we better get to it now."

I hate when she talks that way. Grandpa does it too. They are so morbid, like they have one foot in the grave.

"You aren't that old, Grandma."

"No, but we aren't young."

I sigh deeply.

She must get the point, because she changes the subject. "Looks like you're about done here. Why don't we get some chamomile tea to help us get sleepy?"

"'K," I say, even though sitting here talking with her has already done the trick. I know she is dragging out our time together as long as possible. Like an immeasurable roll of yarn.

While the tea is steeping, there is a knock.

"Who in the blazes could that be?" Grandma shuffles to the door, stretches on her tiptoes to look out the peephole. "Oh good heavens, it's the James boy."

"Levi?" I ask, suddenly alert and embarrassed because I'm sure he heard Grandma through the door.

I slip from the kitchen to the living room and peek out the front window. Is he here to talk to me? To fix whatever happened between us before I fly across the country for a year? My heart thuds through the room when Grandma opens the door. She leaves the screen door closed.

I can't see him but I hear, "I'm sorry to come by so late. I wouldn't have knocked if I hadn't seen lights on."

"Well, it is past midnight." Grandma gives her best disapproving look.

He clears his throat. "Drew left his jacket, and Maggie—" he stumbles over my name, "dropped her book." Grandma opens the screen door to take the items from him. With his mention of my book, our conversation stings all over again.

"I knew they were leaving early in the morning, so they'd probably want their…uh…stuff," Levi's voice says. I can't decide if I want to reposition myself to see him one more time at the risk of him seeing me.

"Well thank you, young man. I'm sure they will appreciate it." The screen door bangs closed. "Have a good night."

As she closes the front door, she turns to me, "Magdalene, you left your book." As though I hadn't been standing there and heard everything.

With a thunk of finality, the door closes.

I lean to the left, knowing he will be there, and he is. In his black leather motorcycle jacket, he stands a few steps back from the door to see me through the window. I cradle the book against my chest, not knowing if I should smile or wave or do nothing at all. He lifts his right hand, in an almost wave, only moving his fingers like he is checking if they still work. I imagine his apologetic eyes shadowed against the street lights.

Even though I can't see him well, I know he can see me in the illuminated room. Nevertheless, I stand frozen to the ground. He is Medusa and looking into his eyes has turned me to stone. He pivots his body, walks to his motorcycle—which takes a while considering my grandparent's driveway is quite long—and grabs his helmet hanging from the handlebar. He swings a leg over the seat, turns the engine over, and is gone.

All while I stand frozen, still deciding if his deep ocean eyes are sorry or sad or indifferent.

I clutch the returned book against my chest, but I notice a gap between some pages. My mouth goes dry imagining a new letter from him, a piece of him I can take home with me. I lay open the book, and between the pages is a pressed sunflower.

"Hey, my jacket," Drew says, coming into the room. "I wondered where that was." He grabs it off the couch, then knocks his shoulder into mine. He reeks of alcohol. "Tea's done."

I ignore him. I don't need any chamomile tea to drain my energy; Levi has left me practically comatose.

Six

I don't go to sleep right away. I can't. I lay in bed—Drew deserves the air mattress tonight—staring at the antique light in the ceiling, wondering what would have happened if I spent the evening with my grandparents. Would Drew have still gone to the party? Probably. Would a drunk Graham have gotten worse? Would Levi have hooked up with Danielle tonight? Or would he still have come here for me?

No matter how many times I relive every possible outcome I can imagine, I will never know. Most nights I drown my thought mazes by reading, but tonight, I don't want to silence them. I want to think through all the possibilities.

What if I had walked outside and talked to him? Our imaginary voices resound in my head. One more conversation before I left town where I admit everything. How much I want him. How he hurt me. I ask him to choose me, to pick me over Danielle, to wait for me.

But I don't even have the courage to imagine if he would say yes.

An off-white telephone sits on the vanity, totally throwing off the look of the antiques next to it, but I pull the phone with its base onto the bed next to me. I dial my mom. I know she'll be asleep and that long-distance charges will add up, but I just want to hear her voice.

"Mom?" I whisper for Drew's sake even though he could sleep through a tornado.

"Hey, Mag." Her voice is raspy with sleep, but I knew she would see the number on caller-ID and answer no matter the time. It's been two days since I last talked to her. "Everything okay?"

"Yeah, everything's good. I know I'll see you tomorrow but I wanted to say goodnight. Sorry I woke you." My voice is small like Robbie's. I wish she could wrap me in one of her full body, all-encompassing hugs.

"It's my favorite way to wake up." I know she's telling the truth.

"How are Dad and Robbie?" I ask, making the call last as long as possible.

"Good. Dad took him out fishing early this morning. They were gone most of the day."

I make a happy sound, so she thinks I'm smiling. "Fun."

"What did you do on your last day?" she asks. I notice she doesn't tell me how her day was. She thinks she's boring, that she only ever does the same things around the house. *A mother's work is never done,* I can hear her sing-song voice say.

"Hung out with everybody." She knows who I mean.

"Hmm," she murmurs. I think she suspects there is more to the story. Or she's just really tired. "And Drew?"

"Yeah. He stayed out with Graham, but he's back now. He's asleep." For a moment, I imagine myself telling her everything.

About Levi. Graham and Drew. Even about Roman Sewell. And I imagine I'm lying in my own bed, my fluffy bedspread wrapped over me, while I curl up against her shoulder. But I know the truth would only hurt her. "Juju brought me back early."

She hesitates. She isn't naïve to Drew and Graham. Sometimes I wonder why she still leaves him here without parental supervision.

"Is Drew behaving himself?" Her tone tries to be lighthearted, but worry lingers behind the nonchalance.

"Yeah," I can't tell her. She couldn't do anything anyway. We come home tomorrow. "I mean, he's Drew, but yes."

She laughs sleepily.

"I just wanted to check in. I'll let you get back to sleep. Say hi to Dad and Robbie for me."

"Okay. I'm hugging you through the phone." She always says that.

"I'm hugging you back." But I wish I really was.

Seven

Our world is still dark while we drive to the airport. Drew turns his portable CD player on and music streams out of his headphones loud enough for me to recognize Eminem's cadence. With his head back against the seat, arms crossed, and eyes closed, he mumbles something about why Mom couldn't book a flight at a normal hour. We don't hear from him again until we pull into the parking garage and the overhead lights beam into his eyelids.

Leaving Michigan is always hard. As hard as Grandpa works us, as strange as Grandma feeds us, they are our home away from home. Leaving reminds me of the unknown. Will we return next year to this same house, filled with the same clean citrus smell, John Deere memorabilia-filled basement and fragile teacups in every corner of the kitchen? Or will there be a grandparent-sized void when we return next?

This time, though, it feels even harder leaving Levi and Juju. I can't explain why. Maybe it's the way Levi and I left things. Without any real goodbye. Or maybe because in a year or two, *everything* will change. High school will be over. New friends will be made. Lives built. And I already feel left behind.

Our grandparents walk us to baggage claim, already bustling with people. Drew and I each have a backpack—mine is generic purple; Drew's is lime green with a white Nike swish—and a suitcase to check.

At the gate, Grandpa puts his bony army around my neck and pulls me close to him. He kisses the top of my head. "Love you, kid," he says, his voice more gruff and full of emotion than usual.

Tears prickle my eyes. I don't pull away. I let Grandpa hold me as long as he wants.

Drew grabs Grandma in a similar way, considering he is the tallest of us all, and Grandma lets out a high pitch, frail sounding, "Ohhh." We all know what that means. She is crying. She digs a tissue out of her little purse while Drew rubs her arms with his broad, basketball hands.

"Go on, now," Grandpa says after hugs, kisses, and tears are exchanged. Drew and I turn around and wave three separate times while in line to board the plane.

Once I find my window seat, I tuck my backpack under the seat in front of me, settle my book next to my thigh, buckle my seatbelt, and stare out the window, imaging my grandparents watching our plane the way little kids do, until it pulls away from the gate and out of sight.

Grunts break out next to me as Drew folds himself into the middle seat, mumbling again about Mom booking the tickets. His headphones are already back on, blending in to his perfectly floppy hair. Long fingers drum his music's beat on the metal armrest, just above the little silver button that will allow my seat to recline if I ever relax on this flight.

My forehead leans against the window, as the sun breaks over the roof of the airport. Rays of light reach out in all directions, but somehow they still miss me.

A tear dribbles down my face without my knowing why. Sure, I'm sad to leave. But to cry? I don't understand myself. Sometimes I think I need a narrator to my own life, to decipher my own feelings. Characters in books have themselves so figured out, and when they don't, they always have big *aha* moments. When will my *aha* moment come?

Warmth covers my hand as Drew rest his palm on mine. I glance at him, where his head still bobs to music I can't hear, then he peeks at me out of one eye. His head-bobbing turns into an offbeat nod, then back to bobbing.

But he leaves his hand on mine a while longer.

***

Emotions overwhelm me when I see my mom at the end of the gate. An older Asian couple walks slowly in front of me, and I want to push them out of the way. I don't know if I have ever missed Mom so much while also wanting to be back in Michigan. My heart has been torn in half and dropped in two states. I ache all the way from my chest to the tips of my toes seeing Mom. A panicked need to run out of this confined jetway to jump into her arms has taken over. I need to reach her; I will split apart if I don't.

The couple moves, and I am in her arms and she strokes my hair. My dad says, "Whoa," because I'm never like this. But I feel even more split apart now that she hugs me, like I can finally release the need to hold myself together. And again, without understanding why, I cry. I hear voices around me. Dad asks

Drew about the flight. Robbie's screechy little voice says my name, but my focus is on my mom's voice in my ear, "Oh, it's okay, love. You're home now." And her fingers rope their way through my hair.

Breathing in deep the scent of her powdery perfume, my body comes back to itself. I finally look down at Robbie's round face and let him crash into me. His arms wrap around my waist and his head burrows into my sternum. "I think you got taller since I saw you," I tell him because he likes hearing that even when it's not true.

Then life goes back to normal. But only for a little while.

Eight

Grandma's laundry detergent scent is indistinguishably attached to all Michigan memories and therefore attached to Levi.

So after I unpack, I hide my suitcase under my bed, zipping up the fresh scent, only to open it when I'm alone, curled up on my animal-print comforter.

I'm not really an animal-print kind of girl, but my mom redecorated my room at the beginning of summer, and she was so excited that I went along with it to make her happy. I didn't really care what my room looked like. I would have covered the walls in old, yellowed book pages, plastered like wallpaper, and floor-to-ceiling bookshelves. But this is fine too.

At least she left my bookshelf standing in the corner, stuffed with every book I can get my hands on. Even my *Babysitter's Club* collection still holds its place. Sometimes when I can't sleep, I slip them from their home and flip the familiar pages, reminding me what the simplicity of childhood was like.

On our only free day between Michigan and the first day of school, Mom squishes in shopping for school clothes. The experience isn't horrible but definitely isn't fun.

"Why don't you try this one on?" she asks every five seconds, holding up some maroon and pink floral, flowy dress.

"Mom, no."

We embody the opposite of most mother/daughter shopping experiences. She wants me to be trendier and dress prettier like Jennie Garth. But what she doesn't know is how even the principal, Mr. Eckhart, stares at my boobs. She doesn't know about the last two weeks of school when all the boys made gestures at me from across the rooms and halls like they were feeling my boobs under the guise of "twisting a faucet." Mom doesn't know Drew didn't do anything to stop them.

When we get home with one shopping bag that includes an over-sized red blazer (Mom's win) and new flannel button-up shirt (my win), I holler, "I'll get the mail." I hop out of the car, run to the mailbox and sift through the junk mail, anxious for a handwritten envelope.

Mom sets the shopping bag on the kitchen counter as I sulk inside, laying the pile of useless mail underneath the phone on the wall. The phone cord falls down in a coil to the floor.

"Nothing in the mail today?" Mom asks. I've never told her that Levi is the one who sends me letters. I don't know how, but Mom always knows.

"Nope." I scuff my Doc Martin soles against the wood floor. A light scuff mark appears that I rub with away with the toe of my shoe.

"It'll come." Mom comes up behind me, moving my long, untamed hair from my shoulders to my back. She brushes her fingers through it. I wonder if she does this because she thinks it relaxes me or because it relaxes her. "Just be patient."

I shake my head. "I don't know if it will this time." I bite my lip, not wanting to turn around and let her see my eyes. They are surely red-rimmed.

"Why do you think that?" Her hand rests on my shoulder, close to my neck.

I study my feet and notice my laces are coming untied. Hanging on loosely, like my heart. "Just a feeling."

***

Ally picks me up for our first day of junior year in her periwinkle Honda Civic Hatchback. Well, she sits in her car and honks. She is always running late and never has time to come inside. When I get to the car, she's still putting on her clear lip gloss in the rear-view mirror. Lip gloss and mascara is all the makeup Ally wears. She's nothing like Juju, but she's my best friend here.

"Are you still pining?" she asks, deadpan, after she smacks her lips together.

"No," I roll my eyes. "Okay, yes."

"Did he kiss you again?" She raises her dark bushy eyebrows. Ally is a beautiful wallflower who refuses to see how pretty she really is. She keeps her curly brown-black hair locked away in a ponytail, and pretty much only wears workout clothes, basketball shorts, and tennis shoes. Not because she plays basketball, per se, but because she (and I quote) "feels most comfortable in them." But I think the truth is, they are hand-me-downs from her brothers.

Obviously, me and my plaid flannels and Doc Martens aren't judging. It's actually another reason Ally and I make great friends. Neither of us care about that stuff.

I answer carefully so I don't break when I speak. "It didn't go like that this time."

"Explain."

I shrug, feeling a piece of me splinter away with the gesture. "Nothing to explain. It just didn't happen. Nothing happened."

***

Apparently, Ally learned to use her car's stick shift while I was gone, because she doesn't stall even once like she did before I left (in the middle of an intersection while driving to Sonic). And I comment on it.

She rolls her eyes at me, lifting both hands off the steering wheel and gear shift to form the "W" for whatever.

"And I see you rewatched *Clueless* while I was gone."

She holds her index finger in the air. "*Clueless* is a feminist masterpiece." I've only heard this a million times, even though Ally seems like the last person who would watch that movie. "All three of the women characters are strong, opinionated, and empowering."

A car-line wraps through the parking lot and down the entrance to our high school. "Stupid one lane entrance, herding us like cattle to the slaughter," Ally grumbles, even though we both know if she'd been on time we wouldn't be stuck in the line with all the parents dropping off the lower-classmen.

Our tires squeal through the parking lot into an open space, earning some nasty looks from parents. I open my door, clutching my backpack in my hand, to hear Christina Aguilera's "Genie in a Bottle" playing from the open windows of the car next to us, a stark contrast to Blink-182 coming from the speakers of my ride.

No surprise that the car belongs to Stephanie Willwright.

Christina Aguilera's belting is cut short as Stephanie turns off the engine and steps out of a shiny new Mustang. She looks like she's stepped right out of a Wet Seal fashion show, camo jeans hanging low on her hips and flaring out at her shins, her black, one-shoulder tank top has a rhinestone star in the middle, right over her boobs. She clearly doesn't care that everyone talks to her chest.

"Hey ladies," she says through full lips and snarky smirk.

"Nice car, Baby Spice," Ally mutters.

Stephanie looks over her bony shoulder and pops out a "Thanks."

As we pass the silver Mustang, the *beep beep* of Stephanie arming the car alarm goes off, and I notice her license plate reads "SWE3T". Ally and I roll our eyes simultaneously.

When my eyes face forward again, I see the school standing tall in front of me. There is a stone at the bottom of my stomach every time I considered going back to that building, to my classes, to the kids who will remember me for one moment that I had nothing to do with, and to see Roman. He's a senior this year with Drew. Why do the halls I walk through daily have to be stained by one memory?

I find myself holding my binder and books in front of my chest like a shield, but that's not unusual. A raucous ensues when Drew and his friends enter the hallway that is a sea of girls in low-rise pants and one-inch midriff-baring shirts. He doesn't say anything to me or Ally. Although that might be a wink as he walks by, which is something.

The day almost passes uneventfully.

Fourth period is Geometry. Ally isn't in this class so I sit alone in the back next to Justin Burns, and he never even looks my way—which I am one-hundred per cent okay with.

Mr. Gonzalez walks in, books stacked tall in his hands and a couple loose papers floating to the ground in his haste. He is a crumpled mess, but I have always liked him. Mr. Gonzalez has a birthmark on the side of his face that he never tries to cover up. While that could be high school suicide, it's impossible not to see the compassion in his eyes while simultaneously recognizing his birth mark. So no one ever laughs at him or makes snide remarks. Also, he is a foot taller than every student, so maybe that plays a part too.

Not even twenty minutes into class, I am painting my nails with white-out, but I glance up when the door opens and an administrative aid from the school office enters. Aides are easily identified by the apologetic look as they enter the class, versus the staff strolling in like they have earned the right to interrupt, and I guess they have.

Mr. Gonzalez is only on the second page of the class syllabus when he is interrupted. The aide hands him a note, he reads it, then scans the class with his compassionate eyes. They whisper back and forth until he clears his throat, and the aide exits as apologetically as she entered. I go back to my white-out.

"Ms. Maggie Thayer?" Mr. Gonzalez glances around the room, waiting for a hand to go up or a voice to respond.

My instinct is to scrunch down in my chair because being called on in math class is my worst nightmare, but I raise my hand.

Mr. Gonzalez scrunches his bushy gray eyebrows together. "Ms. Thayer, you're needed in the office." That's all he says. Simple, to the point, just the way he teaches. But silence engulfs the classroom and envelops me. Everyone stares. So I escape the room as fast as I can, realizing after the classroom door slams shut behind me that I left my books, backpack, everything at my desk. I assume it's a phone call for me or something, so I choose not draw more attention by walking back in to grab them.

Windows line the office walls, and I can see the receptionist talking with a woman whose back is to me, but I know it's my mom. Her pleated khakis and white blouse may not give her away, but the way she stands—with one hand rubbing her upper arm—does. She's worried about something. My breath stutters in my lungs. Something's wrong.

I open the office door with hesitation, and she is in front of me in one step.

"Maggie," she says breathlessly, the way I feel. I know as soon as she turns and looks at me that her news is not going to be good. Her eyes are bloodshot, and her face is red and splotchy. She's been crying, and without even knowing why, I want to cry with her. She wraps her reddened hands around my arms and rubs them, the way she was just rubbing her own. I wonder if she even realizes that's what she does when she's worried. Like a gambler's tell.

"What are you doing here?" It comes out of my mouth more accusatory than I meant.

"I—I wanted to wait for Drew, but—" She peeks down the hall, looking for my brother. When I glance over my shoulder to follow her eyes, nobody is there.

"What's wrong?" I ask, impatient. I don't really care about waiting for Drew. My brother works on his own time frame, and he may take all period to come. Or he may take the opportunity to skip class.

"I—" She keeps her focus down the hall, and I grasp her arm, twisting her to look at me.

"Mom."

She drags her eyes, pooled in sadness, to mine, and my body aches for what she's about to say. A million thoughts go through my mind, all the terrible things she could confess. But I can't land on one.

"Let's go outside," she says, holding my hand with the tenderness of a new mom holding her fragile newborn. Her touch breaks me even more.

I allow her to lead me through the glass-paned doors, down the concrete ramp, to the grassy area canopied by thick trees. Picnic benches sit nearby, and she starts toward them. But I can't wait any longer. I'm shattering with each step, and I don't even know why yet.

"No, Mom, tell me."

She turns. The sun glares in her swollen eyes. "There was an accident." She bites her lip, like she's waiting for the words to push their way out. "Rose called."

My vision blurs. Juju. Levi. Which name will she say? Or both. My body is heavy, unable to hold my head upright anymore. This must be why people sit when they receive bad news. It's the heaviness.

I want to close my eyes when my mom continues speaking, but it takes every ounce of concentration to focus on the next few words.

"Levi was riding his motorcycle on some old roads."

At his name, slow breath releases from my lungs, like the air seeping out of a balloon. Not Levi.

"The wheels went off the road into gravel, and he lost control."

A sound comes out of me, a grunt, that is supposed to be the word "No," but my mouth never opens.

"I know, baby." My mom's long fingers stroke my hair and my shoulders and my arms. Moving from one to the other with nervous energy.

I hold my lips so tightly together, biting them almost, to keep the sob inside. I find some willpower to ask what my mom hasn't made clear, "Is he—?"

"No, no, no," she answers, her hands rubbing up and down on my arms, a parenthesis of comfort around me. "He's in the ICU. It's critical. He hasn't woken up." She speaks slowly, each word a sentence in itself.

But my next words are a ragged demand. "Tell me everything Rose said."

"He flew off the motorcycle…landed on the back of his neck…the force pushed off his helmet…the tests show that his spinal cord is barely holding together…" She sucks in air before she can continue. "He can't breathe on his own." Tears gush down her face at record speed, and I think my tears match their pace.

We face each other, hands entwined between us. I don't know if she's holding me up or if it's the other way around. Maybe it's both. Even together, we are so fragile in this moment that if the wind blew too hard, we would shatter.

"Let's find Drew and go home," she says finally.

I shake my head. "No," I let go of her, even though I can tell she isn't quite ready. But she doesn't fall, and neither do I. "I can't go home. I want to stay."

Mom doesn't understand, but I need to be here at school. The bustling energy of the halls as students move from one class to the other, the droning on of teacher's voices dulling my senses, the rhythm of my pen scratching on paper as I take notes or just draw on the bottom of my shoes. I need this. Home will only reveal more questions.

Before Drew ever shows, I head back to class, leaving my mom on the grassy slope next to the pavement.

I return to Mr. Gonzalez' class, to my books and backpack. He is discussing Geometric proofs, a concept my head has never wrapped fully around, which is perfect. Justin Burns glances at me when I sit, like he didn't realize I was gone. When he double takes, I know my face betrays that I've been crying. But I ignore everything, pick up my pencil and copy down what Mr. Gonzalez has scribbled all over the white board. The lines might as well be a Jackson Pollock painting for all the sense they make. But I copy them nonetheless.

That's when I see I've scratched the white-out from my nails.

I make it to my next class. US History. I make it through roll call and receive my syllabus, when I feel my eyes crossing. In the blurriness, I picture Levi as I last saw him. His hand in the air, waving at me, confused eyes staring through the blinds, his motorcycle in the driveway, his leg swinging over the seat, his black helmet obscuring his face and covering his rust hair.

Then I hear the teacher, whom I've never met, asking me if I'd like to step out to the restroom.

Horrified, I realize my tears and snot are mixing on my chin. I rush from the room. I stop and lean my back against the hallway wall. There are lockers across from me, and for some reason it makes me think of Juju at the hospital with Levi, holding his hand, crying, praying. I wish I was with her.

Or with him, wherever he is.

The sleeve of my flannel shirt is soft against my face when I wipe the tear/snot mixture off. I don't even care that the glossy film left on the sleeve is pretty gross. I run my fingers through my hair, holding it back from my face, taking deep breaths as I make my way to the bathroom.

Three stalls are taken when I walk in, but that's fine because I don't need a stall. I stare at myself in the bathroom mirror, running water over my hands, then splashing it on my cheeks and chin. My mascara hasn't run, which is miraculous. But it's not the miracle I want.

A toilet flushes, and a girl I don't know steps out. She glances at me timidly when she rounds the corner and wordlessly washes her hands, dries them, and leaves.

Another stall opens and out walks Stephanie Willwright. A sliver of her stomach shows between her shirt and her jeans. I would bet money that she has her bellybutton pierced, but I never want to find out. I don't hate her like Ally does, but we haven't ever been friends, even that month she dated my brother.

"Hey," she says, as she steps up to the sink. Her cross-body bag swings forward and hits the counter.

"Hey," I say back, trying to sound and look normal.

The last stall opens, and Stephanie's bff Vanessa Perkins joins us at the sinks.

"We heard about your friend," Vanessa says, looking at me in the mirror as she washes her hands.

I'm stunned. It's only been minutes. Not even an hour. I haven't spoken to a single person. How could they have heard anything?

"Drew told me," Stephanie answers the question glaring on my face.

"You talked to Drew?" The words are muffled, maybe even

slurred, like I've been asleep and am suddenly awake with this information.

Vanessa jumps in to answer. "We saw him on his way out. I asked why he was leaving, and he told me what happened." She smears another layer of frosty pink gloss—four shades lighter than her lip liner—on her lips and pats them on the paper towel she had dried her hands on.

I don't have anything to say to either of them, but I stare at them in the mirror nonetheless. Why would Drew talk to Stephanie Willwright and Vanessa Perkins but not try to find his sister? Did he think Levi was more his friend than mine? Was he even sad?

I check myself and take back the last thought. I'm sure Drew is as devastated as I am.

"Can I just tell you something?" Vanessa asks in her Minnie Mouse voice. She keeps talking even though I haven't answered, "I know this is a really hard for you, but everything happens for a reason."

My blood spikes. Tears are long gone. Maybe Vanessa is trying to be nice, but is she seriously telling me that there's a reason Levi is in the hospital? That God or the universe put him there?

"Excuse me?" I ask, trying to remain calm-ish.

"You know, everything happens for a reason. Maybe God needs another angel in heaven." The words pop from Vanessa's mouth as hard as her hip pops when she shifts her weight.

I want to spit at her. Levi isn't dead yet.

And I can't hold it together any longer. My hand is moving before I realize it. When my knuckles collide with Vanessa's cheek, I think I'm only imagining what I want to do, like Ally McBeal's fantasy scenes.

The shock of pain in my hand announces what I've done. Vanessa's face flings into the paper towel dispenser and shows me how strong my punch was. My face reflects in the mirror when Vanessa's body is no longer in the way and reveals how surprised I am. Stephanie gasps. I forgot she was even there.

"Ahhhh," Vanessa cries, touching her hand to her reddened cheek. "What the hell?" said the girl who just claimed she knew what God was doing. "I was just trying to help," she says, running from the bathroom.

I expect Stephanie to run after her or to say something horrible to me, but she doesn't.

She stands in the corner with her hands in the pockets of her low-rise jeans, revealing the edges of her hip bones. "I don't think Vanessa's lost anyone. I'm not sure anything bad has ever happened to her."

Stephanie's eyes meet mine in the mirror's reflection. She licks her lips and then goes on. "When I was 13, my best friend died of a brain aneurysm. It sucks." She shrugs. "And it doesn't stop sucking."

I rub at the ache in my hand, but it doesn't compare to the ache in my gut as Stephanie talks.

"I wouldn't wish it on anyone."

"Thank you," I say to her reflection.

She nods and leaves me. And I'm alone. My fingers scream at me as I unfold them, but the pain only reminds me of Levi punching Graham, asking me to come with him. I can't shake the images coming at me, so I sit on the musty tile floor and let them come.

***

Before the end of US History, another admin aide slinks into the classroom and my name is called to the office again.

When Mom returns to pick me up, I sit with an ice pack on my hand and a disciplinary note in my lap.

"Maggie," she says my name with a mix of disappointment and utter sadness. My eyes don't reach hers. They fill with tears, but I won't allow will them to spill over.

Mr. Eckhart comes out of his office, and I lift my backpack to my lap, covering my chest. He and Mom speak about me in murmured tones. "One detention ought to do it, but under the circumstances, we thought she might as well go home for the day."

Mom looks over her shoulder at me, as she nods. "I think so too. Thank you." She picks up my backpack, which was packed up for me by the same ridiculous aide. Mr. Eckhart nods at me— or at least at my chest—as I walk out. Nothing is said on the drive home.

Before going to my room, I check the mailbox. Empty. Like me.

I hold detention in my room, not leaving all night, even through dinner, which Mom brings to my door. But I stay in bed, telling time by the shadows and reflections moving across the ceiling. Calculating how much worse the pain of a spinal cord injury hurts than my jammed hand. I accept the pain to have one more thing in common with Levi.

***

We stay home from school the next day too. It's the second day, and I already feel behind. But Drew is probably saying a sweet thank you to Levi for an excuse to skip.

Holed up in my room, I haven't seen Drew since the wink in the hallway yesterday. Since before we found out about Levi. Since before life changed.

My bedroom phone rings loud enough to make me jump in my skin. I reach for the phone, but wince when I try to lift the receiver with my hand. Two of my knuckles have turned purple. Movies make punching somebody look so easy. I picture what Vanessa's face looks like today as she got out of her friend's SWE3T car at school.

I pick the handset up, then pull on the coiled cord to drag the base off my nightstand and closer to me on my bed.

Ally called after school yesterday, but I let the answering machine pick up.

"Hello."

"Hey sis," It's Drew.

Our parents got us our own lines for each of our 16th birthdays. Neither of us wanted pagers, and my dad didn't see the need in us having cellular phones until we could pay for them ourselves.

I answer Drew with a disappointed sigh.

"You wanted it to be Juju," he says.

"Have you talked to Graham?"

"Nope. Nobody. Mom couldn't even hand me my breakfast without crying."

How can he eat? My stomach is a roller coaster.

I shimmy my body down on my bed and curl under my covers. I don't plan on getting out of my pajamas all day. "Shouldn't we call them?" I ask.

"I don't know what we should do." He quickly follows up with, "I don't know what we can do."

"Nothing. We're stuck down here." My voice cracks, and I hate it. "We should have been there, Drew."

"How?"

"Do you think he let some of the air out of his tires like he read in that magazine?" Words tumble out of my mouth now that I have the ear of someone who understands.

"What?" he says the word without the *t* sound. Wha—?

"He was reading that auto magazine and talking about it with Graham, remember? He said the guy in the article let out just enough air from the tires to up his speed and performance, or some crap like that. You don't think he did that, do you? And that's why he lost control?"

Drew hesitates. Which is my answer. But then he speaks. "Nah, not Levi. If it was Graham, definitely. Not Levi." But he doesn't sound convincing.

We're both quiet for a long time, but neither of us hang up. It's weird, I know, but this is the most Drew and I have really talked in a long time.

I finally have the nerve to ask, "Where did you go when you left school yesterday? Mom said you didn't come right home." I have my suspicions. There's a creek on the empty property behind our school. It's a wooded lot, and he goes there sometimes when he ditches class. Sometimes to get high. I hate that he does it. I hate that I'm suspicious of my brother every time he goes somewhere.

He's usually more careful leading up to basketball season, but if he was as derailed as I was from the news...

"I went to the gym."

At first, I think he's lying. But he continues, "I asked Levi one time if he ever let loose partying with Graham. I'd never seen him do anything, you know. He's so straight-laced."

"His uncle—"

"Yeah, I know."

"What'd Levi say?"

"He said he gets a better high from rock climbing and all his stunts than he ever could from pot or acid or whatever else." Drew almost laughs. "'Course Graham said he was full of shit. But I thought, I couldn't get high knowing Levi was—I owe it to him to stay sober."

I'm proud of you, I almost say, but it feels foreign.

"It sucks," Drew says and actually laughs.

"What?"

"Being sober when you wanna get high."

But I don't see how getting high could numb this kind of pain.

***

I'm sitting on my bed when Mom knocks. The leopard print bedspread underneath me is soft and comforting, but I don't know how it is holding me up when I feel like nothing can.

Mom opens the door and comes in even though I didn't answer. I'm staring at the wall in front of me. It's beige to go with the animal print everything and it reminds me of Levi, which makes no sense, but I can't get him out of my head.

I don't notice Mom sit down until her weight shifts the mattress under me. She doesn't speak. Or move. Just sits.

Then I realize why she's here.

"I heard the phone ring," I say. No other five words have taken such effort to say—to open my lips a fraction, to move my weighted tongue, to breathe out words. Incredible Hulk-like effort.

"It was your aunt," Mom says. I wonder if her words are just as difficult to release.

"Is he gone?" I ask. But even I can barely hear the question. The beige wall in front of me is no longer a wall but an out-of-focus painting. It seems like an hour before she answers.

"Yes."

I inhale so loud and deep, like it's the first breath I've taken since I saw her in the school office. Like I just rose above water after freezing under the ice of the frozen lake that Levi used to skate on during winter. And I can't hold myself up any more. I'm not strong enough. I collapse, and Mom catches me between her arms, and she holds me tight against her body. She rocks me the way she rocked Robbie when he was a crying baby. Probably the way she rocked me as baby too.

And I cry. Although, cry doesn't fully express it. I sob in a way that is usually reserved for the bathroom floor when no one is around. I am wrecked all the way through to my toes.

Mom holds me so long that I lose all time and existence. Even after I've cried every ounce of water from my body, she still holds me. I'm shriveled and dehydrated and tired and small. But Mom doesn't let go. And neither do I.

When my voice returns, I say, "I loved him." The words are glass shards in my throat.

"I know, honey. You were all best friends since you were so little."

Even after everything, she doesn't know.

"No, Mom." I work through the rawness of my throat, because she has to understand. "I *loved* him."

Her chest expands against my back as she takes a deep breath. "Oh." The word is small, but she renews her hug. When her arm wraps around me again, I see goosebumps on her skin. "Oh honey."

My words shock me as they spill out in a whisper. "I had this idea," I hesitate, forming my thoughts, "that Juju would move here to go to college. And Levi would come visit, and we would have this beautiful long-distance love story while he traveled the world." I bite my lip to hold in another sob, and I am numb to the pain. "I thought one day, he'd pick me up and take me with him."

Even as I say the words, I don't know if it's what I really want, but this romanticized image in my mind is all fantasy anyway.

"Now—" My thoughts trail off. Mom doesn't say anything. I know she won't bring it up again unless I do. We both sit in a mournful silence. I feel a new tear blaze a trail from my eye over the bridge of my nose around my other eye and onto Mom's lap. How many tears have we all rained down on her? And oh, how she bears it all.

***

When Dad calls us down for dinner, I realize he's had Chinese delivered, which is noteworthy; for one, because Dad typically hates take-out, and two, Mom always cooks. Always. She takes pride in being able to throw together a meal without the help of a recipe. She cooks by taste, the way a musician might play music by ear.

My dad has also set the table—something we rarely do—and even though he ordered in, he is wearing an apron that reads, "Armed and Dangerous." Mom gave it to him for Christmas a few years back. I know he's trying to make us feel better, so I try on my best "I'm okay" face as he sets a plate of Kung Pao chicken in front of me. "Thanks, Dad."

Everyone is quiet as we sit at the table. Dad says a prayer over the food and for "the James' family in this difficult time." I take a deep, gravelly breath wondering if he realizes that I need prayer "in this difficult time," too.

Forks clank. Noodles slurp. Teeth chew. All exceptionally loud. As is Mom's voice as she asks Dad how his day was. They're attempting to keep things normal. *It's not normal!* I want to yell, but I hold the words behind my teeth as I chew the chicken pieces.

Their conversation continues, but I focus on chewing, on breathing, on controlling my emotions. And apparently in that focus, I miss something crucial in the conversation. Because Mom slips something across the table at Drew and me. (We haven't met eyes the entire night. I don't know what else to say to him, and I'd imagine he doesn't know what to say to me either. I'm emotional. He's all control. We're opposite spectrums as usual.)

A piece of paper sits in front of me. "Our flight is tomorrow." She looks quite satisfied with herself as she delivers these words. But they don't make sense to me.

Drew picks the paper up, looking as confused as I feel. His eyes flicker to mine. The pain in them is so deep, it steals my breath. I have to look away.

"No fair." Robbie slams his fork on the table. "They just got back. Why can't I go? I wanna go on an airplane."

"You're gonna stay here with me, bud," Dad says, sounding cheery. He's always an octave too happy, my dad.

They go back and forth, whines and explanations bouncing across the table, but my eyes land on the piece of paper, an airplane ticket to Michigan. The room swims in my vision, and Mom puts her hand on my forearm, her thumb rubbing back and forth in a gentle rhythm. "We'll be there the day before the memorial service." Her smile is off, crooked and warbled, but it is real.

I can only nod.

***

The flight takes forever. At one point, I look over the isle and Drew has his head back against the seat, mouth dropped open in sleep. How can he sleep right now? I'm all jitters and held back tears. I almost hit him the way I hit Vanessa. Until I recognize jealousy disguising itself as anger. I'm not mad at Drew. I wish I could sleep—or even read—right now, turn off my thoughts, my regrets.

My eyes are gritty with the salt of tears, and they ache for rest. So I let Drew sleep. I let him dream of a day when the ache isn't so fresh. Because waking up to remember what has happened is harder than not sleeping at all.

***

Uncle Frank picks us up from the airport in his off-the-lot Yukon. He gets a guy that works at the airport to load our bags on a dolly and take them out to the car, then he pays the guy a hefty tip.

"Hell, I woulda carried the bags for half that price," Drew mumbles to me as we climb into the backseat.

103

I'm nervous to sit on the leather seats, nervous that the buttons on my back pockets will scratch the leather. But Uncle Frank's smile as he closes the door sets me more at ease.

I want to ask about Levi. I want to ask about Juju and Graham. But I catch myself. Like in the game Taboo, a buzzer will sound if I say their names. So Drew and I sit in the back like forgotten toddlers, while the adults sit in the front talking low enough for us to not hear them.

A blur of fields and trees pass out the window, and I let my eyes go out of focus. Until we pass a field of sunflowers. I can't tell which came first, my love of sunflowers or Levi giving me one. I just know they are my favorite, and I'll never see at them the same again.

Everywhere I look is torture. I hold a book in my lap with its pages flipped open, not to read but for somewhere to look other than everywhere. My body knows the turns of every street. My pulse reacts when we pass the main street, where I saw Levi driving just a few days before. And the bookstore.

Uncle Frank takes a turn onto my grandparents' street. I sit up and look over my shoulder, out the back window, confused. "Why aren't we going to the hospital?"

When Mom turns and looks at me, her eyes are wide and bloodshot. She tilts her head as though she's asking, *Do I really need to say it?*

Oh yeah. Levi's not at the hospital. He's at the morgue.

Nine

The sun beams through the giant pine trees in the backyard at my grandparent's house. I feel like I never left, and yet, so much has happened since I last looked out the windows of the sunroom and into the vastness of their unfenced yard. At the back of their property looms my favorite tree, a swing hanging from its lowest branch.

I tiptoe down the flagstone path toward the tree, as though the stones are as fragile as my heart. But this time, under the canopy of branches and velvety green leaves, I don't bring a book. I sit on the uneven plank seat of the swing, my hands folding around the fraying rope. As I lift my feet, I close my eyes, lean my head back. Like I'm a butterfly, flying higher and higher. The heat of the sun warms my face, and I pretend it's the warmth of heaven shining on me. I imagine Levi's face, with beaming light behind. I imagine what his face should have looked like the last time I saw him, smiling at me, laughing, the freckles on his nose scrunching closer together.

Wind blows my hair around my face, tangling the strands together. *Wild hair for a wild heart*, Levi had whispered in the bookstore. I try to remember his voice. It wasn't long ago that I heard it, but the sound already fades from my memory. How quickly will I forget his smile? I keep my eyes closed, the whiteness of the sun shining through my closed lids. But I solidify his face in mind, embossing it in my memory.

Then it fades, and his face from the window remains. His hand in the air. My hand by my side in solidarity. Now in regret.

We never got a real good-bye. Just a partial wave through a darkened window.

I hear his voice saying my name, calling to me. "Maggie," My whipping hair gets stuck in the tears on my face. His voice is louder now, "Maggie."

"Maggie," Drew.

I almost fall out of the swing. My hands slide down the rope and leave that burned feeling in my palms. When I open my eyes, the sun blares like a visual hangover.

"Hey," he says, reaching out a hand to catch me, but I caught myself just fine.

His eyes squint when I stand up. I feel bare in the way he's looking at me.

"What?" I respond with sisterly angst at his persistent stare.

He raises an eyebrow. As though our phone conversation that night made him the type of brother I confide in. But I can see his face now, the face that shrugged off Roman Sewell. The face that left Juju to Graham's drunk advances. So I lift my chin and repeat, "What?"

Drew balls his hands in the pockets of JNCO jeans. "Mom, Frank, and Tammy are picking stuff up for the funeral—uh, memorial service—" His eyes roll at what the adults insist on calling it. Mom says Rose insists on memorializing Levi's life instead of focusing on his death, but I don't see how we can focus on anything else.

My brother keeps talking, like he always does. He's never learned the art of summarizing. "I guess, they're running errands for Rose. Grandpa and Grandma have a church meeting tonight, so they're leaving in ten. I was thinking—" He hefts a sigh. I shift my weight from one foot to the other, crossing my arms, waiting for him to get to the point. Spoiler alert: he's going to leave me here alone so he can go hang with Graham.

"I was thinking we could go for a walk." My eyes bolt to his. And they are as pained as mine. He keeps surprising me. "A long walk. To Levi's."

I almost smile. It will be long, but it will be cathartic.

***

"Did you bring any other shoes?" Drew comments on my Docs.

"No." I kick at a stick in the road as we walk. I should be used to Drew criticizing my wardrobe. "We're only here for like two days."

"You're going to wear those to the funeral?"

I don't look at him, but he knows I'm rolling my eyes. If I rolled my eyes at Drew every time I wanted to, they really would get stuck that way. No myth. Just fact.

"What do you care?"

"Fine."

I pull my denim vest close over my black tank. "I know I embarrass you," I mumble.

"No, you don't." He doesn't look at me or sound surprised. "Your Doc Marten's embarrass me."

My eyes roll again. I kick gravel at him with my embarrassing shoes. He and his Vans kick it back at me. When the gravel hits my bare leg, my head stings more than my leg. My head is in the clouds again, thinking of the gravel under Levi's wheels. I go silent, as does Drew.

We turn onto another street, passing another farm. The long irrigation sprinklers system stretches through the sky over the field. A squirrel skitters across the street several feet in front of us.

"Remember that time we went sledding on the back of that trailer," Drew breaks the silence.

"Ugh. How could I forget?"

Uncle Frank, Dad and Levi's dad, Greg thought it'd be great to hook a giant sled to the back of Greg's truck and trailer. Kind of like a hay ride, except on ice with a sled. And they wouldn't let the kids in the trailer. Only adults and babies. So all of us kids had to get on this giant sled and hang on for dear life. "Didn't Juju fall off?"

Drew chuckles. "No, it wasn't Juju. It was another girl, what was her name? She went to church with them."

"Oh, right." I just remember a girl falling off and all the boys laughing. I was *terrified* to fall off and get laughed at, so I grabbed onto the top of the sled. This was around the same age as the Babysitter Club sweat suit, so I was basically afraid to get laughed at for *everything*. At that age, that's all the boys ever did to us girls. "As soon as they took off, I remember falling forward. I remember I was like laying on the sled, grabbing on to the front of it and never letting go."

"Yeah," Drew laughs. A few steps, a few beats, then he says, "I just remember it was so cold and you didn't have your gloves with you for some reason. And Levi gave you his."

I smile. "I'd forgotten that. They were huge on me."

"That's when I knew Levi had a crush on you."

My face falls and I swivel to look at him. He isn't looking at me. He's staring at the asphalt road in front of his feet.

He knew. All this time, he knew. Even before I did.

***

We're both quiet in reverence as we turn on Levi's street. Is it still his even though he isn't here anymore? I can see the basketball goal mounted over the white garage door where Levi tried to teach me to play after Drew lost his patience. I can almost feel Levi's hand on my back when he would play defense to me. I can see his face, smirking at me as he dribbles, daring me to steal the ball or steal his heart. But I failed at both.

The house is a bustle, so we slip right through. I don't even see Rose or Greg; there are so many people squeezed into the living room and kitchen. Family from out of town. Members of their church. Employees who work for Greg at his auto repair shop. I even notice a journalist jotting down notes in a small notepad.

When we open the back door, I instantly think of all the years we've spent in this backyard, running through sprinklers in our bathing suits, eating watermelon and popsicles, writing in our diaries together. Juju lays on the trampoline. Her hair is a splash of strawberry against the blank canvas.

Drew and I climb on either side of her and lay next to her. Neither of us say anything. I've known Juju my entire life, and I don't know what to say to her. The Levi-Juju bond is something

I've never understood, being that it's so polar opposite to mine and Drew's. But if my pain is a dull ache in every cell of my body, then I imagine Juju's is like being split in half, the way lightning splits a tree, leaving the edges burnt and jagged. The two of them always grew side by side, lived in each other's shadows, so what is left for Juju with Levi's shadow gone.

"I'm glad you're here," she says. And she wraps her left arm around Drew's arm and her right around mine, then puts her hands back on her stomach. But she lays her head on my shoulder. Her pale belly button peaks out from under her flowery crop top. It's strange how she smells like strawberries, even out here—Drew and I probably smell like stale wind and sweat. Strawberries are her natural scent. Graham used to call her Strawberry Shortcake—a way better nickname than Mincemeat—until she got taller than him.

"I wish I'd seen him," I say.

"No, you don't," she responds flatly. "He didn't even look like Levi. Or like anyone. All purple and swollen and tubes. You—" but she just shakes her head instead of finishing. "Be happy with the last memory you have of him."

But I hate my last memory of him.

"I hate mine," she whispers, as though she read my thoughts. Being with her, I feel ashamed at myself for moping about the goodbye I didn't get, when I should be grateful for the little I had.

"They were going to pull the plug. That's how bad he was. But then they didn't have to."

The wetness of her tears warms my shoulder.

"I'm kind of mad at him—for leaving us." I don't know if that's okay to say, but if I can admit it to anyone, it's Juju and Drew.

She exhales. "You have no idea."

Not sure what she means, but I don't have time to ask before Drew changes the subject.

"We should make a slideshow," he says. My guess is that he was on the verge of tears too. "With pictures and videos of Levi, so everyone has a great last memory."

I smile, proud of Drew for such a great idea.

But Juju says, "I don't think I can. Not yet."

So we remain as we are, lying on the trampoline, linked arm-in-arm.

***

Rose asks me to help sift through Levi's room for music to play during the service. Maybe she wants a reason to go in his room and not be alone. I sit on Levi's bed, looking around the room that haven't been allowed to enter since I was nine or ten. As soon as puberty hit, a strict rule was established in the James house: No boys in Juju's room. No girls in Levi's.

Motorcycle posters adorn his walls. That's no surprise. His bed is small, low to the ground, so when I sit on it, I feel like I'm looking at his room from a young child's perspective. He has a desk in the corner and a beanbag chair next to it. A lamp. His stereo. Some racing magazines.

I imagine him sitting at the desk, writing me a letter, blue ink staining his fingertips. Could there be a letter for me stuffed in a drawer, waiting to be mailed?

I lift my eyes to the ceiling where Levi would stare as he lay on this bed. Did he sleep on his back or on his side?

Rose finds a CD. "This is it," she says. "This is his favorite song." I don't know which one it is, but I don't ask. I just smile at her.

How do I know so little about a boy I've loved for so long?

When I pass Juju's bedroom down the hall, there's a lidded box with LEVI written in black sharpie on its side sitting in her doorway.

"What is this?" I ask Rose.

"They're Juju's photos. She said they're all the bad ones she doesn't want anymore." Rose shrugs. "You can have a look if you want. She wouldn't mind. She's throwing them out."

My heart throbs as I carefully open the box, feeling like I'm looking at a secret of Juju's even though I've been given permission. The top layer of the box is all Polaroids. Every single Polaroid photo that Juju had of Levi that is either blurry or hiding his face. I can't believe Juju doesn't want them, but she's never been the type to hold on to things.

One corner that I recognize peeks out from the stack: the photo of Levi, Graham, and Drew on the motorcycles across from the bookstore. I grab the white edge of the photograph and pull it out from beneath the others. Drew and Graham are facing the camera, laughing. Levi profile looks over his shoulder, the corner of his smiling mouth showing.

Underneath it, I see the one of Levi on the beams of the Industrial. The photo that Graham stepped on after trying to get it away from Juju. I stare for a while. Levi's face is smudged from Graham shoe, but I don't care.

I trace my fingers over the smudge of Levi's face, almost expecting the scent of summer to emanate from it, a scratch and sniff photo.

I slip them both in the back pocket of my shorts.

* * *

The memorial service takes place in the auditorium of Stone River High School. Nine months from now, Levi would have graduated in this auditorium. He would have been the guy who pulled some weird prank while walking across the stage. Something stupid that would have made everybody whoop and holler for him.

Instead we're all gathering here to say goodbye.

I pull at the hem of my black dress, even though I'm wearing black leggings underneath because showing bare legs at a funeral doesn't seem right. The dress has little red and blue flowers on it, but it is the only black dress I own.

My fingers tinker with the camera in my hands. Juju snuck it to me as soon as I arrived. "Mom says it wouldn't be appropriate for me to take pictures today. She said I have to sit on the front row and be sad."

I raise my eyebrows at her, thinking of the trashed Polaroids that became my treasures.

"If she knew me at all, she would know that taking pictures would keep my mind occupied." She sighs deep. "I need you to take them instead."

"What—I—No," I take a breath. "I can't take pictures. I'm not any good."

She lays her long fingers over mine—hers elegant, mine stubby. "Just take pictures of what you feel. That's the most important part of photography." Rose hollers Juju's name. "I have to go." She scurries away in her long, flowy dress. The black against her pale skin makes it look like she is the one who died.

I sit with Drew on one side and my mom on the other. My

113

eyes scan the room, looking for what to photograph, what to feel. The James family enters, and hands brush against well-wishers, and I snap a photo. An older woman steps into the isle to embrace Rose. *Snap.* Juju stares at the ground so no one will catch her eye, but she pulls her hair behind her ear. *Snap.* As they reach their seats, in front of the black casket, Greg puts his arms around both of his girls, Rose and Juju. *Snap.*

By the time, the ceremony starts there is standing room only in the auditorium. Graham sits with his family and mine on the second row. He doesn't take his eyes off the ground.

The casket looks too shiny. Too new for a soul as adventurous as Levi. Seems to me, they should have cremated him, let his ashes fly to the heights his body would never reach.

Their pastor gives the eulogy. He tells the story about Levi hiding in the baptismal before music practice and jumping out whenever the pastor passed by. "He got me every single time." Everyone laughs. *Snap.* Levi's older brother, Sam, who married a beautiful Canadian and moved to Seattle, speaks next. He talks about how every morning before school, Levi raced him to the stop sign but always lost. Until the one time that Levi finally beat him. That now, Levi has once again raced ahead and beat him to heaven. Sam chokes up for a moment (*snap*), then raises his head with a smile. *Snap.* Rose uses a handkerchief to dab her eyes. *Snap.*

I see why Juju wanted to occupy herself with this. Instead of my mind focusing on the words, my eyes are focused around the room, roaming, never settling on my own sadness.

Finally, it's over. The pastor directs us to a reception in the high school gymnasium. At the entrance, I am bombarded with Levi. An easel stands with a giant picture of him. One that matches the program in my hand. But I have barely glanced at the program because the picture is Levi's school picture. In it, his hair is perfectly combed and his smile plastered on. A Stepford version of Levi.

Until today I didn't know his middle name. No idea how that's even possible. I've always called him Levi James. But inside the program is his full name. Levi Timothy James.

Looking at it, I wonder how Graham hasn't been making fun of him for having three first names. And yet he never made fun of Levi for anything. Did Graham always know a diss to Levi would get him punched in the face? Maybe it already had. How much of this life here in Michigan have I missed? There's so much I don't know about the people I thought were my closest friends.

For that reason, I find a table near the back of the reception away from the hubbub. Seeing all that I've missed without even realizing it seems like another loss to mourn. Was I naïve thinking that it would always be the five of us? Drew had a life full of friends and parties while I sat at home, pining after life in Michigan. After Juju. And of course after Levi. Always waiting for summer. Always waiting for August.

From the back of the room, I am an outsider looking in on this life that I have missed. As objective as the narrator of a book. Girls in black dresses with pantyhose flit over to Juju, hugging her. Juju smiles her commercial smile, being strong for everyone else instead of the other way around. The same girls drift to Rose and Greg, hugging them. One girl, with curled blonde hair flowing down her back, seems to choke on whatever words she says and begins to sob. It is Danielle. Rose digs a tissue out of her purse and hands it to Danielle, rubbing her arm, lovingly.

A couple guys talk to Graham two tables over. The taller one stands with his hands in his pockets. The other gestures animatedly, then pulls something out of his jacket pocket and passes it to Graham. Graham unfolds a piece of paper, his eyes grazing it, then his arms wrap around the giver, with a couple strong pats on the back.

I don't know any of these people. In fact, I know few of the people here. Even the ones I recognize, I don't know well: the pastor, some of the kids from church, some of Grandma and Grandpa's prayer group friends.

Legs of the folding chair next to me squeal on the gym floor as Drew drags them backward. "You don't have a book hiding under the table, do you?" He slouches into the seat, his long legs sprawl out in front of him, leaving room for nothing else under the table.

I curl my legs under my chair. "No," I say it like it's ridiculous, but I can't say that it didn't cross my mind.

"Then what are you doing sitting over here by yourself? Sulking?"

"I don't sulk. That's you. What are you doing over here?"

"Keeping you company. You look sad and lonely."

"You always think I look sad and lonely."

"But this time, I'm right."

I roll my eyes, because I hate when he's right. And I know he's right.

"I'm just realizing how little I really knew Levi. And maybe how little I really know Juju anymore." My voice is quiet, and in the booming gymnasium, I don't know if Drew heard me.

He stares off at the scene in front of us, as do I. "I guess I'm thinking the same thing. But in some ways, we'll always know

116

them better than these new kids on the block. They don't know what Juju looked like before she turned supermodel. They don't know what Levi sounded like before puberty. And they'll never know that Graham's always been a douche."

I laugh. Guilt pangs my smile, but Levi would have wanted us to laugh at his funeral. He would have wanted a party.

"If Levi could have planned this thing, what do you think he would have done?" I ask.

"He would have had us all rock climbing up the biggest mountain in Michigan or something crazy."

"Yeah," I agree, my lips turn up. "And he would have blared rock music."

"We'd all be wearing his band t-shirts, and he'd be buried with his motorcycle."

"I think he would have been cremated. In a Toilet Bowlers t-shirt."

He makes a grossed-out face. "I guess that's why they don't let teenagers plan funerals."

"You want to get out of here?" I ask my brother, for once knowing we agree.

"Hell, yeah."

We stand at the same time, and the legs of the chairs shriek against the floor again. Heads turn our direction. Graham removes himself from a circle of people, none of whom are talking to him, and starts to walk our way. He looks sharp in a suit with his hair all gelled. I can actually see him as a businessman now.

"You guys bouncing?" he asks when he gets closer.

"Yeah, man." Drew grabs Graham's hand and they do their little handshake thing that I can't ever keep up with.

"I'll come with." He gestures his head backward. "This place is suffocating."

As the three of us walk toward the exit, Juju catches my eye. She lifts her head toward me for a moment. Her hair is pulled back into a sleek ponytail, subtle and glam at the same time. She smiles to the group talking to her, touches the elbow of one girl and her lips read, "Thank you for coming," to them.

"Hey," she says as she takes long strides to reach us. "Are you all leaving me here?" Her eyes are panicked. She glances sideways at Graham, who drops his gaze to the gymnasium floor. I'm about to ask what that was all about, but Juju is already saying, "Wait for me. I'll tell Mom." But when Juju tells Rose, they both return.

"Come back to the house," Rose says quickly and quietly. "We're having an after-reception reception." She winks. "A bit more intimate."

"Are you sure?" I ask, still feeling an outsider.

"Of course. It's for family. And you," she rests her hand on the curve of my cheek, "are family." Then she turns to all of us, still whisper-talking. "Back at the house. I'll get there as soon as this wraps up."

Maybe I'm not the outsider. Maybe family knows each other more than anyone else ever will. Maybe family accepts each other even when we've made horrible mistakes. We can be a part of things that no one else can. At least the important things.

Ten

The four of us—no longer the five—sit on the deck, out of the way. The deck is old and splintered, and the white wicker chairs are faded and hard. But it feels like another home. We sit, quietly. No need for words. Birds chirp and their wings carry them from tree to tree, where the sun flares through the thick evergreen branches.

When Rose and Greg arrive, they aren't alone. There are dozens of James'. We joined them inside, but those who have arrived at the house are buzzing like hummingbirds instead of vultures picking at the dead. There is life here. And laughter.

Juju changes from her lacy black dress to low-rise jeans and Levi's Toilet Bowler's t-shirt that is at least two sizes too big.

Greg passes out beers from the fridge to Sam, Uncle Frank, Grandpa and the other adults. Graham and Drew try to snag bottles, but Greg snags them back. "Nice try."

Rose chats loudly from the kitchen. Her four sisters come in and out carrying *hors'd'eaurves* and beverages. I don't know what to do with myself, so I join them. When her sisters leave the room, Rose and I are alone. I'm leaning on the kitchen island, half-seated on the bar stool and half-standing, as she scrubs down the granite counter.

I straighten the place mat in an effort to help. Grapevines with chunky grapes overflow from a wicker basket in the middle of the island, matching the wallpaper throughout the kitchen.

I watch Rose as she scrubs the counters. Her arm moves back and forth voraciously, so much that her hips shake as does the black skirt flowing down from them. A ruckus of laughter floats in from the living room, but Rose doesn't flinch. My curiosity peaks but I don't want to leave Rose alone. After the last few days, why doesn't she stop for a moment and sit, rest, let someone else take care of her?

The thought brings me from my seat. I go to her side, put my hand on her arm as it moves back and forth, back and forth.

"Can I help?"

She stops at my touch. Her fingers are red and dry. "That's sweet, Maggie." When she turns to me, her eyes glisten. "I have to keep moving. I have to keep working. If I sit, I—I'm not sure what will happen." She drops the rag and turns to me. "Since I have you," she glances toward the doorway to the living room, "there's something I wanted to tell you. Just before—" She hesitates, then continues. "Well, at dinner a few nights ago, we were all talking about what the kids would do after high school. A lot of talk about the future and all, and Greg asked the kids where they thought they would be in five years."

Another cackle, and the front door opens, letting someone new inside, then conversation erupts again.

Rose isn't distracted. "Levi didn't say it at the table. I don't know that he wanted anyone else to know. But later he said to me, 'Mom, I think in five years, I'll be married to Maggie Thayer.'"

My stomach lurches at the words but then it drops with the

sickening memory that he isn't here to make that happen anymore.

"He loved you, Maggie." With that admission, she reaches her arms around me, pulls me into her warm body. She smells of bleach and lemon. "And that makes you family. Forever."

I relish her embrace, wishing it could all be true. Against her shoulder, I ask, "Is there any chance, if you find any letters—?"

"Of course," she says, pulling back to look at me but keeping her hands on my shoulders. "If I find anything at all, I'll send it your way." She releases me and picks the rag up again.

The living room bursts with bodies and laughter. The family stories have moved on from Levi to any story in the last five decades that will make anyone in the room laugh. And it's working. Juju sits in her dad's lap telling a story about when Sam and Levi threw her Barbie doll out the second-floor window, then threatened to toss her out after it.

Sam shares the love seat with his wife. He says, "Never happened," in a dry voice, but smirking.

"It did." Juju stands firm.

One of Rose's sisters one-ups that with a story about a fight with one of their brothers.

Drew and Graham are seated on the fireplace, somewhat removed but still chuckling at the stories. I join them.

From here, I can take in the whole family, many of whom share Levi and Juju's red hair, some of whom share Levi's round eyes. What would it have been like to have called this my family? To have made Levi's five-year plan come true? Sam and Emily exchange a look, his hand on her knee. Levi looked nothing like his brother, but even so, I insert us into the picture. The image I've always had of Levi as an adult has already grown blurry. And I wonder, where does that leave me in five years?

***

Near midnight, Mom tells us we have to leave to get up for our crack-of-dawn flight. Before we leave, Juju holds a bundle of things wrapped in a bag for me.

"Open them later. I've cried enough for one day," she says. Mischief and tears glisten in her eyes.

I don't want to wait a single moment to see what is inside, so the instant my butt hits the leather seat of Grandpa's truck, I open the bag. Tenderly fingering each treasure.

These are the gems I find inside:

- A cassette tape in its clear, boxy case. "Rad Tunes" written in blue ink on the label of Side A, the *s* smudged and smeared by Levi's finger.
- A Toilet Bowlers t-shirt that smells of him, a little bit leather, a little bit motor oil, and a lot CK1 cologne.
- The rest of his bottle of CK1.

What Juju couldn't have known was that I would listen to this mix tape until I had the entire tape lodged protectively in my memory.

Or that I would sleep in Levi's Toilet Bowlers t-shirt that night, and for years to come. Until everyone else forgot where it came from. Except me.

Part Two

10 YEARS LATER
AUGUST 2009

Eleven

The back door opens and closes, but it doesn't register in my brain because I am consumed in a book. Kind of like a dream, when your alarm goes off and it somehow enters the scene where you are dreaming. That's what happens when I'm reading. I lose myself between the cream pages and curled letters of a good book. Characters become my friends, and if an author is exceptional, my family; their travesties and their joys live with me long after I close the last page.

But today, the reader in me is turned off. I am the editor. Like a teacher who marks up the best student's essay with red-inked circles and x's. Except as an editor they pay me to do so, and even though they hurt when they see the markings, my clients are pleased that I have made their work complete, even better than before.

When there are footsteps on the wood floor, the sound breaches my consciousness and takes me away from the black and white words in front of me.

"Long day?"

I jump in my seat at the deep voice behind me. "Oh," I say,

turning in my swivel chair. "I didn't hear you come in."

Before I turn all the way toward Everett, he kisses the crown of my head. I close my eyes and breathe him in, coming back to reality from my stint at editing. I haven't gotten out of the chair for—I look at the watch on my wrist—three hours. Not even for a bathroom break.

When I look up at him, there's a kink in my neck that I immediately rub with my hand.

"Here, let me," my husband says, setting his car keys on the desk to massage my stiff shoulders.

Our wedding portrait stands on the desk next to the computer screen. Framed in place, he stands tall next to me, dressed in his crisp tux and perfectly combed brown-blonde hair. Next to him, I come up to his shoulders, and the pictured version of me has tamed hair and an off-the-shoulder wedding dress that accentuates the one part of myself that I tried best to hide throughout adolescence. But I've learned to love my body, and my brain, since then.

Neither of us have changed much since our wedding picture two years ago. Except that I have added more than a few pounds around my waist and hips. Everett has stayed as lean as he is tall.

I settle a finger to the picture frame, leave the keys and a cup of coffee that sits, now cold, on the edge of my desk, just out of arms reach so that I don't tip it onto the printed manuscript in front of me. I've made that mistake before. Too many times.

"I brought you something," he says, and I follow him the few steps it takes to enter the living room. I already know what the something will be even before I see the tall bouquet of red and yellow flowers in a clear vase atop our coffee table, but I still try to seem surprised.

"The hotel florist came in and replaced them before they started to wilt," he says, the buttons on his black concierge suit and crisp white shirt nearly busting with pride as though he has, in fact, surprised me.

"Oh, thank you," I say, breathing in their familiar scent. I touch the edge of a gerbera daisy that does look as though it is an evening away from browning. The first time he came home with bouquets of flowers that would have otherwise been discarded by the hotel staff, I was charmed. Even the first dozen times. But two years later...

"You don't have to act like it's a surprise." He winks and laughs.

I smile back. "They are beautiful."

Everett kisses me under my ear. "Not as beautiful as you."

But I don't feel beautiful today. My hair is barely brushed and I've been sitting at my desk for hours without any need to put makeup on or much more than a t-shirt and jeans.

He, on the other hand, is dressed impeccably. When we first started dating and he told me he was a concierge, I thought it was an odd job for a guy so young. Then I visited him at work, and he wasn't behind a desk as I expected. He was in the car port near the valet stand, talking to a frazzled mother, her children holding pillows and her luggage stacked next to her like the Leaning Tower of Pisa. Even with his tall stature, Everett's conversation put the mother at ease and made her children laugh. Then he helped the valet put her bags in her car.

He has the same ability to put me at ease and make me laugh. It's the first thing about him I fell in love with.

By the time I turn around, Everett has shed his suit coat on the couch, slipped his shoes off in the middle of our small bedroom floor. If I don't move them or the keys on my desk, then he'll be stomping around the house looking for them in the morning before I'm up.

These are things people don't tell you about marriage, or if they do, you think, that's no big deal. It's so small and petty, it would never get to me. But I'm two years in, and I want to strangle him as I walk behind him picking up every item he has discarded, like I'm his personal concierge.

"Hey hon," he calls from the closet.

"Hmm?" I've learned to limit my words when I'm irrationally irritated at him.

"What's your plan for dinner?"

My plan? Just because I work from home, dinner has to be *my* plan?

I inhale. I don't want to start an argument. All day he makes plans for other people. I want him to relax when he comes home and not have to be the one always making more plans for us. But I also don't know how I can compete with the full service restaurants that he visits regularly in order to recommend them to hotel guests.

"I haven't really thought about it yet," I answer truthfully.

The simple answer would be to go out or order in, but the big bills were just paid and put in the mail, so I know there isn't a whole lot of wiggle room there either.

I swear I hear him sigh, but when he comes around the corner into the bedroom, he's changed into his faded black t-shirt and khaki cargo pants. He's barefoot, fingers running through his hair, wearing his crooked smile, and he looks nothing like the man who just came home. He wiggles his dark eyebrows that don't match his blonde hair at all—his mother says that's because of his German roots.

"I've been meaning to try the new place that opened around the corner. We could walk if you want."

True, our house is just outside the Arts District of Dallas, so tons of trendy places are within walking distance, but right now I find this exhausting.

He steps toward me, puts his hands on my waist. My comfy jeans ride low on my hips and leave them vulnerable to his hands. "Or I could call in the order and go pick it up," he adds, with a kiss to my lips, because I swear he knows what I'm thinking.

"You just got home," *ordering things for other people all day long,* I add in my mind. "I'll go pick it up."

"I really don't mind," he says, and I know he's telling the truth. He enjoys taking care of me.

My shoulders relax. As he looks for the right menu from a stack in the drawer, he sucks in his bottom lip in concentration, the same way he does when he smiles. I've never told him how sexy he is when he does that. I've never been good at verbalizing compliments. It seems odd to say, *The way you bite your lip when you smile is so freaking sexy,* even though my stomach flips every time.

When he grabs his phone to dial, I look around at the mess he's made in the ten minutes he's been home. I see his socks on the floor of the bathroom. Water droplets are splattered on his mirror. I go behind him and clean it all up, willing myself to be okay with it because he's taking care of dinner and because I love him more than I love a clean house.

I want to get a few more minutes in on my work. I'm close to the end of my first edit, and I hit a stride this afternoon, which is why I lost track of time.

"Mr. Lange," I hear the voice chime through the phone. His reputation proceeds him, as usual. Someday, I hope his salary will match it.

Everett turns his charm on high speed as he places our order. He puts his hand over the speaker and whispers to me, "Do you want the tempura fish or shrimp tacos?"

"Shrimp."

He nods and repeats the order into the phone.

When he leaves, I rattle around the kitchen cabinets looking for clean dishes. We don't have many dishes to begin with (except all that fine china we got for our wedding), and what we have is piled high in the sink since the dishwasher broke. But it's not going to take him long to get around the corner and pick the food up. He always gets the best service from restaurant owners who know his occupation.

I feel guilty that he is taking care of dinner, so I decide to make it up to him. I hurry to scrub the piled-up dishes. I throw placemats down and set the table, complete with our usual fishbowl centerpiece filled with a candle, sea shells, and starfish collected from our honeymoon. Most of our two-bedroom house has a beach vibe. Because we live so far from the beach, I attempt to bring vacation to us. Ice cubes settle in their glasses just as Everett walks through the door with bags of food in hand.

He places the bags on the counter and begins to pull the containers out. "I thought you were going to keep working," he says, surveying the table.

I grab the containers of food, take them to the table and plop in my chair. "I wanted the house to look nice for you," I say with a smile, but I feel deflated. I wanted to keep working. Why did I think I had to do all of this instead?

Looking at me with soft eyes, he tilts his head toward me. "You didn't have to. Just you being here makes the house nice. That's all I want." In two strides he crosses the kitchen and has his hands on either side of my face, kissing me. His breath fills my soul and relaxes my bones.

As the tension in my body releases under his touch, he smiles, pulling his bottom lip between his teeth. My stomach flips, but all I say is, "I love you." And it's true. Right now, I don't need dinner or work, I only need Everett.

***

"You won't believe who checked in this morning," Everett says between bites.

My finished plate sits on the table in front of me. I place my dirty fork and crumpled napkin in the middle of it. "Who?"

"Colt Bradley," he says with a crooked grin, then takes another bite of his tempura fish taco.

"The basketball player?"

There are plenty of perks to Everett's job, but his meeting celebrities and sports figures makes my brothers undeniably jealous.

Everett nods, but his mischievous expression says there is more to the story.

"He wasn't in his room for 30 minutes before calling down and asking me to find him an escort."

My eyebrows raise. This isn't the first time that he's had this request, but it's always a surprise when it's a celebrity with a squeaky clean reputation.

"At least this one's not married." That's happened before too.

Of course Everett is bound to privacy per his contract. But still.

"True." He wipes his mouth with a napkin and adds an *Mmm* to his next bite. I am certain Everett will list it in his guest recommendations. Although, that's never a guarantee just because the management is nice or even when the food is comped. Everett takes pride in his honest recommendations. It's his concierge code. "I got a hefty tip out of it."

My response to his story is dampened by the new pile of dirty dishes. I doubt Everett will notice them. Concierges make plans, but they don't clean up after them.

"I'm telling you, you're in the hotel version of *The Devil Wears Prada*, and your hotel clients are Meryl Streep."

The landline phone rings a shrill tone. Everett reaches for a napkin for his greasy hands.

"I'll get it."

"So you're saying I'm the Anne Hathaway character."

I smile as I pass him, "But prettier."

I grab the cordless phone in the corner of the room, leaving Everett chuckling to himself. "Hello."

"Good evening, Maggie."

The first syllable of the female voice chills me. It's Leslie Cohan, one of the hotel managers.

"Is Everett available?" Leslie croons, over-enunciating his name. I hate the way she does that.

"Yes," I say bluntly. All the joy of the evening evaporates. I hate that she calls my husband this late. I hate that she calls my husband at all.

I bring the phone receiver to him. "It's your girlfriend."

He grits his jaw at my statement. We both know it was loud enough for Leslie to hear.

"Leslie, hi," he says with clipped words, then walks into our office—my office—and closes the door all but a crack.

We've discussed getting rid of our landline, and now I know I'm ready. A cell phone could be put away and wouldn't shrill through the house in the middle of dinner so he could run off to his work wife.

With my office occupied, I can't work, but I don't want to clean the kitchen *again*. Instead, I scrub off my makeup and throw on my pajamas, slamming every cabinet and drawer along the way. Our home is small enough that he can hear me.

Even though the manuscript I'm editing isn't in my hand at this moment, the words are in my head. I try to focus on them. My process usually takes two edits, but sometimes even a third after I let the book marinate in my thoughts. I'm thorough. Some would call me a perfectionist. But it's a privilege, really, to have someone's words in your hands, to help them hone their creation. Often, my thoughts aren't in the real world but in the book world, even when the manuscript is elsewhere. But my irritation with Everett and Leslie is too acute. Every second he's on phone with her burns me.

When I'm done in the bathroom, I stomp into the kitchen. I pick up the first plate and hold it in both hands. Is this my life now? Feeding him. Cleaning up after him. Playing second fiddle to his work. Although I suppose he is often second to mine.

In my mind, I play out the same argument we've had so often it circles around us like a vulture.

Did she get what she needed?

Yes.

Was it really so urgent she needed to interrupt dinner?

Maggie, it's my job.

Why won't you just admit there is more to it than just work?

Here we go again. Nothing has ever happened. You're jealous over nothing.

No, I'm mad that you are oblivious to her. That you don't trust what I see in her.

My blood pressure rises at the argument we're about to have. I use the dishtowel to hand dry a coffee mug. The mug feels sturdy in my hand, and for just a moment I wonder how bad it would be if I hit him over the head with it. Would it give him a headache and knock some sense into him, or would it actually hurt him and make him bleed? I don't want to make him bleed...I don't think.

I create an excuse to storm into the office and make my presence known by slamming the mug down on my desk where it usually resides.

When I push the office door open, Everett swivels around in the chair toward me. His hair is rumpled, and his dark eyebrows are threaded together. I don't want to soften. The angsty side of me wants this argument. I advance to the desk and deposit the mug in place, albeit less aggressively than planned.

He catches my hand and mouths, "I'm sorry."

I don't pull away even though I'm still irked.

Chatter squawks from the receiver, but Everett moves the mouthpiece back so he can whisper, "Problem with a guest request. It's big money."

I give a sympathetic nod.

With a slight tug, he pulls me onto his lap. Eyes locked on mine, he says into the phone, "Leslie, let me pause you right there. I don't see how there's anything I can do about this tonight." He leans in and nuzzles my neck. Goosebumps prickle my arms.

"Why don't I work on it first thing tomorrow?" he says to

the phone, as I wrap my arms around his neck. "Yeah—Sure. Yeah, I get it." His shoulders deflate and he shakes his head.

I don't storm out or make a scene. I quietly get up and leave the room. He tried. The problem is I want the argument. I want to be petty. I'm still upset that Leslie called, that he chooses his work over home. But if I bring it up now, I'll be the wife who picks a fight. Nobody likes that wife.

***

I lay down in our bed, the pale blue paisley comforter thick on top of me, even though it's August, in Texas no less. Tonight, it is my shield.

Everett opens the bedroom door and slips through the room without a word. He knows I'm not asleep, but he pretends that I am, just as I do.

The first year of marriage was supposed to be the hard part. Merging two lives together, learning each other in new ways. But our first year was a breeze. Year two hit like a hurricane. I don't know how it happened. We woke up one day and things were more comfortable and less comfortable at the same time.

I've always been a good editor, from college to my first day on the job to working on my first best-seller. I know how to make things look the way they should look, move words around in the correct order so they flow smoothly off the tongue. But I don't know how to be a good wife. Even though I want to be, far more than being a good editor.

Everett turns to the nightly news on the television in our room, slides between the sheets, throws the comforter off of his side of the bed and onto mine (maybe he's trying to heat me out), and in minutes, his breathing turns heavy and slow.

As soon as I am confident that he's out, I roll over and watch him sleep. His eyes flutter behind his eyelids, his chest rises and falls with each deep breath. He's asleep without even trying to talk things through with me, without fighting or yelling, without any effort toward me at all. I want to slap that sleepy glaze right off of his face. I want to yell and cry. I want him to yell back and tell me I'm overreacting, that he loves me more than anyone. That Leslie could never be anything to him other than a co-worker. That I have his heart entirely and wholly. That he would never choose anyone else over me.

Instead I roll back to my side and close my eyes.

Twelve

I wake to the sound of Everett scrounging around for his keys even before I open my eyes.

"They're on my desk," I mutter, through a sleepy slur.

"Oh yeah, thanks." He walks to my side of the bed and kisses my forehead. "Have a good day."

"You, too." I half speak, half groan.

This is our every morning. Well, it's not always the keys, but everything else is the same. He won't bring up what happened last night if I don't. And really, what's the point? So I won't either.

Instead of going back to sleep, I throw back the sheets and sit up. I look around the bedroom. The walls are a buttery yellow, covered with canvas beach photos from the only trip we've taken: our honeymoon.

It's a small room, inside a small house, that I adored when we bought it, but now I'm suddenly claustrophobic. The walls seem closer than they ever have. The door is seriously four steps away, and from there the kitchen is maybe six steps further. Everything is closing in on me.

As I put my feet on the blonde, wood-grain floor, I can

predict exactly how today will go. From Everett's obligatory kiss on my head to the moment we lay down.

Was this really what I wanted for my life?

The day we bought this house, the realtor handed me the keys, and right there in the middle of the title company, I jumped like a little girl. They laughed and took a picture with Everett, me, and our glowing smiles. The house seemed perfect. The beige siding and white trim with a cute little porch and hanging swing that I swore I would wake up and sit on every morning. Every little bit was perfect for us. We hung a sign over the door that read: The Lange's.

Now the sign, along with the enthusiasm, is sun-faded.

My day is a fog. The air is thick around me, even as I sit at my desk to edit. I look at the manuscript in my hands. Someone else's manuscript. Someone else's words.

Aren't you tired of letting everyone else write your story? I hear the statement in my head, a familiar voice, but I push it away.

After a while, my head hurts and my eyes burn. I decide to take a bath, relax, reset my head. I don't know what's going on with me today, but I have to shake it.

As I sit in the bath, I notice my belly before it submerges underwater. I have gained a few pounds since being married, even more than the freshman fifteen. Working from home with a kitchen six steps away has not served me well. Nor has Everett's constant restaurant outings. I push my fingers on my soft stomach. I haven't had a baby yet and my midsection is already like the Pillsbury Doughboy, minus the giggle.

I step out of the bathtub, dripping on the floor, and turn my radio on, hopeful that familiar lyrics will fill my head instead of these poisonous thoughts. The tuned-in station is instrumental, but it reminds me of Everett's hotel, so I change it to the pop station. Katy Perry blares through the speakers. I settle back into the bath, with music that is less relaxing but at least I can sing along.

"You are listening to 105.1 KXPX," the radio DJ chimes, "on this beautiful summer day, August 26th."

I sit upright, the water running down my chest, droplets splattering from the edges of my hair back to the surface of the water.

That's it. August 26th. My subconscious knew the date even if I didn't.

I drain the water, grab my towel, and dry off haphazardly. My skin is damp as I pull on my slouchy jeans and yellow halter top. Then I rush to the closet, climb awkwardly on top of the dresser to reach the high shelf. There are a handful of brown moving boxes that we never unpacked, and I don't know which one I want. They are marked with things like "Office supplies" and "Crafts" that we don't currently need or have room for. But I don't remember which box I packed it in, so with my hands stretched above my head, I grab the first box, pull it down to the dresser and sift through it.

Most of these things could be thrown away, but I'm not here spring cleaning and I don't want to get sidetracked, so I shove everything back and replace the unwanted box on the shelf then move to the next one. It takes far too long, but I finally locate the purple photo box with gold handles. My heart pounds in my chest. My mom gave it to me full of body lotions and sprays for some birthday.

The lid shifts, so stuffed with photographs and papers that it can barely stay closed. I'm out of breath by the time I climb down from the dresser. I hold the purple box between my palms like the Holy Grail.

I rush to my bed, pull the lid off, holding my breath as though dust will fly off this relic that hasn't been opened for so long. When I remove the lid, the scent of Japanese cherry blossom lotion is still encapsulated. Inside are papers, so many papers. From the days before texting, when we slid notes under classroom desks and handed them off in school hallways. When the internet was so new that we still thought to mail a letter on actual paper. These are the treasures in this box. The silly words of high schoolers that held the value of jewels.

On top is an 18th birthday card Ally crafted for me on construction paper. I laugh out loud at the card that I had forgotten. Each page opens to another celebrity photo cut out of a magazine, the likes of shirtless Nelly with his pants far below his boxers and floppy-haired *Good Will Hunting* Matt Damon. Ally had drawn little word bubbles over each celebrity's head, filled with birthday messages for me.

A collection of origami-folded notes cluster together and maybe one day I'll read through them, but right now, I am focused. I sift through the papers, until I find them. The letters. Each one carrying my name drawn on the envelopes like graffitied walls. The paper feels thin between my fingers, worn from being held by a teenage girl's hands, read over and over, kept between pillows and sheets to be reread again after dark.

Under the stack of envelopes—I'd forgotten how many letters there were—are the Polaroids. The photos have faded with time. Instead of the face I am searching for, I find only profiles and lens flares.

"Who's that?" Everett's voice is over my shoulder. I hadn't

heard him walk up. When did he get so stealthy? And where had the time gone?

"Oh, it's just a boy I knew a long time ago," I say with nonchalance. "I found it in a box in the closet. A bunch of notes from high school, actually." I'm not lying. I'm just omitting the part where I searched with desperation. "Like this birthday card from Ally." I show him the homemade card. He met Ally a few times early in our relationship, when she visited from Boston to see her family and, once, for her brother's graduation.

Everett chuckles as he flips through the purple construction paper. "They don't sell cards like that in stores!"

My husband moves along to the closet. His belt buckle clanks in the other room as he changes out of his work clothes. I prop the lid back on the box and slide it under our bed.

Just a boy… I think. What he doesn't know is how much this boy has shaped who I am. How much I am changed because of this boy. So many unexplained things in our lives, things that seem so insignificant to my husband, are all reminders to me of this boy.

That email address I had to spell for my husband over and over when we were first dating, the one that I now use as my junk address because I can't let it go, that email address was an inside joke with this boy.

My passwords are made up of mixtures of our nicknames together. Which makes for a secure password, because nobody knows about him. My pin number is the date of his death. I don't talk about this boy. I haven't told my closest friends about him. I haven't been back to his home or to talk with his family, hang out with his friends, who used to be my friends.

I pretend it didn't happen. That this boy didn't mean

everything to me. That this boy wasn't my first love. I pretend this boy didn't crush me and leave me broken and damaged, taking years of my life to care about someone new. That I had imagined right now I would be married to this boy instead, imagined my life entirely different than it is. I don't tell anyone those things.

I just hide them among passwords, pin numbers, and junk email addresses.

Still, this boy has been with me every day for ten years.

Thirteen

Everett carries something in his hand when he comes back in the room. I recognize the pink and white box from my favorite bakery around the corner.

"I brought you something. And it's not hotel flowers." He winks before he leans in to where I am seated on the bed and kisses me on the lips. "I'm sorry for how last night went."

Before taking the box from him, I say, "I'm sorry too." I think I am anyway. I want to be. I open the box, and there is my favorite strawberries and crème cupcake just as I suspected. I dip my finger into the cream cheese icing and lick it.

He pulls one single sunflower from behind his back. "And this," he says. "I said no *hotel* flowers."

I draw the long stem in to my heart. The round face of the flower stares at me. Yet another thing I haven't told Everett: why I love sunflowers so.

"Did you forget about dinner?" Everett asks, taking in my state of dress.

"Tonight? I don't have anything on my calendar." Seems like I would have noticed the date if I did.

The annual ache honors Levi. It honors Juju and her loss. It honors Rose and Greg, moving on in life with two living children instead of three.

Everett gives me a strange look. "We have dinner with Eric and Becca."

I sigh, remembering the entire conversation when we planned this. I fix my ponytail so it looks sleek instead of messy, and I add chandelier earrings to dress it all up. I change into a royal blue dress with a thick patent-leather black belt in the center that serves absolutely no purpose.

Becca is probably the only person who could take my mind off of the past right now. She is light-hearted and laughs at everything, and I love her for it.

We meet Eric and Becca—whom Everett and I have coined the faux "celebrity" name of Berica—at a quaint new restaurant that serves an array of European entrees and what smells like the most delicious pies I've ever been in the presence of. We have reservations, even though a place this small usually doesn't give out reservations. Enter the perks of Everett's job. As soon as he gives his name to the hostess, everything changes. My guess is the staff was prepped with his name and the typical "Give him the best service you've ever given anyone in your life; your job depends on it" speech.

While I have yet to regret getting amazing service from a restaurant, Everett suppresses a sigh when the staff perks up at the name on our reservation.

Eric and Becca, or Berica, are seated on benches just inside the entrance. They are holding hands, nuzzled against each other as though they are keeping each other warm in freezing weather. Her engagement ring glitters even in the restaurant's dim lighting. I remember those days, when the infatuation runs alongside the love. Sometimes I even miss them.

When Becca sees us, she hops out of the booth and wraps her arms around me. She's a hugger, and usually I'm not, but right now, I could use the warm embrace. I lean into her. As she pulls back, she squints her eyes at me, "You okay?" she asks in her British accent that I adore. Sometimes I ask her open-ended question just so she'll talk more.

How she knows something could be up is beyond me, but her superpower is empathy.

"Uh huh," I answer behind my thin-lipped smile.

"I don't believe you for a second, but I'll let it go for now." She whispers so only I can hear. "Later."

I nod, then follow the hostess to our table and slide into the booth next to Everett. I don't want this night to be about me or what today represents for me. I want to be able to push it aside and enjoy dinner. But the fact that it's been ten years shakes me. So much has happened, and Levi missed all of it.

As Becca scoots in the booth across from me, she flips her hair over her shoulder so that she doesn't sit on it. Becca's second superpower is her Rapunzel hair. I don't know exactly how that becomes a superpower, but it just is.

The waitress brings the bar menu over, with a reflective smile and a nose ring, however it's clear that she doesn't know whether Eric is the concierge she should impress or Everett. My husband isn't going to make it obvious. "I'll just have water."

"Who cares about the drinks menu when there's a pie menu?" Becca says, laughing with the waitress, then ordering a cocktail.

"Ah!" Becca shrieks as she stares at the menu. "You have mincemeat pie?"

The waitress stops and returns to our table. Her bright red lipstick frames her smile. "We do. There's a story behind it, but I won't bore you with that."

I stare at her. *You have no idea,* I want to retort, but it will make no sense to anyone because my young Mincemeat nickname and story is yet another thing about myself that I have not shared. Of course, I don't have a clue what the restaurant's mincemeat pie story is, but I guarantee mine's worse.

"Have you tried mincemeat pie?" Becca beams at me with her big, brown, excited eyes.

"Oh, yes, I have," I answer, trying to appease her so she won't place the order.

"It's actually a traditional Christmas dish, but who cares! I haven't had one since being here in the States," Becca says. Then to the waitress, "I'm from Wales."

"No kidding," the waitress says, but I can't read if its sarcasm or not.

Everett leans toward the waitress. "Have you ever had anyone order the mincemeat pie?" he asks with a smirk.

She bites her red lip, but the lipstick does not rub off onto her teeth. "No, never." She laughs a little.

"You simply have to try it." Becca is still going.

"Alright, we'll be the first," Everett says. "Bring us the mincemeat pie."

My stomach grumbles in what could be perceived as a growl but I recognize as a dreaded groan.

Still, Becca isn't finished. I don't know that I've ever seen her so overtly excited. "Change my drink order. Do you have a port wine or maybe some sherry?"

They confer while I am desperate to think of an excuse why I can't eat the pie. I refuse to tell my story. It took years to shake that nickname, and ever since we gave Berica their name, they've been trying to nickname us as well. I cannot hand them this foolproof ammunition.

When the pies come out, I'm in worse than expected. They are little individual pies. Eight to be exact, the size of mini-muffins, with a star-shaped crust atop each and a shake of powdered sugar. They're cute, I admit. My excuses evaporate and seeing Becca so excited makes my guilt less palatable. That's right, my guilt tastes like mincemeat pie. Becca passes out two pieces for each of us.

I remember a trick my mom used on Robbie when he didn't want to eat his broccoli. She'd have him plug his nose before he put a bite in his mouth to hide the taste. Then he'd chew with his mouth wide open, only unplugging his nose after he'd swallowed. I think Mom even made it into a biology lesson for us, showing how the sense of smell and taste work together. Mom could make anything into a lesson.

As I sit with two mincemeat minis in front of me, I try to work out how I could plug my nose without anyone seeing. This night could do without another memory of growing up with Levi...as much as it could do without my throwing up mincemeat like when I was eleven. Before I can finish my thought, Everett picks up an entire piece and throws the whole thing in his mouth. One bite. He chews, makes a "huh" face, then swallows. "Not bad," he says.

What?! I want to crawl under the table.

"Now sip this sherry. They pair together brilliantly," Becca says. She has her knife and fork in hand, attempting to cut her bite-size piece even smaller.

147

When Eric takes his bite, he doesn't look as pleased as Everett, but he eats it nonetheless.

I'm in a nightmare. They're all looking at me to take a bite next.

"I've tried mincemeat before. It's not my favorite. You can have mine, Becca, since you love it."

Of course she objects. So I bite into the soft crust and textured filling, trying my best to keep my face from utter disgust. After two almost-gags, I swallow the chunky, mushy mess in my mouth without vomiting. I call that success.

Becca trills with laughter. "Now drink this." I down the sherry like its water after cough syrup, then smack my lips.

"It's an acquired taste for some." She's still laughing. "Good on you for trying anyway."

The taste left in my mouth, regardless of the sherry, is exactly how I feel about this entire day.

***

The parking lot streetlights loom above our car. Clusters of bugs swarm under the light like dancing dust particles. With the moon providing a backdrop, it is oddly magical.

Everett opens my door for me.

"Thank you," I say, barely glancing his way. But in that glance, his expression catches my eye. His dark eyebrows are knit together, furrowed lines appear in his forehead that I don't remember being there this morning.

The door closes on my thoughts, so I wait until he strolls around the back of the car and opens his own door. His keys jangle in his hands as he folds himself into his seat. He takes a deep breath that matches the breath of the car engine coming to life.

I swallow, the aftertaste of mincemeat lingering, even after dinner. I should have known this conversation was coming. I could feel it in the atmosphere like rain before a thunderstorm.

"What's going on with you today?" Everett beats me to the starting line. I'm not sure that has ever happened. "Is this still about Leslie calling last night?"

"What?" That catches me entirely off-guard. My mind is in such a different place already. "No, no, that's not it. I mean," I press my fingers into my brow bone, pushing away the headache this talk is already becoming. "That's not all of it."

"But the phone call *is* part of it." He lays his head back against the seat's headrest, his blonde hair blending in with the taupe leather. "Maggie, how many times do I have to tell you—"

"It's not about Leslie, okay?"

He stares at the car's ceiling. "Then what is it about?" The breath in him whistles out quietly, deflating him like a flat tire. "Are you unhappy?"

A month ago I would have answered with a definitive *no*, but if I'm honest about the last few days, I'm not so sure.

My hesitation answers for me.

"Maggie," my name fractures in his mouth. When I meet my husband's eyes, he is the nearest to crying I have seen him since the day he proposed to me.

"Unhappy isn't the right word." That is a horrible way of deflecting, but if I tell him the full truth, I'd have to explain a side of me that Everett wouldn't even recognize. I'd have to admit that I am pining after a boy who died and a version of me that died with him.

"What is the right word then?"

"There's just a lot going on right now. It's not that I'm unhappy. Maybe discontent." As soon as the word passes over my tongue, I know it is accurate.

Everett rubs his fingers into his neck. Me, the pain in his neck. "Discontent with what exactly?"

"Life."

He scoffs. "I thought this was what you wanted."

"It was. It is. Look, I don't even know what I would change. Or if I would change anything at all." I stumble over myself; my thoughts are so cloudy. "I think maybe I'm in a confusing head space. Today was a weird day."

"What happened today?"

This is my chance. I bite my lip trying to get the words to come out. *Today is the ten-year anniversary of the death of one of my best friends.* It's a simple sentence to say but complicated to deliver. I prod myself, *Just say it, Maggie.*

I shrug. "Nothing in particular." Why can't I tell him? Here he thinks *he's* doing something wrong, but it's me. I don't want him to think that I wished I had married someone else. That he is a close second place. That would hurt him even more, wouldn't it? I don't want him to look at me differently.

What is wrong with me that I can have everything I have ever wanted but still look over my shoulder longing for what I left behind? I sit next to a man who loves me with his whole heart, and whom I love deeply. Yet I'm wishing for more. Guilt slips out of me like tears. How many people have lost everything they loved or never felt loved to begin with, and here I am living a postcard-picturesque life and I'm still wishing for something else. My heart always wanting something it doesn't have.

"What can I do?" Everett asks.

"Nothing. I'm sorry I'm so off. I just—" I shrug, "Maybe I just need some time."

"What kind of time?" In his face, I see what he thinks I am implying.

"Oh, no. Not that kind of time." I grab his hand across the car's console, reassuring him. "I'm not going anywhere, and I don't want you to go anywhere. I just need to figure some things out for myself. Why I'm feeling this way. What I want to do differently. I promise, it's nothing you've done or not done."

Everett tilts his head with a smirk to lighten the atmosphere. "Really, Maggie? 'It's not you, it's me.' I haven't heard that since high school." We both chuckle.

"I love you," I say, meaning every syllable. I grab his hand and kiss his palm. "Can we go home now?"

His hurt expression has hardly changed, but he nods and puts the car in drive.

***

I wait until he is asleep to pull the purple box out from under the bed.

After I undress him and let him undress me. After we make love and he smiles at me as though he believes me, but I still see uncertainty behind his eyes. After he kisses me and rolls on his side, with his bare back to me, and heaves the deep breath of sleep, that's when I pull out the box.

I gently tug on its gold handles, pick it up and tiptoe bare feet across wooden floors to the office. Sitting on the floor, I curl my legs under me as I lift the lid again. Walls and rooms stand between Everett and me, but I still work to make little noise.

Opening up these memories, remembering what the 17-year-old me thought life would become, all the possibility, all the hope, I wonder what she would think of 27-year-old me.

Maggie Thayer of 1999 was cautious but hopeful. She wanted life to crack the shell of safety. She wanted to observe interesting people and write about them; to expand the borders of her mind, not stay put and build new borders. She saw the world brimming with wonder.

Would she look at Everett and see safety? Would her face sag at the pile of books I have edited rather than written?

I summon an image of my husband beneath the sheets, his rumpled hair, the slightest bit of the day's scruff on his chin that will be shaved clean in the morning.

We are only two years in to a lifetime of marriage, if I've already lost the stomach full of butterflies, then what will happen at five or ten years? Does every one give up a piece of themselves in relationships? Is that normal? Should it be?

I picture my mother while I was growing up, wearing old clothes so that we could have new ones for school, mopping the floors after we trekked in mud, choosing family vacation destinations instead of quiet ones with Dad. What else did she give up for my dad or for us kids? She and Dad are still married, happy and ready for grandchildren, but was there a time that she was discontent in her decisions? She has never said, and though we talk nearly every day, I've never asked.

These aren't the sort of questions you ask out loud.

After Levi, I didn't date for a couple years. I couldn't. Every face was held against his. If I moved on, a shadow might be cast over my feelings for him, and I couldn't let that happen. I went to my senior prom stag, dancing the night away with Ally, pretending I wasn't disappointed to be there alone. My first kiss after Levi was in college with a guy named Jordan, whose hair was too gelled and lips too dry. Another guy I dated had no ambition beyond what party he would attend that weekend. One guy (whose name I don't remember) asked if I'd tried Kama Sutra before the appetizer even arrived. I didn't stay for the meal.

On those days, I would come back to my bedroom, pull out this purple box from beneath my bed and sift through the pages of these letters. I would remind myself of who every guy had to match up to: Levi. The proverbial deck was stacked against every man. Until Everett.

He was the only man who felt like a warm blanket on a chilly day. He felt like home.

I returned after our first date to the purple box as always, returned to Levi's letters, but I didn't find as big of a gap between the boy of my childhood dreams and the man who had just dropped me off on my apartment's porch. Those first few months almost felt like cheating. Cheating on the memory of Levi. Somehow cheating on my future with Levi that would never happen.

Until one day, I forgot to pull out the purple box. I forgot to remind myself what I was missing. Because I didn't feel like I was missing something anymore. I had Everett.

Life metamorphosed into chasing the next goal. Get the job. Marry the man. Find the home. Here I am standing in this life that checks every box. I have found everything I'd hoped to find. But now I wonder, is it enough?

Parents and family and friends, they walk through the valleys with us, so they are happy wherever we succeed. But our own disappointments are the hardest to overcome. Over time, they look less like disappointments and more like grooves that we settle into. The day in, day out, monotony of life. Quicksand that pulls you in deep before you realize it's a place you didn't want to be.

I'd had dreams of being a modern day Jo March. Never needing a man to validate myself but finding a husband who complimented me instead of completing me. Writing manuscripts until my fingers calloused. Creating stories from my depths that moved people to tears.

But in the end, I was Beth, scared to step out of the ordinary. I was Meg, following in footsteps of tradition.

In front of me, the office floor is covered in unboxed letters and unearthed dreams.

Guilt crashes in to me as I think of Everett, lying in our bed, unknowing, dreaming of our future together. I want that future. Just as much as I question it, I want it. I want to see our babies, meet them, hold them, see his beautiful features mixed with mine, our expressions and emotions melding into a little human being. I want to know the man Everett will become, and the woman he will encourage me to be.

But I don't want to be sitting in this office ten years from now, wondering if I made the wrong choices.

Yet I know, if I continue the way I am, I'll still regret something.

How can any of us ever know if we did the right thing?

If I had run out the door with Levi instead of watching him on the porch waving at me through the window, would I have had the chance to see him grow up, to marry him, to share a home with him?

If I had taken Drew home to my grandparents and had that special dinner with them instead of staying at the field party, would the five of us still be knit together in friendship?

If I would have returned to Michigan even once after the funeral, would Juju have lived out her plans instead of giving them up?

I want it all. I want both sides of this future I see. But I can't have it, can I?

The letters sit atop the pile now. His handwriting reaches out to me. Linear, clean lines. Always in blue for some reason. The top envelope has lightning bolts drawn across the front. I remember Mom—the only person in my world who knew Levi wrote me letters—saying, "I don't know how those letters get to you with so many drawings on the envelopes. I pity the postman." I can still see her smirk as she sneaked the letters to me.

I touch them with the tips of my fingers ever so softly, as though the ink might smudge my fingertips blue. Even with my gentle touch, I can feel the deep indentations in the paper. I conjure an image of Levi bent over the envelope as it lays on a motorcycle magazine, while he fills the lightning bolts in, drawing short strokes back and forth.

Every letter he sent me was covered with doodles. They weren't amazing drawings, but they were masterpieces to me.

Around the lightning bolts is my name and address in crisp letters—Maggie Thayer—and his return address: From the redhead who lives up north.

Reading it, I smile, just as I did the first time. A wintry postage stamp rests in the corner. On the back of the envelope, over the fold, an entire scene is drawn. A motorcycle in the rain—or maybe snow—under a lamppost. This must have been the response to the letter I'd sent to him recommending he read *The Chronicles of Narnia*.

So this is what we did before the internet and Netflix, I muse to myself.

My breath draws sharp when I handle the last letter he wrote. Well, the last letter he mailed me. Crazy me, ten years later, is still wishing for another letter to be discovered.

Next to the pile of letters, I lay out Juju's Polaroids. I squint, desperate to see Levi's face. I don't remember the color of his eyes. I mean, I know they were green. But how green?

I know his hair was a rusty red. He had freckles, each one I loved one hundred times more than he hated. He smelled of gasoline and motor oil covered up by CK1 cologne.

Underneath the faded Polaroids is a copy of his last school picture. The photograph Rose and Greg had enlarged and framed at the funeral. A copy was printed in Juju's yearbook to honor the loss of a beloved student. It's a nice picture, the way I imagine Rose and Greg wanted everyone to remember him. But it's not how I remember him.

I only remember glimpses of him in motion. An overexposed face staring at me on the dock, then jumping in to the pond instead of kissing me like I wanted him to. A kiss and a touch in a bookstore. Little moments captured here and there. But even those memories fade, same as the Polaroids.

I grab my landline phone and drag it down to my lap, lean my back against the wall and dial the phone number that I still have memorized even though we don't have to memorize phone numbers anymore.

The line picks up after two rings.

"Hey," Juju says. The edges of her lips make a parting sound through the receiver.

"Hey," I say back, reminiscing on the times we talked late at night, twirling the coiled phone cord around index fingers. Back when long-distance phone calls cost by the minute and we had to squeeze all our chats into five or ten-minute increments. "You good?"

She takes an over-sized breath. "I am. Yeah."

Juju and I talk every now and then. We are friends on Facebook and post old throwback pictures together for each other's birthdays, but we are an abridged version of the friends we used to be. Since August 26th when everything faded.

And I haven't been back to Michigan since.

The place that once felt like home turned into the one place I could never visit. I was afraid of what it would be like without him. Afraid to see that everyone else was moving on when I couldn't seem to.

I've only seen Juju once in ten years. At my wedding.

She didn't come to Texas for college like we talked about. She stayed at the University of Michigan, close to home and her parents. She played soccer through college until she graduated. She'd grown more responsible, less fanciful, with every year. It was a bit heartbreaking to watch, honestly, because I'd always counted on Juju and Levi to be the ones to bring adventure and excitement into my world.

"Ten years," I whisper into the phone.

"I know. It seems like ages ago and yesterday at the same time."

Juju isn't married, which still flabbergasts me. When she came down for our wedding, I chided her about it. Who knew I would get married before my supermodel friend, Juju James. Her strawberry red hair has turned more auburn. And I wonder if Levi's would have followed the same path.

"Do you think he'd be bald and fat?" Juju asks, keeping it light as always.

I laugh into the phone. "Definitely not fat. He'd be that guy rock-climbing across America, or whatever new dangerous fad he found."

"But he'd have to wear a bandanna to cover his receding hairline," she adds. I fake a chuckle.

"How are your mom and dad?" Thinking of Rose after the funeral, scrubbing the counters even when they were already clean.

"They're really good. Mom and I took flowers out to the graveside at the crack of dawn this morning. Dad couldn't go because he had work. I think he went later. I mean, Mom didn't break down or anything. She's still fixated on heaven and seeing him again someday. She really focuses on celebrating his life and those of us that are still here," she hesitates. "I know she'd love to see you. So would I."

"I'd love to see you guys too," I say, truthfully, but change the subject before Juju can pin me down for more. "How's your dad's auto shop?"

"It's still putting along. He actually just promoted Graham to manager."

"Wow."

I still can't picture Graham working on cars and motorcycles the way Levi had. And I can't imagine Uncle Frank being happy about it either. We all imagined Graham being this high-powered, money-making businessman like Uncle Frank. But when Graham was kicked out of college from all the partying and drugs, Uncle Frank and Aunt Tammy paid his way through rehab. Twice. After he was released, Graham found comfort in the familiar and the easy going, which Greg James has in vast supply.

"I don't think Graham would be doing as well without your dad," I say.

"Yeah, Dad is hoping to pass the shop to Graham one day. It'd almost be like keeping it in the family."

"You don't seem happy about that."

"I'm not sure."

I don't know what to say to that, more proof of the big black hole Levi left that turned everyone into something they weren't before.

"So, how was your day?" Juju jumps in at my pause, feeling the tension. "You didn't wallow, did you?"

"No," I lie. "I was working on a book all day. Then Everett and I had dinner plans with some friends."

"Berica?"

"Yeah," I laugh that she remembers their couple name.

"How's the book you're working on? Is it riddled with errors that you are solving with your magic editor wand?"

I feel a draw toward my desk. Often when I can't sleep, I sneak in here and work. "This one's actually not bad. It's a historical mystery, and I've only noted a couple holes in the story."

"Can't wait to read it." After a pause, she adds, "When are you going to write your own?"

Why does this question haunt me so?

"Maybe it'll be the same year I come up to visit you."

"Oh no," Juju squeals, "Don't let it take that long!"

When our laughter rests, Juju is the one to get quiet. When she finally speaks, her voice is soft. "I miss you."

"I miss you too."

"But seriously, I miss you here. I lost Levi, then slowly I lost every one of my best friends." Her words pierce through the phone line. They strike me in every nerve. "Come back. Just for a visit. Bring Everett." She is pleading now. "Mom and Dad would love to meet him. And your grandparents would too." She knows that's a bruise.

"Sometime."

"Promise?"

"Yes, I promise." The lie slips through my lips with ease. I've been making this promise for ten years.

I start to place the phone receiver back in its cradle, when I hear Juju saying my name through the speaker.

"Maggie," her voice is a ragged, high pitch.

"Hey, I'm here."

"There's something—" she swallows, hesitating. "There's something I should have told you a long time ago. I think—I think I was waiting for you to come here again, to tell you in person. I don't know. But now it's been so long that I'm afraid you'll hate me for not telling you."

The metronome of my heart beats faster. "Juju, what are you talking about? You're freaking me out."

"Levi didn't die the way everyone thinks."

Fourteen

Blood pulses in my ears, the sound throbbing over Juju's voice. I have to focus to hear the words she says. And I still barely understand them.

"What do you mean Levi didn't die the way everyone thinks? Juju, what happened?"

"I told everyone that I drove up on his accident and found him. But I didn't. I was there, Maggie. And I wasn't alone." The words choke her on their way out.

"Tell me, Juju."

But I don't want my world to shatter all over again, even though I can feel the plaster of it cracking already.

"Graham called and said he wanted to meet up at the Industrial for a last hurrah before his senior year. I thought it was going to be a big party, that's what I told Mom. Levi was at work, and I assumed Graham had called him and invited him too. But Levi came home from work before I left."

I picture Levi, as best as I remember him, standing clad in his work uniform, name tag and all, casually asking where Juju was heading all spruced up.

"I thought he was joking. I asked him if he was coming, but he hadn't gotten a call from Graham." She hiccups between scenes. "I didn't know why, but Levi jumped on his motorcycle and raced to the Industrial. I was so confused because he wasn't in his right mind. I tried to catch up, but I got stuck at a red light." She catches herself before letting her emotions escape. "Of course, Levi didn't wait for me. He didn't want me going at all. When I drove up, their motorcycles were the only one's there. Just Graham and Levi."

What Juju had thought would be a whole group was only Graham waiting for her.

And after what happened at the Industrial when Drew and I were in town, then at the field party...

"I would have thought the same thing Levi did," I tell her.

She is quiet, but surely she agrees.

"They were already inside. I could hear Levi screaming at Graham from the parking lot. The door was open. You know how that place is, it's so close to other buildings and houses. I didn't want anyone to hear them, so I closed the door behind me."

Levi's letters and pictures still scatter the floor in front of me. My eyes blur over them while I picture the vacant building we'd been in a decade ago. I may not be able to remember the exact shade of Levi's eyes but I can see the fire in them the night of the field party. I remember Juju telling me that if he knew about what happened with me and Roman in the school hallway, he would drive all the way to Texas to handle what Drew wouldn't. Instinct tells me what Juju's about to say.

I am in her mind as she purges the story from her thoughts into mine. Even though the words are coming through the phone, I hear them as Levi's words to Graham, "You think you're going to invite her here all by herself? Did you think you were finally going to bang my sister? Is that your big hurrah?"

A push. Graham stumbles backwards, tipsy from a couple beers but not drunk like in the field, so he can hold his own this time.

"Don't be stupid, Levi." Arrogance steeps each of Graham's words.

"Did you think I wouldn't come? You think because we're 'bro's' that I'd just sit back and let you touch her?"

"That's not what—"

Another push. "Shut the hell up and listen for once."

"Levi, please. Just calm down." Juju's voice echoes off the concrete but doesn't seem to reach Levi's ears.

He points his finger in Graham's face, both still bruised from the beating in the field. "You forget I know who you are, Graham, and I know what you've done. I won't let you do it to my sister."

Those words startle me out of my imaginings. "What was he talking about Juju?"

"I don't know what he was talking about. I never asked," she whimpers, crying. She hates crying. "I still don't know."

"What did Graham do?"

"They were going back and forth. Graham was trying to defend himself, saying Levi had it all wrong." When she inhales, her nose wheezes.

I hold my breath. I don't want her to say what I think she's about to say.

"Levi had Graham by the collar. He kept shaking him, yelling at him."

I can hear their voices in my head, and I wasn't even there.

"Graham finally got his hands under Levi's. He pushed him." Our breath and voices stay suspended in the miles between us. "He pushed him really hard."

"Who?" Maybe it's cruel, but I force her to say it. "Juju, who pushed whom?"

"Graham. He was just trying to get Levi to let go. But Levi tripped backwards and hit his head on the concrete. When he got up, he was swaying back and forth." She pauses a beat. When she starts again, her words are laced with tears. "I knew something wasn't right, Maggie. I told Graham to leave, to let it go. But I couldn't stop Levi. He jumped on his bike and followed Graham. I don't know where they were heading, but I got in my car and followed them. Levi was driving so reckless, trying to run Graham off the road or cut him off. Then I don't know, his tire just went into the gravel and he lost control."

I lay my head against the wall behind me. Every muscle in my body is taut, and I can't manage to relax any of them.

I remember my mom telling me how his body flew the opposite direction of his motorcycle. How his helmet popped off his head the moment he landed on the back of his neck, nearly severing his spinal cord. I remember how I pictured it all in detail, just as I am now. Except when I pictured it before, he was alone.

"I slammed on the brakes because I thought I was going to hit him." Juju gasps for breath and then again between her words, "Graham was running—toward me—when I stood over him."

I'm in her head again, staring at Levi's crumpled body on the concrete. Her shriek is stifled by her hands.

"You have to leave, Graham."

"Juju," Tears thread Graham's voice.

"Now, Graham. You have to leave now." She stands and looks him in the eyes. Always a pillar of strength.

"But—"

Juju stretches her arm out to him to keep him at a distance, to protect him from seeing those sage green eyes, already darkening. "Too many people were at the field party. They heard what you said. They saw what Levi did to you. If anyone finds you here, smells your breath…Graham, you have to leave. I'll take care of him."

Trembling as he goes, Graham stumbles backwards to his motorcycle. She hears him whisper, "I'm sorry," under his breath. Juju listens for his motorcycle engine to start up, then drive further and further away.

She breathes life into her big brother. Watching *ER* for years at least taught her not to move someone with a neck injury—she knows it is injured by its horrible angle—but she can't go for help without leaving Levi. There is no other choice. She runs. Not down the road, but into the neighborhood nearby. "Someone call 911!" She cries over and over, as loud as her throat allows, hoping the same people who emerge from their homes to help have been too caught up in life to notice the other motorcycle that just left.

A woman comes running, the fabric of her yellow skirt floating behind her, and she hollers that her husband is calling 911. Juju spins her story of an adventurous brother and his high speed loss of control.

"They all believed me. They didn't have any reason to not. Everyone knew the way Levi always pushed the limits. I told Mom that we'd waited for Graham but that no one ever showed."

"Oh Juju. Why didn't you ever say anything?"

"I couldn't."

There was a time when Juju and I could tell each other everything, but Levi had become the secret between us.

"It wasn't Graham's fault, Maggie. He didn't do anything."

Levi seemed to think otherwise, and it cost him everything.

"It was just an accident," Juju says, but I can tell there is more. "I'm as much to blame as Graham."

"No. You are not." I wish the phone and distance would disappear so that I was next to her.

"Graham and I never spoke about it."

"You've held this all alone for so long. How could you not tell me?"

"It's wrecked his life enough, don't you think? I didn't want to do that to anyone else."

I was good at secrets. I could have been there for her, but she didn't even give me the chance. I'm mad at Graham for taking her from me as much as taking Levi.

"Maggie, I had already lost Levi; I couldn't lose Graham too."

We all lost something that day. We lost each other. If she had shared the heaviness of the secret, it could have bonded us together in a new way.

The silence we sit in stretches out the darkness. Then her quiet voice passes through the phone.

"Don't hate him," she pleads.

But I don't know if I can make that promise.

"Don't hate me." Juju adds. And I hear my heart break.

**

I hang up carefully, like the sound could wake Everett. But I'm not ready yet to go back to this life.

When I flew home after the funeral, I left so much behind. A second home. A family. A vision of myself I barely recognize. I had to learn to be human again.

My grief didn't always make sense. I didn't lose my brother the way Juju had. Levi and I had only ever kissed, and yet my soul was entwined with his. As though pieces of me were broken the moment he crashed. Like the gravel embedded in his body had embedded my heart, altering my very existence.

Without him, I didn't know how to go back and see all the places he had been. To go back to my grandparent's home, look out that window, see the ghost of him on the porch, with his hand in the air.

But it had all been a lie.

Yes, Levi was still dead. But maybe things could have been different if I had known the truth. But my best friend had lied to me. She'd lied to everyone.

Except Graham. All this time, Graham had known her better than I had. The one person who shouldn't. Her lie hadn't saved him. We still lost him to drugs and alcohol. Now, he was working in Levi's exact job, taking his place. How could Juju forgive him, not to mention stay silent for him?

I fumble through the purple box next to me and retrieve the mix tape labeled, "Rad Tunes" in Levi's handwriting. I dig further into the box until I uncover the Walkman saved for this one cassette tape. I push play and lie down, curling my body around the mounds of letters and photos. The headphones adjust against my ear, with a crinkly sound of the foam over the earpiece. The first track begins, just as I remember: Pink Floyd's

"Wish You Were Here."

By the time Syd Barrett calls us lost souls in a fish bowl, my face and neck are wet with thick tears. I feel more lost now than ever. Going back to Michigan seems like the only way to find my way again. Remind me of who I was. Convince Juju that the truth could save us.

Even though I'm not sure yet if Graham is worth saving, but he shouldn't be powerful enough to ruin us all.

I don't believe we are too far gone. Even if Levi is. Maybe we can still break out of our fishbowls.

Fifteen

My eyes are closed, but the sun glows bright through my eyelids. I must have fallen asleep, but I don't actually remember. With heavy eyelids that don't want to peek at morning yet, I feel the bed next to me. It's empty. Everett must be getting ready for work, so I will do as I always do and lay here until his good-bye kiss.

Bedsprings squeak under my weight as I adjust my pillow. Our mattress is only two years old, so it shouldn't be squeaking already. One spring jabs between my ribs, as though it's trying to keep me awake. I groan at the valiant attempt.

No idea how long I stayed in the office last night. Did Everett find me and bring me to bed? Will he ask me about the letters and pictures?

The stirring of my questions convinces me to open my eyes. My faces feels puffy, like the morning after crying to a sad movie. Then I remember the call. Juju. Graham. The lie. I groan to myself and the new world I have woken up to. Morning glares at me and my vision is blurry with sleep. But I see the outline of something I don't quite recognize. A vanity. I don't own a vanity.

My eyes squeeze shut then I peel them open again. They are less blurred this time, and the vanity still stands in front of me, tilted at the angle of my head on the pillow. A doily rests on its wood surface.

This is all vaguely familiar. Where do I know this place from? It's like a bed and breakfast.

I didn't have that much to drink at dinner last night. Why am I so confused?

Something reflects in the vanity mirror. A porcelain doll that I recognize. I am instantly awake, aware of every breath I take, every tingle in my nerves. If I roll over and the doll is still there, I'll know where I am.

A breath leaves my lips slowly as I urge myself to move. I roll over. The porcelain doll is there, blonde hair with scarlet lips and a puffy blue dress. But not just one doll, there is a brunette one on the window sill and one on the rocking chair with a parasol in hand. I bolt up. I'm in grandparent's house. Theirs is the only house I would actually walk into with this many dolls. All of the blank eyes are on me at once, staring at me with dead expressions. I almost scream. Then I laugh at myself for almost screaming.

My hand goes to my head feeling for a hangover. Or even a head injury at this point. But there isn't one. I sit up stock straight, and the bed creaks. That bit makes sense now. Grandma's guestroom bed has creaked forever. No wonder she made us kids sleep on it.

A face meets me in the vanity mirror. My dull brown hair is up in a frizzy ponytail—I haven't worn it up at night since I was a kid. My under eyes are unlined. My fingers press into my cheeks, which feel tight and plump. Then I notice my unmanicured nails. There are no lines in my hands, no wrinkly knuckles, and no wedding ring.

"Holy hell," I say aloud. I've never had a dream feel so real.

My stomach churns with a mixture of bile and hunger. Leaving this room opens the potential of running into someone and speaking with them. But I need to understand where I am. *When* I am. Just thinking that makes me want to throw up. If I consider that this is anything other than a dream, then I'm insane. A bubble of excitement resides next to the panic. I can't decide between the two. So I pinch myself. Isn't that what you're supposed to do to wake from a dream? Nothing happens.

I swing bare feet over the edge of the bed. Wood floors should be beneath me, but instead I place my feet on something soft, squishy, moving.

"What the hell?" Drew barks. "Damn, Maggie, get off me."

There lays my big brother, on the air mattress we used to take turns sleeping on. Shaggy-haired, smooth-faced Drew.

The last time I saw him, he had a dark goatee and the beginnings of a beer belly.

A delirious giggle seeps out. "Sorry. I didn't know you were there."

"Whatever. You embezzled the bed out from underneath me." He rolls onto his back, hairless chest exposed above the blanket. His mouth hangs open after speaking, the way it so often did. I'd forgotten that.

"Embezzled. That's a big word for you so early in the morning."

"Shut up." But his words are already slurred with sleep. Then he is out.

I wish I could fall back asleep as easily as he had. But I'm also relieved that I don't have to sit and talk with him. Oh god, teenage Drew talked so much.

An idea occurs to me. I lean down in Drew's ear and whisper, "Drew, what year is it?"

He swats at me like I am a swarming mosquito on a summer night. But I am a determined, lost girl.

"This is a dream, Drew. What year is it?" I try again.

He mutters and mumbles, "I don't know. 1999. Go away."

1999.

What the hell?

***

"Ohmigod. Ohmigod. Ohmigod. Ohmigod. Ohmigod." I can't stop saying it. I can't stop pacing on the tile floor of the bathroom. In my grandparent's house. In Michigan. In 1999.

I've never had a panic attack before, but right here in this bathroom, there is a good chance I am having one. Who wouldn't if they fell asleep as an adult on their office floor only to wake up a teenager in their grandparent's home?

I pinch myself again, because honestly I can't think of anything else to do. My grimace is caught in the mirror, but I keep on pinching, using my nails this time. Harder.

Pinching doesn't work, but I've left myself with two fingernail-shaped indentations on my arm that are sure to bruise.

"Okay, so it's a dream I can't wake up from," I say aloud to my teenage self. With every word, my hands flail around. "I just have to go about the day and try not to act crazy. Or think about how I'm stuck here." I stop and look at myself in the mirror. "This could be fun. You can do this," I say sternly to my wide-eyed reflection.

"You don't have a choice," my reflection says back.

Between the letters and talking to Juju before falling asleep, plus the mincemeat pie at dinner, I shouldn't be surprised to wake up in a dream about my teenhood in Michigan. But I've never been so aware of a dream before.

Interaction is inevitable, I decide, so I take a deep breath, puff out my cheeks, blow the breath back out, and thrust the door open.

My feet take me into the hallway without my input, the way they do in a dream. Then I'm in the kitchen next to an armoire of teapots and teacups with various patterns.

Grandma sits at the round breakfast table with her back to me. Her weathered hand is carefully holding her teacup. It's the Old Country Rose china pattern by Royal Albert. I know this because she sent Everett and me a set for our wedding, even though she couldn't come. Her doctor doesn't let her travel anymore since her heart started acting up. Plus, she couldn't bear to leave Grandpa in the home alone with only the nurses. She was concerned he wouldn't remember why she was gone.

I haven't seen either of them in about six years, and my heart thumps against my ribs as I look at her slight frame seated in front of me.

Her brown hair is curled under at her shoulders but still messy in the back from sleep. She doesn't hear me walk up behind her which gives me time to work up the nerve to say her name, have her turn, to see her face.

"Good morning, Grandma," I stutter.

When she turns around, I see how young she looks. I mean,

she still looks old, but younger. Weathered but not threadbare. Now I see how taking care of Grandpa has aged her in the last decade.

"Oh, good morning, Magdalene. Did you sleep well?"

That was the million-dollar question, wasn't it?

"Not really. I had some weird dreams," I answer, looking around the room, grappling for anything that could tell me the day or remind me of what has been going on.

"You're up early for being out late last night. Will you join us at church or would you rather stay home with Drew?" She asks, as her hand warbles to bring her teacup to her lips.

"Church?" I ask, buying time to evaluate if staying home with Drew would be more trouble than going to church with my grandparents and all of their friends. "This morning?"

"It's fine if you want to stay home from church so you can go out with your friends this afternoon," she says. The teacup clangs against the saucer as her hands trembles.

"My friends?" I repeat, still watching her hands as she rubs one palm. That must be her arthritis setting in.

"Yes, your friends, dear. Juju James and that brother of hers and your cousin." She stands and narrows her eyes at me. "Do you need a cup of tea to caffeinate that brain of yours?"

I chuckle, trying to remember how I might have laughed as a teenager. I am no longer awkward the way I was at 17, and I have a feeling that could get me in trouble in this dream world.

"So?" Grandma stares at me.

"Friends. Yeah," I punctuate with a nod, but inside I'm having trouble keeping my thoughts straight.

"Yes," Grandma corrects. With a sigh, she shuffles to the sink, washes out her teacup, dries it, and returns it to the cupboard. I watch her every movement, aching with how much I have missed her.

When she turns, I haven't moved a centimeter. She raises her thinning eyebrows at me. "Are you feeling alright?"

"Yes, I'm fine." I smile. "I think I will go to church with you and Grandpa this morning." It's been so long since I've seen them that I realize I want to spend as much time with them as I can, even if it's only a dream. I want to reach for her and hug her even now. But by the look on her face, I know she would think something was gravely wrong with her granddaughter—which I guess is true—so I refrain.

"Oh. Alright, then. Grandpa and I would enjoy that." She treads by me down the hall, then turns to add, "Don't forget, this afternoon is the Homegrown Festival. I'll invite Ms. James to drive with us if you'd like."

My smile drops and decade-old memories streak across my mind. The Homegrown Festival. Of course.

I know what day it is.

Today is the last day I saw Levi James alive.

Sixteen

Tiptoeing through the bedroom to the closet so as not to wake Drew, I grab my clothes. I remember exactly what I wore on this day, and I don't have to rummage around for long since there are half as many clothes of mine in the closet as Drew's. My Doc Marten's rest in the corner. I smile at them. "Hello, friends," I whisper, before grabbing them up and tiptoeing back to the bathroom.

Slipping into my teenage wardrobe is like dressing up for a '90s costume party as Claire Danes circa *My So Called Life*. I mean, she was my style icon. The bob haircut, plaid flannels, the Doc Martens. My feet meet the soles of these boots with a comfortable welcome, returning to one of their favorite places in the entire world. I tie the laces, wrap the flannel sleeves around my waist, then glance in the mirror.

Actors talk about fully becoming their character when they don the costume, the makeup, the hairstyle. They look in the mirror and have become someone new.

But I have become someone familiar.

***

A sweet aroma overwhelms me as the door opens to the donut shop where my grandparents stop before church. A sugar high could seep into my blood stream without taking a single bite.

Grandpa buys me an apple fritter, calling it my favorite, apparently remembering something about my childhood that I don't.

But I don't care that I don't really like apple fritters or that I haven't had this much sugar in I don't know how long. Because I am standing next to my grandfather, looking him in the eyes. He doesn't say a lot—he never has—but it's more than I've heard his voice in years.

He was diagnosed with dementia four years ago. Well, back in my real life he was. And he has hardly spoken to anyone except Grandma since. She says he barely even talks to his nurses. So standing next to him, listening to his clipped words that come out like grunts, accepting the apple fritter from his strong, calloused hands, I take in every moment I can. He's wearing his boots and wrangler jeans, even on the way to church, but dressed up with a nice button-down and no John Deere hat.

A couple of farmer friends that I don't remember are seated at the circular table next to us. The room is bright, the patrons are cheery, and my grandparents know every single one of them. My grandmother is in her element, flitting from table to table, talking to the little girls on their way to Sunday school, a family from their Bible study, a young man she hired to mow the lawn when Grandpa was down with the flu earlier this year.

I used to hate the way they would take us grandkids out to do something "together" and then spend most of the time talking to people they see in town every week. But now I feel nostalgic. It's an odd feeling to have nostalgia *while* you are living through something.

I bite into the warm apple fritter that is bigger than my hand. My tongue tastes the glaze before my teeth even sink into the rich batter, thick with apple pieces. The sugar rush will hit in seconds and I refuse to think about how many calories I'm about to intake, but then I'm 17. This what being a teenager is all about. So I eat the entire fritter.

I lick my fingers as we head out the door for church, and everyone says goodbye to my grandparents—and to me by proxy—like we are town celebrities. I smile and wave at people who know my name but whom I don't remember ever meeting.

"Dear," Grandpa says in his husky voice and gestures a thick finger to his upper lip as though he is wiping something off.

"Oh," I say when I realize what he means. Raising my hand to my own upper lip, I feel a thick clump of glaze left behind. I brush it off with a laugh. "Well, Grandpa, that's just how much I enjoyed it."

"That's nice to hear," he says with a chuckle.

My reaction is a surprise because my 17-year-old self would have been mortified to have passed through the room and spoken to people with something on her face. Just as mortified as my 27-year-old self would be to have eaten an entire apple fritter.

Wherever I am, this is the best of both worlds.

***

Growing up in church was never a hassle to me. Sure, there were plenty of times I wanted to sleep in on Sunday morning, but I didn't really mind. I liked church. So I don't mind attending the service with my grandparents.

Grandma and Grandpa's church is a bit different than the church our family attended. Their Methodist church still has pews, hymnals, and stained glass.

When we step through the doors, everyone I see has gray hair. I am greeted with a vigor that says they haven't had a young person visit in a while. Granted, wardrobe-wise, I stick out like a goth chick at Billy Bob's.

I follow my grandparents down the red-carpeted aisles to their pew—the one they sit at every Sunday. Might as well have their names plated on it. As we sit, the sanctuary fills up, and a few younger families enter.

The pastor walks to the podium and picks up the microphone. I remember him being so old, but now that I look at him, he's probably only 45. He might be one of the youngest men here. The starched collar of his buttoned-up shirt under his suit coat squeezes against the skin of his neck.

Before a word has left his mouth, he clears his throat into the microphone. "Good morning," he says. "Welcome," he gestures into the seated crowd, "It's good to see you back in the house of the Lord, Darryl."

Another gray-haired man nods, and a few people in the crowd murmur their agreement.

I melt into the pew so he doesn't notice me and call me out. I may not actually be 17, but even now, that would be mortifying. Thankfully the pastor moves along to a lengthy prayer that includes blessings over a sickly congregant and the upcoming weather.

"Amen," the entire crowd says, and I add my quiet *amen* a few seconds behind. When I open my eyes, the musicians and singers meander on to the platform, instruments and microphones in hands, respectively.

I am surprised to hear an electric guitar, though the volume is turned low, and electric drums playing hymns along with the organ. The organist is as you would expect her to be: glasses, cardigan, pantyhose, and a bun. But there are also two young women singing.

The biggest surprise, however, comes when one singer sways to the music and gives me a brief view of the drummer. A flash of red hair. *No way,* I think to myself, but the metronome of my heart quickens. I step nearer to Grandma, and I see him.

Levi.

My knees lock, and I stand as still as possible, willing him to glance my direction, to see me. I stare so hard that my eyeballs start to hurt, and then I stare some more, hardly blinking or breathing. I know it's a dream, but I no longer want to pinch myself awake.

I had dreams about him after he died. A lot of them. But he rarely ever spoke in the dreams or I woke up just as he was about to. So now that Levi has appeared, I want to make this dream last. I can't wake up until I speak to him, see him up close, hear his voice. Remember the shade of his green eyes.

With death, you think the hardest part is the void they leave aching like a phantom limb. When you pick up the phone or start to write a letter, only to realize they aren't on the other end to receive it. It is the worst conceivable pain.

Until you start to forget. The sound of their voice, the rhythm of their laughter, the gait of their walk. The way your name sounds in their mouth. I've forgotten it all. All I have is the curve of his letters. But now—now I can embed him in my mind again.

The drum beat thunders through me, as though it's the only part of the music playing. In between two beats, his eyes shift and he sees me. He smiles like he's laughing, and I match his smile. A giggle bubbles out of me, but I bite my lip when Grandma gives me the side-eye. Laughter and anxiety and the need to run to him and hug him all boil inside my belly. It takes everything in me to stay in place. He winks and twirls his drum stick in one hand between the beats. I can't take my eyes off him. I won't.

Eventually the music ends, and he leaves the stage. I lose track of him then. I don't see where he sits in the crowd. My leg bounces up and down while the pastor speaks. Grandma notices at some point and places her hand on my knee to calm its movement. As the service seems to finally be coming to a close, ushers stand—which is torture because the usher on our pew requires a cane to raise himself from his seat—to pass the offering plate, and my foot begins to tap.

The pastor takes the platform again. "Now for a closing benediction song." My eyes flit to the drums, but Levi isn't there. There are no drums or no electric guitar for this song. Only the organ and the voices. My eyes flit around the room in an effort to spot him. I even turn and look over my shoulder, which is a big no-no to Grandma and evokes a *tsk* from her.

Over my right shoulder, three or four rows back sits Juju. Strawberry hair floats in layers—a long version of "the Rachel"— toward the shoulders of her flower-patterned dress. She wiggles her fingers at me and mouths, "Hi." I didn't even remember the James' family went to church with my grandparents. I lift my hand in a return wave. But I still don't see Levi. Juju is seated only with her parents.

Seeing her, though, makes my heart soar. Oh how I have missed my best friend.

I right myself, facing forward. All anxiety passes after seeing Juju's face. This dream, it feels too real, but I sit in it, welcoming whatever's next.

The benediction song ends, the pastor prays another lengthy blessing over his congregation, and I pop out of my cushioned pew as soon as he utters the words, "You are dismissed." I refrain from running toward her—running in church would certainly earn a finger wag from my grandmother. But before I can get to Juju, he's there. He saunters over to her, hands in the pockets of his corduroy pants.

In two short strides, I'm next to him—I nearly jump on him—and I hug him big and deep. The kind of hug I usually reserve for my mom. All enveloping.

"Whoa," Greg James says over my shoulder. Ms. Rose is giggling. The couple exchanges a knowing look. They are both so happy, their posture light.

"Hey Maggie," Levi says in my ear. And I think my heart might have stopped for those milliseconds. I instantly remember his voice. I remember everything about him.

In this dream state, I don't care what people think anymore. All inhibitions fade away. So I hug him the way I always wanted to but never got the chance. "Oh my gosh," I say, tears prickling my eyes, but I command them to stay put. Dreams let you get away with a lot, but there is no way I could explain tears in this moment.

He laughs and wraps his arms around my back, not as tight as mine are, but still there. When I inhale the smell of him, I laugh. Just like summer.

After too long, even dream-me realizes it gets weird, but I take my time letting go. I smooth out the button-up shirt he's wearing, my hands grazing over him. He face is flushed; I imagine mine is too.

That's when I notice Juju staring. One eyebrow is raised to point in a way that I've never been able to do. Her lips are parted, and frankly, she looks like she's posing for a picture in a magazine.

A laugh bubbles out of me. Partly because I'm so happy to be standing here with her and Levi. But another part of me realizes this is the first time she is seeing me fawn over him. I try to control my smile. "It's just—I just—it's been so long—" I giggle. "I've missed you. Both of you."

"Yeah, yesterday was a long time ago," Greg says, and Rose swats at him.

Levi's gaze falls to his shoes. He's blushing but also chuckling. His laugh is throaty and full of heart. And I remember it instantly.

I return my eyes to Juju, and she remains frozen.

"Oh, come on," I say, pushing on her shoulder, then pulling her to me and wrapping myself into her. "Is that what you wanted? Were you jealous?" I say, with too big a smile, as we pull back from each other. But it worked. She's smiling.

"Duh. I'm the best friend. If anybody gets a hug, it should be me." And just like that, she's my Juju.

I think of all the things I could tell her. Things that we've spent hours talking about late at night or over the phone or through emails and Instant Messenger. I want to grab her and tell her, I'm actually making a living reading and editing books. I want to tell her all about sex, because I know she'll hold on to her virginity until her junior year of college. I want to rub it in her face that Lance Bass of N'SYNC is gay, which I always knew, and that Justin Timberlake is the one who makes it big, not JC Chasez. That Ross and Rachel do get back together. I know we'll have these conversations in the next few years, but wouldn't it be such fun to tell her right now.

"Alright, love birds," Levi says to me and Juju, and we both roll our eyes. I'm officially 17 again. "I gotta go."

I want to reach out to him, but I don't.

"I wish we could be there," Rose says.

I don't ask where because I'm assuming the 17-year-old me already knows.

"I know," Levi says to her. "It's fine."

She touches his arm in her maternal way. "It's not fine." She tilts her head. "But it's business. And I know you'll do great."

He nods, then kisses her on the cheek. "Love you, Mom."

I'm a puddle, right in the middle of the aisle.

As he leaves, I realize he's talking about the Homegrown Festival. My 17-year-old self didn't know he was playing, and now I wonder why I didn't find out until I saw him on stage. Either way, though, I know that however this dream turns out, I will always picture Levi as he was today, on the drums smiling at me. I will fight for that memory, to never let it fade the way too many others have.

***

Grandma invites Juju to drive with us. I know from memory that she meets me at my grandparent's house but still takes her own car. But it's a dream, right? And dreams take their own direction.

Standing in the living room of my grandparent's house waiting for Grandpa to finish up a couple things in his barn before we head to the festival, I'm sad that I've never brought Everett here. That he's never had the chance to meet my grandparents. I never shared these memories with him, and while this dream feels so real, I keep waiting to wake up, so I can tell him about this crazy dream I had. But that means telling him about Levi and Juju.

He's never pressed me to know why I stopped coming up here. He never knew me and Juju as we are right now. He's only known the faded version of Juju, the girl who retains the title of best friend without having to show up. I'm sad Everett never got to know my grandfather when he could warm you from the inside out with only a couple of words. That Everett has never seen this house that Drew and I spent countless hours fixing up, or the golf course that my family helped build and run over decades. Why had I let something from so long ago stop me from experiencing it with him and making new memories?

New memories. Going to church with my grandparents this morning tells me that I don't have to live today the exact way that it happened. I can hug my grandpa again and maybe in real life, he'll feel it.

Standing in my worn-in Doc Martens on this wood floor that Drew and I helped install, I am making new memories, even if I'm the only one who knows it. When I wake up from this dream next to Everett, I will tell him everything. Then we will plan a trip to visit, like we should have long ago.

***

The Homegrown Festival is just as quaint and cute as I remember it. It makes me wish for small-town living instead of being smack-dab in the middle of a big city.

This morning was spent trying to figure out what day it was and doing something new. But being here, exactly where I've been before is even weirder. We arrive at the festival exactly the same way. I couldn't have told you what song was playing or what the band looked like before today, but being here again, I recognized it all immediately.

It's shocking how much I have forgotten in ten years. I thought I'd remember everything. I thought I would remember people's names, my favorite place to eat, movies that came out. At this age, everything is so important, so critical to life. But being here is like reading a yearbook. With every turn of the page I say, *Oh yeah, I remember her.* A constant state of *déjà vu*.

Juju and I walk through the vendor tents, and I remember feeling like it all came so naturally to her. But as I watch her, she's just like anyone else. She asks questions of the vendors, simple questions, how long they've been making soaps (or whatever their product is), if they've always lived around Stone River, if they have kids. She doesn't have some special talent. She just cares. It comes natural to her because their answers matter to her. These people and their stories, they matter. She nods when they tell her something interesting. She laughs at a silly story about their children. She can make friends with anyone because she feels so deeply. And I wish I could feel things the way she does.

Until I remember how her bright eyes faded to gray after Levi died, and I take it back.

When we stroll to the next booth, I snap out of my lull. I'm not that 17-year-old girl spending all of my moments attempting to be someone else, observing how they talk or act or move. No, I'm a grown women—albeit not in a grown woman's body—who has found who she is.

The booth in front of us has interesting repurposed items. A drawer sits on display, but it's no longer a drawer. There are four feet attached to the bottom, making it stand on the table. The outer wood has been painted, and the inside of the drawer has been decoupaged with book pages. I touch the smoothness of the pages that don't feel like pages at all.

A woman behind the table—I'm assuming she is the creator—steps toward me and smiles without a word.

I glance up and ask, "How did you get an idea for something like this?"

The woman adjusts the oval-shaped glasses on her nose. She looks far too young for the streaked gray hair she wears. "I like to see the potential in something that others view as broken or useless. I can give it another life." Her hands follow mine to the drawer, feeling along the smooth surface.

I see the price tag attached to one of the feet. It reads, "Hannah."

"I name them all. Maybe it's silly, but I have to call them something while I restore them." She shrugs and a strand of her braided gray hair comes lose. "The desk she belonged to was broken. So I gave her love. Sanded and smoothed some of the roughness, and I repainted her. But you can see she still has some scars showing." She points to some gashes in the surface of the wood beneath the paint and varnish.

"I love the old book pages too," I say, remembering how I once wanted to wallpaper my room with pages just like this.

The woman adds her agreement in a hum. "She belongs with someone a lot like her. A little broken, roughed up, mix-matched, but beautiful inside and out."

When our eyes meet, I wonder if this woman knows what's happening to me. Like she's my guide through this strange dream. I search her eyes and almost ask in a whisper that only she can hear. Then she looks away and my trance is broken. She's probably only trying to make a sale.

I start to move on, noticing that Juju is far ahead of me, but I turn back to the woman and say, "I hope the right person finds her." And I catch up to Juju.

The folk band is ending their set when we return to the grassy area where my grandparents chat up a family from their Sunday school. I only vaguely remember them but I do remember the conversation that's about to follow. My memory is triggered as soon as I hear a guitar tuning and drum cymbal clang. I turn to look at the stage, this time knowing what I'm going to see. Levi grins at me from behind his drums, as though he knew that I was going to turn and see him even before I did. I smile back and this time I wave.

"Isn't that your twin brother?" Grandma says behind me.

"It is," I hear Juju answer, but I don't turn. My eyes stay locked on Levi's as though he has magnetized them. He twists a knob on his drum kit without even looking away from me. Then he picks up a drumstick and twirls it with his fingers just as he did at church this morning. I'd like to think that he's showing off for me, but I don't think that gesture takes much skill. What do I know?

While the Toilet Bowlers play their cover of "I Wanna Hold Your Hand," a little girl tiptoes up to Juju. I remember the idea of this little girl, but I don't remember her face until I see it. Same with some of the guys in Levi's band. It's strange.

"This is my friend Maggie," Juju is saying. "Maggie, this is Alice."

The little girl pulls Juju by both hands, giggling and twirling in the grass to the music. Their trills of laughter are contagious. "Dance with us," Juju says, and I distinctly remember not dancing. Why didn't I? I guess I didn't want people watching with their judging eyes and critical opinions. Now I glance around and no one is watching. I was the only one who cared.

I slip my shoes off to match their bare feet, and feel the velvety grass beneath my soles.

Next thing I know, they grab my hands and we are twirling, spinning, swinging each other around, laughing. When the song changes, we don't stop.

There is something freeing about dancing with a child, all inhibitions are gone because the only important thing is making the little one smile bigger and giggle louder. Even the adults around us are laughing now and more people have started dancing. The joy of a child is contagious like that. Maybe we all want to remember the carefreeness of childhood, to forget judgments and comparisons, to just twirl and dance and laugh. To feel free. Even for just a moment.

Tendrils of hair stick to my lip gloss when I finally stop spinning with Alice and Juju. We are laughing and dizzy, nearly falling onto the grass beneath us. The heat of the sun warms my back and face. I turn toward the music and see an unobstructed view of the stage and the drummer. He's staring at me, not smiling. Bewildered.

A gaggle of girls have flocked to the stage, swaying to the

music, making themselves seen. And yet the drummer is watching me. I clasp Alice's pudgy hand and ask, "Do you know this song?"

She shakes her head, and I think that's a shame because I grew up hearing all the Beatles songs. "It's a pretty easy song to learn. You wanna run up there by the stage with me?"

Tangled, blond curls bounce when she nods her head.

I gesture to Juju and the three of us rush the stage, still barefoot and laughing. Some of the girls glance over their shoulder at us with competitive eyes. There is Danielle. The girl I can't forget about. The first time I saw her here, she wasn't concerned with anything but Levi. But the way she looks at us, I'm not sure that's true this time. No matter, because Juju and I sing along to "When I Saw Her Standing There" at the top of our lungs. Before long, Alice is singing too, all three of us in a different key.

The lead singer of the band, I don't remember his name, laughs into the microphone and bobbles his head ala Paul McCartney. Each of the guy's stage presence shifts from showing off for these girls to legitimately having fun.

We stay for the whole Toilet Bowlers set, even though Alice teeters back to her mom after one song. I don't glance at Danielle again. Even if she is only here for Levi, I'm not. I'm here for Juju, too. For my grandparents, for Alice, and for me.

But her presence here, the timeline, the set list, even some of the conversations being exactly how I lived this, is making me question that all of this is a dream. But if this isn't a dream, what is it? And why am I here on this exact day?

Seventeen

When the music wraps up and the next band is getting ready to play, Graham and Drew pull up on Graham's motorcycle. This is the first I've seen of my brother since our interaction this morning, and I'm waiting to see if Drew looks at me funny after my asking him what year it is and telling him it was all a dream.

And Graham. When I see him, I'm startled. His face is unlined and hairless. He's so young. The way I remember him only when looking through pictures or home videos. But I am disgusted at the sight of him. This is the Graham who killed Levi. The Graham who couldn't control his drinking or his mouth. Or whatever else.

I want to warn Levi to stay away from him. I want to scream at Juju for not telling me about him. I want to beg her not to keep something so devastating from me.

Drew dismounts from the back of Graham's motorcycle. Seeing him reminds me of the Polaroid photograph of the three of them riding.

My head starts to spin when I realize that we aren't supposed to be here. The first time around, I was so hurt seeing Danielle that Juju and I left the festival early. We didn't see Graham and Levi until afterward when they were driving on the main street. *After* she bought her camera.

If this isn't a dream, which seems outrageous but somehow plausible in this moment, I have to keep the timeline right. I can't lose that photograph. I see the picture of the guys in my mind. I need her to buy that camera.

I'm reeling, trying to figure out how to get us out of here. An ache emerges in the center of my skull as I summon the sequence of events to memory. At some point, Graham invites us to the Industrial. I think that's why they stop in front of the thrift shop to talk to us. That's when Juju snags the photo of them. The iconic photo of this day that I have to ensure is taken.

I'm having all the Marty McFly feelings from *Back to the Future* when he and his siblings are disappearing from their family photograph while his parents miss their first dance. If I had the photograph in my pocket right now, how much of it would have already faded away?

"Juju," I say too loudly and she jolts. "Let's get coffee." Although by the pitch of my too excited voice, it doesn't seem like I need any more coffee.

"Okay," she says, but her trajectory doesn't change. She's still headed straight for the guys. "Let's just say hi first."

I groan inside. As soon as we speak to them, they'll have no reason to stop to heckle us on the main street and the picture will fade.

My arm jerks toward hers, tugging on her forearm. "C'mon Juju, I want coffee!" I attempt to sound like an angsty 17-year-old instead of a desperate 27-year-old. Her pony-tailed hair swings in my face as she turns toward the guys and keeps walking. I tug a little harder, then cut her off, hollering toward the guys. "We're getting coffee, come find us when you're done."

The three of them show they hear in their own way with nods, waves or Graham's consistent flip-off. And I drag Juju toward the coffee shop. When my boots and her white Keds hit the cobblestone of the street, only then do I exhale in relief. Even though I think our timeline is a little off now, I know I can work it out.

Coffee first. I drink my coffee black now, but I remember from pictures that I ordered an iced coffee. When Juju orders vanilla, I order the opposite, a caramel iced latte. Because that's the way we were then. Almost the same with a different flavor.

The barista—although I'm not sure they're called that yet— calls my name and hands me my drink order. Juju snags a drink of my caramel, leaving a ring of frosty pink lipstick on my straw. I wipe it off with a napkin because there wasn't a lipstick ring in the picture. Maybe it's hyper-sensitivity to not change these photographed memories. But just in case.

As we walk out, nostalgia washes over me. The bookstore is next door, and I feel it drawing me. There is a cell-level connection between me and bookstores. But this bookstore is different. This is *our* bookstore.

"You can't pass a bookstore without going inside, can you?" Juju says, biting her straw. As she says it, I tingle with *déjà vu*.

"I'm always more at home inside a bookstore." I shrug. Then thinking of the time shift we've created, I add, "You don't have to come in if you don't want to."

She shrugs, the pony-tail of her hair brushing against her shoulder. "I'll catch up with you in a bit." She winks and turns on her heels.

I enter the bookstore like I'm in a vortex. Maybe I am. I don't know what books came out this year, so I'm walking into an upside-down world. What authors are on the best-selling lists? What books are even out yet? My brain is too overloaded to calculate pop culture right now. But the back wall is drawing me to itself, a Maggie Thayer magnet. I inhale that smell of old book pages and coffee grounds, and I am transported to the day Levi kissed me.

I know how silly it is to still pine after a few days of teenage romance, a few secret moments that didn't last. Especially because I know true romance. The kind that sweeps you off your feet, that looks into someone eyes and sees an adoration that you would sell all your possessions to experience again but you don't have to because they are right there by your side promising to never leave. That's the kind of love I have waiting for me when I wake up from all of this.

And yet, my heart still races standing in the shadow of the bookshelf where Levi first kissed me. First loves don't always evaporate with time. They saturate the heart and hold on for dear life long after they've ended.

My trance is interrupted by Juju jumping on my back. "You gotta come next door with me. I found something." She kisses me on the cheek and hops down, expecting that I'll follow, and I do. Because this, I remember in detail. I know more about cameras now than I did before, but I let the whole scene play out exactly as I remember it. Juju and the thrift store sales guy with the ameba-shaped hairline go back and forth about the classic Polaroid camera, and I act just as disinterested as I did the first time, except that I'm listening more carefully.

"Let's see if this baby works," Juju says, then flips it around to take a photo of us together.

Here I am looking into the viewfinder of a Polaroid camera, while in 2009 I am used to carrying a cell phone with a camera in it. We still have to flip the phone around at just the right angle to get our faces in the shot, but when it's too close or over-exposed or misses our faces entirely, we can delete it and try again.

But I've missed this: the art of the snapshot. The blurry, high exposed photos with our natural faces instead of posed ones.

The photograph pops out of the camera, and Juju squeals. When the picture finally appears within the thick white square, there we are just as I remember. One wild and carefree. The other guarded and unsure. I think of us as adults, and how we have met in the middle as we've grown. I've blossomed and she's subdued. And I wonder how much of that is because of Levi's death.

Revving motorcycle engines sound from the street outside, and panic streaks through my belly. I know where they're going, but there's no way I could explain that to Juju. My feet itch to take off for the street, to beat the guys before they drive away.

Before Juju's transaction is complete, I hip-bump her. "Hey, I'm gonna wait outside."

"Okay."

I step outside sipping on my iced latte, casually making my presence known. Within seconds déjà vu has enveloped me again. Drew clings to Graham on the back of his red Harley. Even knowing it was coming, I can't help but throw my head back in laughter. Like laughing at an episode of *Friends* even though I've seen it at least twenty times. No matter what Graham has done or is going to do, this scene doesn't get old. I push my hand against the glass door of the thrift store and holler between fits of laughter, "Juju, ohmigod, come out here."

"What?! No!" Juju shrieks as she sees the two of them looking like a chimpanzee mom carrying her young on her back.

Laughter gives way to relief as Juju snaps the photograph. Juju is still laughing, and I want to join her but my throat is thick. The scene in front of me only confirms that I'm probably not in a dream. There are too many sequences in play, too much of my personal control for this to be a dream. Which only leaves me with more questions. I don't know what's happening to me, but I do know what's going to happen next.

"Meet us at the Industrial," Graham says over the engines.

One place I never wanted to see again. I would have been happy if they'd torn it down. But I have to go. Even though this is where it all begins.

My hands go clammy against the plastic cup I'm holding. Why would I want today to play out the same? Today leads to terrible things. But I've already changed part of the day. Going to church with my grandparents wasn't the original story. Seeing Levi and Juju there. I've changed the story already. Could I change more? I gasp audibly.

"You okay?" Juju asks, her touch delicate against my elbow.

"Oh," I stutter over words. "Yeah, um—" Pedestrians cross the street leaving the Homegrown Festival. I point toward them. "I just remembered that my grandparents had plans for Drew and me tonight."

"We don't have to go with the guys. I can take you back."

"Uh," I stall, because my brain is busy sorting through the next few hours like cold case files in a ten-year-old investigation. If we skip out on the Industrial, the whole Juju and Graham debacle won't happen. Then we won't go to the field party. Or we could still go to the field party and it'll be great because the whole Juju and Graham debacle didn't happen. And maybe, just maybe, at the party I could give Levi some sort of warning without really telling him it's a warning.

Maybe I could save him.

But if we skip the Industrial, Drew will still be there and I'll have to explain to Grandma and Grandpa why he's missing. And I will probably miss the field party once I'm back at my grandparent's house, which means I don't get a good-bye with Levi. Not that the existing good-bye really counted anyway.

What if I make all of these changes, and they mean nothing? What if Levi still dies, and I never see him again after these moments on the street just now? Can I risk that?

"No," I finally answer Juju. "No, we can go." I pat the back pocket of my jeans. "Let me just call Grandma and let her know." When I find my back pocket empty, I pat the rest of my pockets feeling for my cell phone. Too many seconds go by before it occurs to me that we don't have cell phones in 1999.

When I glance back at Juju, her eyebrows are arched at me. "You want to go inside the store and call them, or—"

I shrug. "Oh, no, it's okay. Maybe we just won't stay long."

"Okay," she says, dragging the word out in suspicion.

Sitting in her green Volkswagen Beetle, driving down Chicago Street brings me back. The rounded ceiling of the car feels high above my head, like a clown car that could fit twenty clowns sitting on top of each other. A plush gerbera daisy in its bud vase sits attached to her dashboard, and I brush my finger against it. I haven't been inside a VW Bug since Juju's.

Original 1999 me didn't know what to expect at the Industrial. I didn't know it was an abandoned building in the middle of town. I didn't know it would turn from an innocent hangout to uncomfortable near-assault.

I sit in the tan leather seat, driving toward a different kind of uncertainty. I could say something. I don't know what I could say to impact Levi enough. To warn him about the field party or tell him to never return to the Industrial. The dashboard daisy bobs along to the rhythm of the drive like a nodding head. *Say something.* I imagine it saying in a sweet, mousy voice. *Don't let him die. Tell him.*

What could I say without sounding insane? Or ominous. The thing is, Levi knows what he's doing is dangerous. Rose, Greg, and Juju, they've all told him to be careful, that he could break his neck—I cringe thinking that so flippantly. Part of what he loves is the adrenaline in the danger.

We've all thought Graham was the junky, but its turns out Levi's the real junky. He just does it legally.

"You're so quiet. Did something happen at the bookstore?" Juju asks out of the blue. Although, I haven't been paying much attention, and when I come to, we are pulling into the parking lot of the Industrial. I haven't spoken since entering the car.

"No." I shrug, placing myself back in the moment. "I think I'm just sad to be leaving tomorrow. I'll miss you guys so much."

"Ah, don't get all mushy on me. You know I don't like to cry," she says as she puts the car in park.

"So this is it?" I look around. For ten years, this building has been in my dreams. And in my nightmares. I never thought I'd be back here.

"Yep." She jumps out of the car, clicking the keyless lock on her key chain. If she knew what this building held for her today and days to come, she wouldn't have such a pep in her Ked-clad step. I follow behind her, her crown-high ponytail swinging back and forth with every step.

The motorcycles stand empty, propped up by their kickstands, which means the guys are already here, "picking" the locks. My stomach still churns, even knowing we won't get caught.

"Is this really a good idea? There are so many people around." I feel like there's a spotlight on us. Maybe it's just me.

As expected, Graham pipes up, "What are you, chicken shit?"

But Juju comes to my rescue. "It's okay. We do this all the time." Her voice quiets in my ears; I'm not sure if she's actually lowered her voice or if the pounding of my heart has drowned all other noise out. "Graham sort of has an *understanding* with the local cops."

Nothing she says will quiet the voice screaming, *Don't set foot in there. Don't let them set foot in there.*

The air gust from inside the building slaps me in the face when Graham jimmies the door open. All of the imaginings I've had of this building rush into my mind. I suddenly feel all alone, standing among my friends.

I stare at my feet as everyone passes me to enter the shell of a building. Dampness reaches my nostrils, curling my stomach until I think I might throw up. My downcast gaze scans the concrete beneath me for any signs of where Levi's head hits. I know that's impossible because it hasn't happened yet, but I feel like the Industrial perhaps charted across time with me. Of course the concrete is covered in dark spots and stains, leaving no possibility of deciphering between them. And I don't know if he left behind blood from his fall anyway. Down the road, though, I know the pavement is stained. Or will be.

I step inside the building, against my own will. Graham claims his corner with a stash of beer. Juju lays out her quilt. Levi climbs the arm of one of the loading docks, unable to keep his feet on the ground.

"This place is tight," Drew exclaims, popping the top of his first beer. I want to scream at all of them. I want to tell them that this place changes everything. That from this moment, we have a chance to fix it.

Drew and Graham huddle together, sucking down their beers, and I'm almost more disgusted with Drew now than I was all those years ago when he let Roman get away with all his crap. My brother, the coward.

It feels like penance being back here, watching my friends live carefree. Is that the lesson I'm here to learn? To not be the carrier of Graham and Juju's secret? For a friendship that has lasted our entire lives, it's sad to know how many secrets we've kept. I remember when I thought the only secret between us was Levi and me. And in the end, that wasn't much of a secret. This one, though, tore us apart.

Their voices carry, chattering like normal. But I can't find normal in this place. I've tried all day to act like everything was fine, like I'm 17 on summer break loving life, like this is the first time I've lived through each moment. But I can't do it here. The little box inside me that I've padlocked with all the secrets is splintering.

I force myself to speak, "So we're just supposed to sit here," I say, standing over Juju on her quilt. My voice carries more than I want. One more thing I know I don't want to change is the last photo of Levi standing up there in the rafters. If I play my cards right, maybe I can keep Levi's face from being smudged, destroyed by Graham like every other part of Levi.

"Better than just sitting at home."

I scoff.

"We don't have to stay," Juju says. The confusion and concern on her face in the car hasn't changed. I can't hide my bizarre attitude from her.

I toss my cross-body bag onto the quilt and sit down. My tailbone screams at me. There is no way to get comfortable.

Levi jumps onto the concrete steps, reaches up for the ceiling beams, and even though I know he'll make it, I cringe. "What is he doing? He's crazy." As the words come out of my mouth, I realize they are the same words I said before. Even though it wasn't on purpose. "That's not going to hold you," I tease, because I know it will.

A wry smile, my favorite of all of his smiles, reaches his mouth. "Why don't you come up here and join me?"

I shrug. "Okay." I jump up from my spot on the quilt. Up in the air with him has to be more comfortable than sitting on the concrete floor.

"Maggie!" Juju shrieks. I hear the guys laugh in the corner. Drew has already started on another beer. I climb the bare scaffolding stairs, deciding to stop paying any more attention to the two of them.

"A brave soul," Levi admires. He stands on the thickest beam across the ceiling. He has one hand on another cross beam.

I reply with a wink. I don't know what's gotten in to me, but this seems like the only way to combat the nausea from being in this building.

"Grab on to that one." He points to a part of the bolted-down scaffolding above where I'm standing. "And put your foot there to boost you up." This feels like a horrible idea. I'm smarter than this, and yet my heart racing inside my chest gives me the will to do as he says.

I'm reminded of the time Everett took me to an indoor rock climbing gym on a date. I think he'd run out of ideas for new places to take me, or maybe he notices my eyes linger whenever we passed a rock climbing gym and misunderstood my grief for interest. I remember the cheesy grin on his face when we pulled into the parking lot. I probably disappointed him with my blank stare. All I could see was Levi. Hear his voice from today. *The best place was out in Grand Rapids.* I didn't know which place it was. I just remember him saying that, and Graham's snarky response. *He hasn't been* real *rock climbing though.*

As I boost myself onto the beam Levi suggested, I remember the conversation I would be having with Juju down on the ground. I don't recall what we said, except that it was about Danielle. She was so important back then, and yet she's barely crossed my mind while I've been here. The feelings I had about Levi choosing her instead of me were so strong and so real, but even in this room, in this time, they are only a distant thought. Seeing her at the festival, her blonde hair, her platform shoes, her focused attention, none of it evoked competition or envy in me.

As an adult, I have often caught myself thinking teenhood and high school was a simpler time. But being here, I chide my older self. Instead of simple, everything here is colossal. Every hurt, every smile, every glance has meaning.

When you don't know how everything is going to turn out, you don't know which moment to hold on to tightly and which to let pass by without notice. But I know better this time around. I know to live in every moment I have with Levi.

Do I live that way with Everett? I don't think I do.

"Don't be scared," Levi says. He stretches out his hand to me even though it's impossible to reach.

"That flimsy beam isn't going to hold both of us."

He smirks and bounces his legs, making not only the beam he is on but also the ones attached to it bounce and shudder. "I think it will."

"That's not funny." Even though my laughter says the opposite. I know he wouldn't put me in danger. "Aren't you afraid of hurting yourself?" I look down for a second, then bounce my eyes back up to him. "Or worse?" I ask with a knowing bubble in my throat.

His smirk remains. "We all die, Maggie. Don't you want to have stories told about you after you die?"

"Sure. Stories about how I lived so long."

"I bet none of those books you read are about people who sat around doing nothing." He tells me where to put my foot next, then my hand.

White knuckling the vertical beam of scaffolding, I step up, my foot shaking a little until I find my balance. I don't answer him for fear that I'll lose concentration and fall.

"We only tell stories that are worth telling. So why wouldn't we live our life worthy of a few?" He tilts his head back in a way that would throw my balance off entirely, and stares at the metal ceiling as though it is a vast sky spotted with stars. "One day I'm going to touch the ceiling of this building. I haven't figured out exactly how to get there but I'll do it eventually."

"I'm not going any higher. There's nothing to catch me if I fall."

"You have to be surefooted."

Even this high, I barely notice what's happening on the ground below. It's quieter up here. Maybe this is why Levi prefers his feet to be off the ground. Up here, it's just the two of us. For the first time since I've been here.

"I'm going to document it when you fall," Juju hollers at us with a nervous laugh. "Smile for the camera." She holds the boxy camera in front of her face. From here, I can't hear the click or the gears as they work, but I see the white square photograph pop out of the front.

That's the photograph. The last picture of Levi. And now I'm in it, the two of us forever frozen next to each other.

Levi breaks connection with me and swings from one beam to the next all Tarzan-like, then thuds with both feet solid on the ground. "Lemme see that."

"Levi, don't leave me here," I holler, nervous for more than one reason.

I know what happens next. I see it all unfolding, but I'm stuck up here. I can't stop it. The gears are already in motion. I chose the wrong moment to be spontaneous and join him up here.

"Juju," I say as I carefully step down from the scaffolding to the lower rung. My anxious heartbeat is telling me to hurry, but my unsteady feet are reminding me how high I am off the ground with nothing to catch me. Juju doesn't hear me call her name over her laughter and squeals.

By the time I'm steady on the ground, Graham already has her by the waist while she holds the photograph high in the air with one hand. His face is next to hers, and he's saying something in her ear that I didn't notice before. Her free hand goes to his forearms as they press into her breasts. But Levi and Drew still think they're playing around.

"C'mon, Shortcake, you wanna show it to me."

My stomach roils at Graham's slurred voice. A flash of pale

skin shows from her bare midriff as her shirt rides up. I can see the underwire of her nude bra. I think that's when Levi realizes it's no longer fun. I watch his face turn from heckler to protector, his eyebrows reach in to each other. But he still doesn't say anything.

The photograph falls as Juju flails, and I'm left debating if I try to stop Graham or if I save the photograph from trampling. It was special when it was only Levi, but now, this is the only photograph I have of Levi and me together without anyone else. Juju kicks her legs in the air and I cannot get around them to snag the picture.

"Seriously, let her go," I say to Graham but he and Drew only laugh more. A kick makes its way near Drew, as he sidesteps it, his shoes lands on the photograph before it is fully developed. And I know in that moment, that it's ruined. My heart sinks. But I step closer to Juju, put my hands on Graham's forearm and scratch at him.

"Stop!" Juju says, and Levi goes into action. In one motion, he has pulled Graham's arm down, freed Juju, and pinned Graham's arm behind his back. Graham spins around to free his own arm and swing at Levi, but in the process, Juju falls to the ground with an *oomph*. I skitter to the floor next to her, picking up the photograph before any more harm comes to it and grabbing Juju's hand to help her up. She allows me to help, but clearly doesn't like it.

"Dude," Levi says to Graham, who stumbles back a few steps.

I imagine it happening right here and now. Levi yelling. Graham defending himself first with words then with action. Levi falling against the concrete, then swaying as he stands up and rushes Graham. But then I'm back, in the present if you can call it that.

"What the hell, Graham?" Juju says, brushing off the seat of her pants. I hand her the photograph after dusting as much of the dirt as I can get off. With a slight limp, she trudges to her quilt, snatches it all up in her arms, then heads out the door. "Why do you have to ruin everything?"

"I was just messing around," Graham says, his eyes have gone from drunk and vengeful to sober and humiliated.

She never even turns to look at him, only mutters a few curse words at him and throws a free hand in the air to flip him off. The door slams behind her.

I start to follow, remember my bag, and grab it. I don't want to ask Drew to come, but I know I should. Even though he didn't show me any consideration, I don't want to be like him or Graham.

Drew has already grabbed another beer when I say, "You're drunk." I forgot what a horrible drunk he is. I haven't seen him drunk in so long. "We should go."

His head hangs over the beer in his hand. "You go on." No animosity, only brokenness.

I do as he says. I follow Juju. And Levi follows me. At the door, I stop him. The waning sun brightens his face. Daylight is refreshing after being in shadows and the dark hue of the Industrial with light only breaking through the foggy glass. I don't want to leave him with Graham. I don't want to leave him period. But I need to be with Juju. And I haven't decided how much of this day I can or should alter.

"They shouldn't be alone. You know that will only lead to trouble."

His face inches closer to mine. "They'll be fine." Green eyes pierce through me, envelope me, swallow me. I memorize every fleck in them. I want to tell him to run from this place and never look back. "I want to check on Juju," he says, without taking his eyes from mine. "And you."

Our hands are both on the door and for just a moment they touch. I don't pull away. Instead I inch my fingers closer to his, speaking to him through my slight touch. I feel his thumb trace the edge of my index finger, and I forget to breathe. I forget where I am or where I was going. I sink into his insignificant, monumental touch. Tiny moments were always ours. They were all we ever had. So reliving one is like reliving a lifetime of romance in one touch. Breathless and outside of time.

A clattering beer can stirs me. I glance at our fingers, overlapping on the steel door. It takes a steel will for me to say what I have to say.

"I'm fine," I stutter. "I'll take care of Juju." My lips are the only part of me that moves. "I'll take her to my grandparent's house. They wanted to do something special with Drew and me, but he's clearly not in any condition to see them. So I'll take her."

"I'll come with you," he says taking steps over the threshold and out into the fresh air with me. The breeze blows his hair into his eyes. He's pulling keys out of his pocket, and I should stop him. But why. He could come with us. I see a flash of him sitting at my grandparents table eating dinner from the country rose china, looking out of place and at home simultaneously. What would it hurt?

But Drew. I don't care for a second if something happens to Graham. Even though guilt surges through me as soon as I think it.

I shake my head, more at myself than at Levi. Shaking my

imaginings far, far away.

"If you go with Juju, I'll stay with Drew, but someone has to stay with him. He can't get on a motorcycle like that."

"I'd rather stay with you." His thumb finds mine again, but this time it doesn't stop at my index finger. He sweeps it across the back of my hand, then his other fingers move between mine, tangling themselves together.

I swallow everything I want to say and do. I know what is supposed to happen here, and I don't want to pick a fight. My words, even my breath, stutter out of my mouth.

"What about Danielle?" I ask him, wishing I didn't have to but not seeing an alternative. It'll keep him here. I will not trade Levi's death for Drew's, even if I somehow can save Levi. "I saw her at the festival. You're still with her, aren't you?"

No matter what words come out of my mouth, I don't let go of his hands. I'm sending mixed signals all over the place, but that's what being a teenager is all about, isn't it?

He hangs his head, studying our hands. "It's complicated."

"Please don't," I whisper. The words mean so much more than I could possibly explain to him.

"Maggie."

"If I lived closer it would be different, right?" He was always right about that. Everything would have been different if I lived closer or if my family had never moved from here at all. I'm learning all over again what it's like to have little to no control.

A horn honks behind me, then lays on louder. I drag my gaze from Levi—beautiful, pain-filled Levi—and I see Juju with her hand on her car horn. I pinpoint the moment her face transforms from *Come on, let's go* to *Oh my god, what are you doing* when she sees our hands and our proximity.

I panic, release Levi's hand, and forget all about where our conversation was going and why. All I see are Juju wide eyes and her glossy lip parted in shock.

Of all of the things I've wanted to alter, this wasn't one. I step toward Juju's car.

But Levi pulls me back, his hand catching mine, not caring that Juju watches. "Wait," he says, then words tumble out his mouth that before took so long to pull from him. "Danielle was what everyone else wanted for me. And you were all the way across the country, and I caved. I know it wasn't fair to you or to her. But it was easier than fighting."

The words I imagined saying every time I replayed this conversation for a decade slip from my lips. I hold my head up and say, "I wanted you to fight for me."

Then I go to Juju.

***

"What. The. Hell." She draws the words out before my butt has graced her passenger seat.

I take a concealed deep breath, then roll my eyes to play it off. "I know. First Graham then Levi."

Her face remains blank. "Please tell me I saw it wrong."

My eyes bounce back and forth between her face and her console where the Polaroid of Levi and I sits fully developed. I don't want her to catch me staring at it. Certainly not now. I return to her steady stare. I've been caught, and my limbs know it as they tingle and grow heavy. "What if you didn't?"

"How long?"

I just want her to give some expression to let me know what

she thinks about it instead of looking at me like she's had too much Botox all over her face. "Last year."

"That's why you asked me about Danielle?" Before I can answer, her back straightens. I can see the light bulb blink on in her mind. "You're the pen pal."

I swallow a lump.

"Foreign exchange student, my ass," she grumbles. A few wild strands of red hair are pulled out of her pony tail from the exchange with Graham, and they match the wild look in her eyes.

There is no way to keep deniability, so I concede, "Look—"

"Have you slept with him?"

If I had water in my mouth, or even any saliva in it, it would have spewed out my mouth or my nose onto her windshield. "No!"

Eyebrows raise, asking again.

"I didn't." My delivery is an octave too high, but it's still the truth. "You know I couldn't have kept that from you."

Her expression doesn't change.

We drive out of the parking lot, without Levi stopping to tell us about the bonfire. I don't know how I can work it for us to get there now. And knowing what will happen there, I don't know if I should.

Eighteen

Pink stains the sky, painted with thin clouds, as we pull up in front of my grandparents' house. Neither of us have spoken. Juju's silence reminds me of all of the reasons I didn't want to tell her about Levi.

My grandfather's truck is in the driveway and my stomach sinks a little that Drew isn't with me for whatever Grandpa has planned. I've wondered for a decade what was waiting for us.

Juju parks but doesn't unbuckle her seat belt.

"Please come in with me," I beg. "Tonight is my last night here. I don't want to leave with you upset."

I have become so accustomed to being 17, I've almost forgotten that I don't know if I'll wake up here in the morning.

Tonight is my last night in Michigan, certainly, but when I lay my head on the pillow tonight, will I wake up back in my beachy bedroom with Everett at my side. I don't know if I have changed too much.

At the thought of Everett, my insides knot. What am I doing? Playing around with Levi, tangling my fingers—and emotions—with his, when I have a husband miles and years away.

"I've noticed things." Juju's eyeline is bound to the dashboard, not looking at me while she speaks. "I could have guessed. But I assumed if what I was seeing was for real that you would have told me. I mean, why wouldn't you? The two closest people in my life wouldn't be lying to me, right?"

A sound takes shape in my throat, but when I open my mouth, I am empty.

Juju unbuckles her seat belt and turns off the car in one swift motion. "I was right, and I was wrong." She leaves me in the car.

I hate that I've messed things up. I hate the betrayal in Juju's eyes. Why couldn't I leave everything alone? "Please," I beg after her, but she is already knocking on the front door, saying hello to my grandparents, hugging them. When she looks at me, her warm smile has returned, but there's a veil of insincerity over it.

"Where's Drew?" Grandma asks, looking behind me, expectant.

"Oh, I think he's going to a bonfire," I answer, unthinking.

Both grandparents grunt in different ways of disapproval. "Well, come in girls, you don't have to wait to be invited." Grandma waves us in.

"How'd you know about the bonfire?" Juju asks.

On the outside, I shrug. But inside, my heart accelerates at my mistake. "I guess I heard the guys talking about it."

"Grandpa bought all of your favorite ice creams and pulled out your favorite board games." Grandma points to the coffee table stacked with boxed games, and the kitchen island has bowls and toppings lined up. "I hope you like ice cream," she says to Juju.

Juju lifts her head, beams her smile, and answers, "Ice cream makes everything better." I think that's pointed at me.

We binge on banana splits until our mouths are frozen, and the four of us play a game of *Sorry!* that Grandpa wins. It's funny to me that these were the big plans I've spent ten years missing. It could seem anticlimactic, but instead it's perfect.

Here I am with my grandparents, creating entirely new memories, and have successfully kept Juju from the bonfire and from Graham. Maybe that is what I came here for. Maybe I prevented Levi's death.

But I can't help feeling I have messed everything up. Sure Levi might live, but Juju might never forgive me for lying.

And Everett. Oh Everett. Had I erased him from my life entirely? What will this version of my life look like? The unknown is the scariest thing of all.

"Magdalene," Grandma sounds worried. "You have gone utterly pale. Has the sugar hit your stomach all at once?"

My mouth is too frozen to speak, but not from the ice cream this time. I hadn't considered what my choices would do to Everett. Not seriously. How could I alter a life to exclude the man I love?

"I'm sorry," I stumble over my words. "I—Grandma, if you could go back and change something terrible that happened, even if it meant losing something good, would you do it?"

"Well," Grandma fiddles with her wedding rings. She ponders the question longer than I expect, and I almost follow up by asking *what* she would change if she could. She finally answers, "I suppose it depends. I choose to believe that when we accept that we cannot change the terrible, that's what births the good. If you remove one, you almost certainly would remove the other."

I chew on the inside of my lip. I suppose I've agreed with her all along.

"What is this all about, Magdalene?" Grandma asks.

"I don't think I can say."

Grandpa interrupts as though he knows I can't reveal what has suddenly bothered me. "What is this bonfire I heard about?"

"Oh," Juju says, looking at me, almost concerned. "It's a farewell-to-summer bonfire over at Prairie Grove Farm. Levi and Graham thought it would be great to take these two on their last night, but you know Maggie would rather spend the night with both of you."

Everyone's attention turns back to me, and by their faces, I must still appear sickened.

"Well," Grandpa checks the grandfather clock in the corner of the room, "I'm turning in, but it's early yet for you young people. Why don't you both head over to Prairie Grove. That sounds like a good time."

That's the most consecutive words I've heard Grandpa say in decades, but I still have to protest. "No, that's really okay. I don't mind—"

"Nonsense," Grandpa grunts. "Go with your friends." He stands, adjusting his belt as he does. Then he kisses the top of my head. "Thank you for coming home tonight."

Oh how my heart aches that I missed this the first time around.

If I wake up tomorrow in my own bed at home, if I never come back to Michigan, then this is the last night I spend with my grandfather. Unless I've saved Levi and changed the course of the next few years, then maybe I can change the fact that I haven't returned here in a decade. But there's nothing I can do to change the dementia that will descend on my dear grandfather.

Tears sting my eyes.

If I save Levi, I save my chances of seeing my grandparents again, here in their home. But in doing so, I likely lose Everett.

How can I want things to be the same and so different at the same time?

I squeeze Grandpa with both of my arms wrapped around his waist. "I'll miss you."

"I'll miss you too, Maggie."

Then Juju and I leave.

***

When we pull up to the Prairie Grove Farm, the field is smaller than I remember, like so many people say when they return to their childhood home, but the party is just as hopping, even though I don't think people say that anymore. This morning, I woke up in a fog, but these memories are as potent as if I was here last week. I sling my canvas bag over my shoulder and hop out of the car.

Juju wraps her arms around mine, and she kisses my t-shirt covered shoulder. "I've thought about it," she says so only I can hear. "And I love you two together." Then she winks at me. "My brother and my best friend," she says, quoting a scene from our favorite show, *Friends*.

"I'm glad you're not mad," I breathe. "I don't want to lose either of you."

She bounces off to get us drinks.

A glance at my watch tells me that we are walking up at least an hour later than we originally did. I'm not sure what to expect. I scan the crowd for the guys. My hope is that Drew came to his senses and took Graham's drunk ass home.

The stereo plays Blink 182, bodies jump, and voices sing the lyrics above the music. Girls stand around the bonfire. And I see Danielle. Her tiny shirt, short shorts, flowy blonde hair. I don't remember her being here the first time, maybe it's because we are arriving so much later. I see red hair next to her, but can't tell if the fire is distorting the colors. Until I see Levi making her laugh.

I pivot in my boots, the grass giving way underneath me. It was a mistake to come here. I don't want to be jealous of Danielle but the feeling snakes through my veins. I'll find Juju and we'll leave. I should have left it all alone and never shown up.

"Maggie," he calls after me. I want to ignore him, but he catches up to me and takes my hand.

"Dance with me," he says as he spins me toward him. He's wearing a mischievous grin that I've rarely seen.

"No way."

His grin drops.

"I saw you talking to Danielle." I try my best not to, but I know I sound like a jealous girlfriend. "I don't get you, Levi. I've spent my life pining after you, waiting all year to see you. Then I get you for a sliver of a moment, and you choose someone else."

"That's not how it is."

My head tilts, asking for the truth.

"Not at all," he says, with a sadness that we share for different reasons.

"Then you don't see how she looks at you. You don't see what I see." The argument is familiar, natural even. Not like the conversations of ten years before, but the arguments I've had with Everett about Leslie.

It's like a veil lifts from my eyes. I was never concerned that

Everett would choose Leslie over me. This was a wound that had been opened years before Everett by a boy named Levi. A boy who never chose me and I spent the next decade longing to be chosen above any other woman.

Everett had chosen me. He had never wavered from his choice, and he said it to me over and over even though I wouldn't believe him. I loved him, yet I questioned him. I thought I didn't trust him, but the question was never about him. The question rooted in a seed Levi had planted. It's not Levi's fault that I saw myself as inadequate learned to be second place. I supposed, Levi only exacerbated my own disbelief in myself.

"I'm not your August fling, Levi. I can't be that person."

"You aren't."

"I know it would have been different if I lived here," I say.

"I want it to be different now."

"But it isn't. I still live across the country. And she's still here."

He squeezes my hand and draws me closer. "I chose you."

I've waited so long to hear him say those words. But now I don't even know if it's what I want to hear anymore.

Over his shoulder, the firelight glitters across Danielle's glowing skin. A scene from every CW show I'd ever watched. She isn't looking at us. She's already laughing with someone else.

I'm too old for this.

I purse my lips. "Juju knows everything."

"All the more reason to dance with me. No more hiding."

I remember my line, "I don't dance." Even though I've learned how to dance in the last ten years.

"Everybody dances."

The bag on my shoulder bounces between us as he pulls me

close. He loosens it from my shoulder and lets it drop to the ground.

Could I have this one night, this dance, as a final good-bye? Standing here, swaying to "Wonderwall" by Oasis, Levi is in my ear singing that maybe I'd be the one who saves him. Chills prickle my skin even with the bonfire so near. I let myself be in this moment. I let myself forget who I am, where I am from. I forget the things I don't want to remember. I am here, now, swaying to the music, in arms that feel like they are saving me as much as I might save them.

Juju clears her throat, coming between us as she always has, but this time there is a sparkle in her eye. "Look at you two."

Levi opens his mouth, but his sister shakes her head. "I like the look of this." She whips her hair around with a bounce to the music, then throws an exaggerated wink over her shoulder as she says, "But don't go getting all nasty."

With a sway of her hips, she disappears into the dancing crowd.

I return my attention to Levi and the smirk that won't leave his face.

"We should have done this a long time ago," he says.

"Dance together?" I know exactly what he means, but I'm being coy.

"Well, that, yes." His arm squeezes my waist against his. "But also, tell everyone. What were we so afraid of?"

"Ridicule. Mockery." Then I let the truth slip out that I maybe didn't even realize until this moment. "Breaking up. Hating each other."

"That," he narrows his eyes at me, "would never happen."

My lungs are heavy, trying to breathe through the thunderous beating of my heart. I feel nothing but Levi. I hear nothing but his voice. Nothing is in focus but his face.

I lift my chin and smirk between closed lips, the way I've learned to fake confidence. "Are you saying you'd marry me, Levi James?" I tease.

"I'm saying I would," he answers. No hesitation. Full confidence.

The smirk melts from my face. I hadn't expected him to answer. I thought we were flirting, playing around, but Rose's voice rings through my ears, a distant memory of her confiding that he thought he'd be married to me within five years. It feels like a dream that you almost believe is real life.

Our swaying has come to a halt when he grabs my hand and spins me, my eyes attempt to stay locked on his all the way around.

"Someday," he adds when I return to my original position. "But until then," he lifts a hand to my face, his fingers brushing my neck, my ear lobe. His mouth moves closer to mine, asking a question in their proximity. My lips part, answering.

That's when the voices infiltrate our realm, and everything stops, like a record player screeching to a halt. It's happening, even though I didn't want to acknowledge it.

I grab Levi's hand, the one that still rests against my face. I hold it there, hold him there. "Levi,"

But his attention is already drawn to them. Graham's slurred voice. Juju's unflinching response. His whole body turns toward them, the same as everyone else in the crowd.

I squeeze his hand tighter, even as he's trying to pull it away. "Don't," I say, but I've lost my grip on him.

"Hey," Levi interrupts Graham.

I don't understand how Graham is even here. The time frame is completely off. I thought I had fixed it.

"You're embarrassing yourself, Graham."

"Not as embarrassed as you when I finally bone your sister."

And like that, Levi slips away from me. Again.

This time I try to stop him. Even though no one else helps. Not even Juju. "Levi stop." I grab at his back, as he lunges at Graham. "Stop!" I shriek, but his arms are faster and stronger than me. Over and over against Graham's face.

Like an instant headache, memories that aren't mine crash through my head. Levi lying in the gravel, his neck ajar. Graham's slurred speech, pushing Levi onto the concrete of the Industrial. Juju crying over the phone, finally confiding a decade-long secret.

If I can't stop Levi, then maybe he should just finish it. Until Graham can't talk back, until he can't get up, until he can't hurt anyone else.

My hands pull back from the fight, but they are shaking uncontrollably. I stumble backwards.

Levi quits as quickly as he began. His shoulders quake in heavy breaths. His hands are painfully red, broken, and bleeding. Small droplets of blood splatter Levi's shirt. My mind is like two universes colliding trying remember if there was blood before. I feel responsible, somehow, for this time being worse. As though Levi read my thoughts and knew I wanted Graham to die. *Instead of Levi*, I justify to myself, but it doesn't make my admission less shameful.

I can't catch my breath. My chest is heaving and the ice cream from earlier feels like it's coming back up.

Destiny's Child is jumpin', jumpin' through the speakers, but no one moves to the music. Levi works out a way home for Graham, just as he always did. I want to shake my head, scream in protest, because now I want Graham to drive home. I want him to put himself in danger. I would rather attend Graham's funeral than Levi's.

All of this anger doesn't become me, I know. I'm not good at playing God, pretending that if Graham drove home that he would be the only one in danger, thinking I know the future, even though everything I do to fix things only makes them worse.

The crowd dissipates into the backdrop of the party, as though a fight at a field party is an everyday occurrence in Stone River. I don't know anymore; maybe it is.

Levi trudges toward me, and even though I want to look in his face, to take us back to the moment just before Graham's voice rang out, I can't look at him.

No doubt he thinks it's because of his actions just now, but I can't tell him that I wanted him to keep going until he killed Graham.

"I'm sorry, Maggie," the words leak out of him as painfully as if they were tears. He leans his forehead on mine, slumping against me. "Oh god, I'm sorry," he breathes.

"I know," I answer his breath with my own. I think I'm crying. Maybe he is. I only know that as we stand here, we are one.

"Come," he says, low so that only I hear, "with me." The breath of each word flutters my eyelashes, heats my blood.

Oh, the memories come flooding. This one moment, I have relived over and over. But it's so different now. What would happen if I took his hand when he reached for mine in just a few moments?

When I don't respond right away, his fingers entwine with mine. A familiar current runs through my entire body, originating in those fingers. But the current feels wrong.

I want to save Levi, but Everett's face fills my mind. I can't give Everett up just to rediscover one moment I lost so many years ago. It wasn't fair to him that I kept so much from him. How could he have known my spirit was being crushed beneath the monotony of our life? If I could get back to him, I would tell him everything. I would explain how this one decision at a field party made me both discontent and equally afraid of the future.

Levi is waiting for my answer. I shake my head against his.

"I can't…"

Before I say more, Levi's wounded fingers drop and his forehead pulls back just enough to study my face, the current between us broken yet again.

"Why?" he whispers, almost a whimper. But he doesn't wait for an answer. "If you're afraid of what they'll think—" Both of his hands cup my face, and I can smell the blood on them. He sounds desperate now. Not at all like Levi. "Aren't you tired of letting everyone else—" He drops off.

I shake my head against his hands. I don't know if I can do whatever should be done right now. I can barely see him for the blur of tears.

He drops his hands and steps back from me. "Well I sure as hell am tired of it." His eyes blaze at me, disappointed, betrayed. He turns from me, silhouetted against the bonfire.

"Don't go, Levi. That's not what I meant." My voice raises with each word. Juju starts toward me.

No. This isn't how it is supposed to go. I am two people, in one body. I don't want to be here anymore. I don't want to keep ruining things. I pinch myself on the soft, sensitive skin under my armpit, trying to wake up. But this doesn't feel like a dream anymore.

"I wanted you. I chose you. But," He studies his hands, like they are the reason I'm not going with him. He doesn't understand, and I can't tell him the truth.

"Levi, please," I don't even know what I'm asking of him.

But he's already stalking away.

"This isn't how it's supposed to go," I say as a tear drips down my neck. I don't know what I want anymore. I don't know anything.

Juju shoves Levi's shoulder on her way past him. "What the hell did you do?" She's at my side, holding my elbow, wrapping her arms around me. "Maggie, what happened?"

Levi watches us leave, his expression pained and confused. Exactly how I remember it.

And just like that, the timeline to his death is back on track.

Nineteen

Juju's car stops while my eyes are still closed. When they open, we are in my grandparent's driveway. I'm not sure how we got here so quickly. Juju must have driven like Drew.

Together we saunter to the bedroom so I can pack. A perfume of regret hangs over me. More and more regret. I thought I came here to fix the regret, that if I lived through it again, I'd do it better this time, that I would be able to right all the wrongs. But somehow I've made it worse. I know where this story leads.

The bedroom smells of laundry detergent as Juju helps me pack in near silence. Only the music of Savage Garden fills the space. Being in this house feels safe. At least I know what's happening here, where Grandma has piled up my clothes, folded more pristine than a retail store.

Juju puts the suitcase on the bed, and I robotically place the stacks of folded clothes in the cavernous case. Both of us seem too drained, too tired to talk. Maybe I can convince Juju to spend the night, one last night. Because based on every movie I've seen, my guess is that when I wake up in the morning, I'll be back home in 2009, living out whatever changes have occurred here. Or I'll wake up and find out it really was a long, elaborate dream. I'm not sure which one I'm hoping for.

I'm not sure of anything anymore, except that I don't want to crawl in this bed and fall asleep alone.

Juju plops on the bed, curling one leg under her. "My brother's an idiot." Because this is clearly what has been on her mind.

I follow suit and sit on the bed. The bed springs retort under me. "He's not an idiot," I say, because I don't want to remember saying anything bad about him. I don't want to add to the regret.

"What did he say to you?" she asks.

"He didn't say anything wrong. He just—" I shake my head, because I don't know how to finish.

She nods like she understands even though she can't possibly. "Well, boys are idiots. I could have taken care of Graham. It wasn't a big deal. He was just drunk."

My heart races at the mention of Graham. I recall what she told me over the phone last night even though it seems like a different lifetime, the words that Levi shouted at Graham. *You forget I know who you are, Graham, and I know what you've done. I won't let you do it to my sister.* What did Levi mean?

So I ask, "Why did Levi turn on Graham so quickly? He just went from dancing with me to beating on him."

Juju's eyes flutter to mine and then around the room. I can't tell if she's hiding something. She's my best friend, and I can't tell. All of these secrets between us, maybe they are the real reason we fell apart.

"I don't know," she shrugs. "He's not usually so emotional. Maybe you opened his emotional flood gates."

She's being so flippant about this. It's not like her.

"Has Graham done something to you before?" How have I not asked her these questions? My attention was so caught up in Levi that I overlooked my best friend in the process.

"No," she says, and I think she's sincere. I think.

"Have they been in fights before?"

"Probably. I mean, they're boys."

I bite my lip, trying to gauge how to plant seeds of distrust in her mind. "You should talk to Levi. Maybe you guys need a break from Graham for a while. Like a clean break after we leave."

"Yeah, like we could get away from him in this town."

I shrug. "You could try."

"What if I moved to Texas after graduation?" she delivers, again like she's been thinking about it forever.

This sounds familiar, and the conversation progresses like I remember, just with a little less energy and a lot less giggles.

Grandma says if it was any other night, Juju could spend the night, but we have to get up so early that she doesn't think it's a good idea. I wish I could explain, but begging has never worked on my grandmother.

In the driveway, we wrap each other in a best friend forever hug that squeezes tears out of my eyes. She is the only person that I'm okay with seeing me cry over something that seems so silly.

"You're going to make me cry," she says when we pull away from the hug, then she pulls me in again.

I don't want to let her go. I don't want to wake up in a world where we haven't seen each other but a few times in a decade. I don't want to leave her to live through what's about to happen or to the truth she's about to hold all alone for ten years.

So I say it in her ear, or at least what I can say without her wanting to have me committed. "You know you can call me at all hours and tell me anything." Then I pull back to look into her bloodshot eyes. "Anything. Call collect. I'll pay."

"Of course I know that." She squeezes my arms. "And you can do the same." She sighs and rubs her eyes without smearing the makeup that is still magically in place at this late hour. "I love you."

"I love you too, Juju," I say as she gets in her car. I watch her drive off, and turn to see Grandma standing in the window watching as well.

"She's a good friend to you," Grandma says when I join her inside.

"I wish I was a better friend to her."

"Nonsense. You are a wonderful friend." Grandma takes my hand in hers.

I shrug. "I haven't always been." Not lifting my eyes, I add, "I'm going to finish packing." Dream or not, my hands needs something to do right now.

"I'll make us some chamomile tea to help us sleep."

While the tea is steeping, I hear her shuffle down the hall and see her peek in the bedroom door.

"You can come in," I say.

I move the last bit of clothing into the suitcase so she can sit on the bed. "I don't want to leave," I say as I sit next to her.

"I never want you to leave. But all things come to an end."

"I'll miss you." I'm somber knowing how she will begin to slow down and slowly lose bits of Grandpa.

"I'll miss you too, Magdalene," she says, kissing my hand.

Some moments are frozen in my mind, to be replayed like a movie reel over and over. This moment, sitting on the bed with Grandma is one of the few moments where I can watch my life play from outside my body through the reflection of the mirror. And I lay my head on her shoulder just as I did ten years ago.

The first time I did it for her. This time I do it for me.

There is a knock on the front door, loud enough to hear through the halls. And my heart yo-yos between my stomach and my throat when I realize who is knocking.

"Who in the blazes could that be?" Grandma says, pulling herself up from the bed.

I don't know how I could have forgotten what was coming. If I close my eyes right now, I would instantly see him looking through the window with a hand in the air, waving the only goodbye we ever got. Only willpower keeps me from bolting toward the door.

"Check on the tea, will you?" Grandma says to me as she leaves the room.

I'm grateful to have a reason to follow her, to position myself where I can see his face.

"Oh good heavens, it's the James boy."

I swallow. My throat is dry, but I've already forgotten about the tea. I hear his voice, and my insides clench.

"I'm sorry to come by so late. I wouldn't have knocked if I hadn't seen lights on."

"Well, it is past midnight." To the average ear, Grandma sounds grouchy, but my tuned granddaughter ear knows she's smiling inside.

He clears his throat. "Drew left his jacket, and Maggie—" he stumbles over my name, "dropped her book and bag." I hear the screen door open, and I imagine running through it and grabbing him around the neck the way I did at the church this morning. Because this might be the last time I see him.

Unless I'm wrong. Unless, somehow I have changed things. But it doesn't feel like I have.

"I just knew they were leaving early in the morning, so they'd probably want their...uh...stuff," Levi's voice says.

"Well thank you, young man. I'm sure they will appreciate it." The screen door bangs closed.

"Have a good night," he says.

Then Grandma turns around and sees me in the doorway. "Magdalene, you left your bag." She hands me the canvas bag weighed down with a book. I pull the book out and see the gap between pages, held apart by a lone sunflower. Grandma catches me eye and gestures her head to the side, raises her thinning eyebrows. I smile at the twinkle in her eye.

I dash to the window, hoping Levi hasn't already turned away. The world moves in half speed, so I have no way to gauge how long it has been since the door closed. I move the sheer white curtains to the side and look out the window, hopeful.

There he is. The porch light illuminates him like a spotlight. He doesn't see me at first. His eyes are still fixed on the front door, like he's willing it open. Or maybe he's thinking of knocking again. But I watch him in his natural habitat. If he turns this way, he'll see me. If he turns the other way, what will I do?

Then he's facing me. His expression changes about twenty times, from confused to expectant to sad to hopeful. But I have no idea what my expression is doing, I'm so lost in his.

He lifts his right hand and wiggles his fingers in the wave I've held onto for a decade. The sleeve of his leather jacket looks too big for his arm, that's just the style, but I am suddenly aware that we are only 17. Levi is still a boy growing into a man.

I raise my hand to match his wave. I've always wished I had at least done that. Without even realizing it, my palm touches the window, reaching for him. My hand leaves its imprint on Grandma's clean glass.

This is my last chance. It was always my last goodbye, but now I know, it's my last chance to change that goodbye.

If I do this, if I make a move, it changes everything.

I run down all of my options, but there isn't enough time. I can't possibly foresee what any of my moves will become. But as long as I stand here, holding Levi's stare, I'm holding us in place. We aren't moving forward toward a known or unknown future so long as my hand presses against this window and my eyes focus on his.

I want to tell him I'm sorry, to tell him that he's misunderstood everything. I want to tell him not to go to the Industrial, not to chase after Graham. I want to tell him everything I've thought to say every time I reread his letters or looked at those Polaroid pictures.

His lips are parted like he wants to say something too but no part of him moves.

So I move. I don't look back at my grandma. I don't say a thing. My hand move from the glass. I feel the door handle twist in my palm. I hear the creak of the screen door, and my feet land on the porch.

"Hi," I say.

"Hi," his hand is down by his side now. "I just came by—"

I interrupt him. "Ask me again."

"What?" he asks, confused.

"Ask me again." Because I always wanted to answer differently. "To come with you."

A few seconds pass before recognition crosses his face.

"Come with me." Then he puts his hand out, palm up, fingers right there in front of me.

I place my hand in his. My other hand still carries the book he brought me, holding the last thing he gave me against my heart, like I can hold him there.

I turn to see Grandma in the kitchen with her teacup. Her lips lift just a bit and she begins her shuffle down the hall.

One hand stays wrapped in his, and I set the book down just inside the door then close it behind me. I grin at Levi, and he grins back. Then we take off toward his motorcycle. We climb on the bike together. I wrap my arms around his chest, holding on tight. My heart thuds against his back as I lean in to him, because our timeline just took a major plot twist.

Twenty

There are things we should be afraid of, and there are things that we fear erroneously. I have feared never seeing Levi again. I have feared the unknown. I have feared risking it all. I have feared too much for too long.

Levi and I ride under canopies of trees, down roads that loop like ribbons around farms and ponds. I have no idea where we are, but out here, the stars are like a million little lighthouses in the sky.

This is the first time I've ridden with Levi. My mom was too cautious to let me on the back of a motorcycle with a teenage boy, no matter how I begged.

You would think I would be nervous riding on the vehicle that ushers him to the end of his life, but I'm not. I feel safer riding with him than with my feet on the ground all alone.

I lose track of time among the beating wind in my hair and the roar of the engine vibrating through my body. Until he slows and turns down a smaller road, more like a trail. The ground is bumpy and gravelly. The branches of the trees on either side of us reach out for my arms and my hair.

The motorcycle comes to a stop, and he puts his feet firmly on the ground. The engine quiets, then Levi dismounts. He reaches his hand out to help me down. My first instinct is that I can do it myself, but I let him help me, for the sake of taking his hand again. I slide off the seat and plant my feet next to his.

We are completely alone for the first time ever.

I can think of nothing to say, and apparently Levi can't either, because we both stare at each other for seconds that feel like minutes. We see each other through the headlight's beam. I feel naked in front of him as he stares back at me. Maybe I even blush because he winks at me then goes into motion. He takes his leather jacket off and lays it over the seat. He's changed his clothes since the field party. Now he wears a baggy, striped shirt. I wonder what he did with the shirt splattered with his and Graham's blood.

He unlatches the lock on one saddle bag of his motorcycle. Then he pulls out a quilt, with white, red, and gray triangles stitched into a diamond pattern. He tucks it under his arm and pulls out a Meijer's paper sack, a little crumpled up at the top. When the saddle bag of his motorcycle is empty, he uses his foot to close it. "Can you latch that? Thanks."

Eyeing his stash, I say, "You had all of this in there." I point to the motorcycle. I'm stating the obvious, seeing as I watched him pull everything out, but I'm stunned with the memory of how this night went the first time around.

"Yeah," he says with a wink. From the bag, he draws out flashlights, turns his on, and tosses me the other. "Come with me."

Come with me. Those haunting words.

"This was always the plan," I whisper, mostly to myself though.

"I guess. If by 'always' you mean for the last couple hours." He walks forward with long strides and in a few seconds he disappears into the trees. "C'mon, Mincemeat."

My insides flutter and my light follows his. I should have known Levi James would take me on an adventure.

"You're taking me hiking?"

"If you consider walking on flat ground to be hiking," he chuckles.

I do, but I don't say so.

"When you're looking to have a midnight date in Stone River, you have to improvise."

"Do you want me carry that?"

"Nope. We're close." He nods in the direction of more trees. I don't ask; I just follow.

We are quiet for a few moments, only our footsteps and the wind in the trees sound. Then I see where we are—the pond behind Graham's house. I've never seen it from this side. There is the tree with a rope tied from its branch so that we could Tarzan-swing into the water, and the dock as it leads to the backdoor of Graham's house. Familiar but backwards.

He smiles that smile that crushes my lungs and expands my heart. How does he know? How could he know that this view, from this angle, is just like this night with him? Same, but different.

"We had to have to a first date. A real date." He puts down the crumpled sack and lays out the quilt in an opening where there are fewer tree roots emerging from the earth. "And what better place than where we have spent the most time together."

My whole body warms. How could he know everything when I feel like I know nothing?

He waves his hand over the quilt. "Sit." And he joins me.

From the paper sack, he pulls out two Styrofoam bowls and

two plastic forks. I try to arch one eyebrow, but I've never been able to. He reaches his index finger out and touches my brow, lightly lifting it into an arch.

I gasp a laugh at the gesture that had long been forgotten. What a joke it had been that Juju and Levi could raise one eyebrow, as could Graham, but Drew and I couldn't no matter how much we tried. After enough ridicule, when they would arch their eyebrow in skepticism or disapproval, Drew and I would use our index finger to raise our own and match their expression.

"I forgot," I say amid laughter.

He tilts his head. "You forgot?"

I let out a last breathy laugh and look to the pond. "I forgot how quiet it could be out here."

Another plunge into the paper sack emerges with a container of sliced berries and a tub of yogurt dip.

"How did you do all this?"

"Well, I like seeing you surprised. Not a lot surprises you."

"I think that has changed recently."

"Really?" He narrows his eyes but lets the comment go.

We pop the lids and dig in, dipping the fruit and taking full juicy bites. For a second I think he's going to feed the fruit to me—is that what boys think is romantic? I hope not—but he doesn't.

This side of the pond is so quiet we can hear each other chewing. We have one night together. Am I really going to waste it being too shy? That's what 17-year-old Maggie would do. But I'm not 17.

"I don't want to ruin the night you've planned, but are we just going to sit here and not talk about what happened at the party?"

"You're different. Ever since that hug at church." He peers at me with those deep green eyes.

"You're changing the subject."

He laughs. "No, I'll answer whatever you want to ask. I'm an open book, and you like those."

I laugh with him.

"But really, what's different?"

I shrug. "I guess I didn't sleep well. It was a long night."

"Hmm," he grunts, popping a yogurt dipped strawberry in his mouth. "What do you want to know?"

I have so many questions, but I know exactly where to start. "Why'd you turn on Graham so fast? What happened between you guys?"

"We haven't been close for a long time. I mean, we've hung out while you all are here, but I haven't hung out with him for so long."

I had no idea. "Why?"

"We don't have anything in common except motorcycles." A few leaves crackle under him when he adjusts his legs. He's wearing motorcycle boots that closely resemble my Doc Marten's. "Honestly I don't even know what he's into other than partying. But I know he doesn't come to my shows, and if you haven't noticed, he disses everything."

He's treating this lightly, but his bright red knuckles tell a different story. "Did something happen with Graham and Juju?"

He shifts his body for longer than necessary, then attempting to sound casual asks, "Why?"

I wish he would quit stalling and be honest with me. "Because we were talking—I thought we were having a moment—and as soon as he started arguing with Juju, I couldn't get you back."

A patch of yogurt sits in the corner of his lips and he wipes it away. "It bothered me," he pauses, raking his fingers through his hair, "the way he treated her at the Industrial and wouldn't leave her alone. I didn't like it."

"Enough to do this." I caress my thumb over one of his knuckles. His hand doesn't flinch, but his jaw clenches. "I know this isn't date talk. I'm sorry. We just don't get much time alone—or any time alone—to talk."

"I know." He digs a couple water bottles out of the paper sack and hands me one. After taking a substantial drink, he says, "It was Danielle."

I pause with the water bottle centimeters from my mouth.

"She's the one who told me what Graham does."

My eyes widen with every word. "Like what?"

He picks a couple sticks out of the dirt beyond the edge of the quilt. "It was some of her friends. He didn't attack them or anything. I would have gone to the cops if he'd raped somebody."

I am as still as the water in front of us. The woods are so quiet that I feel like Graham could hear us from across the pond.

"Lifting up their skirts and grabbing them in places he shouldn't, stupid shit that he knows he shouldn't do." Levi shakes his head in slight motions as if it's tremors. "I felt like a jackass for not noticing. But after she told me, I couldn't look away anymore." He rests his elbow on his bent knee, staring toward the water. "I've see how he looks at Juju, but I thought there was a line. So the way he picked her up and wouldn't put her down at the Industrial—" he stops himself. "I wanted to beat the shit out of him then. I had to distract myself doing all of this." He waves his hand over the picnic in front of us.

"Why haven't you told Juju?" If I can convince him to tell her, then hopefully she won't meet Graham there in a few days.

"Danielle asked me not to say anything."

"That's ridiculous. Why?"

"She said her friends were embarrassed. For all I know, he's done it to her and she just won't admit it."

"Or she's scared."

"Yeah. Well, maybe Graham's the one who's scared now."

"So that's why you did it."

"For all of them. However many there are."

I bite my lip. "You need to tell Juju."

He sighs.

I rest my hand on his, careful not to touch the split skin. "I wish more people saw how deeply you care."

His fingers move against mine, like we are magnetically charged. "I never wanted you to think I picked her over you. I would never do that."

"Oh, more great date talk." I laugh. "We really don't have to talk about her."

"I know. But I just wasn't sure where you were at. We never talked about it. We had moments here and there, but I didn't know—"

Why had I never said anything? I always picked a book over anything else, always hoped he would make the move. Always afraid. Always waiting.

He continues, "I know it was unfair for me to decide for both of us. I should have said something, asked or something. But if I had known," he shakes his head, then leans in to me, touching his forehead to mine. "I'll always choose you."

Now he chooses me. Now he says it. When it's too late.

"I shouldn't have made you wonder where I was at." I inhale

the courage to say what I never could. "That first letter was supposed to be a declaration."

He squints, because I'm still not being clear enough.

"I never really wanted a pen-pal. That letter was me asking you out. And every letter after was like a long distance date." I smile at him, remembering how I would run to the mailbox looking for the next letter, wondering if he did the same thing. "I probably should have made that more clear."

He puts his arm around my waist and scoots me closer to his side. "That would have helped."

"Thank you for bringing me here," I say, leaning my head into his shoulder.

"Oh, we're not done."

My eyes shift up to his.

"If we only have one night for a real date, we're going to make it one helluva night."

And we do. Only have one night. Unless…

Twenty-One

"I don't want to break in to another place, Levi."

"We're not breaking in," he says with a smirk that says he has everything figured out. He holds up a little key chain with a lone key hanging from it. "I work here."

"What? I thought you worked with your dad." This little trip is teaching me so much.

"I do both. I can only work here at the beginning of summer because of band camp and all the other stuff in August, but I'll start back in September."

Was I included in all the other stuff in August?

"This one time, at band camp…"

He rolls his eyes at my *American Pie* reference.

"Oh, you've heard that one before."

"Only every day since the movie came out." He unlocks the door to the Stone River Lanes bowling alley. A light flickers.

"It's still funny though."

"Okay, Ms. Babysitter's Club."

I hold up my index finger between us. "Hey, I learned a lot from those books on how to make money. My friends and I started our own babysitter's club, I'll have you know." I step over the threshold into the quiet building. The manager's office is on the right; the concession stand is ahead of me.

"Hmm," he says. "Did you buy your own BSC sweat suit with all that money?"

"Oh, that stupid gray sweat suit will haunt me forever."

Levi locks the door behind us, and steps in front beckoning me to follow him.

"This is where the Toilet Bowlers got their name," he says as we pass the bathroom.

"Gross."

"You think I'm joking."

"Please, tell me you're joking."

"Maybe." He makes it to the counter in a couple strides, lays the keys down with a clink, then adds, "It'd make a great CD release party, though, right?" He turns on the disco ball in the middle of the bowling alley. Rays of light splay everywhere as it starts its rotation.

Music springs from the speakers with a demo recording I've only heard once.

I point toward the ceiling speakers, wanting to be right but not quite sure. "This is you."

"Well, not just me. The Toilet Bowlers."

I laugh like I always do when he says their name so seriously.

"C'mon," he says as one bowling lane comes to life. The mechanical arms set the bright white pins down in their homes.

There are ten lanes, but Levi has only turned on the one under the disco ball.

He stops me right under the ball, the lights beaming above us, glittering through the air. "It's not a bookstore, but I don't have a key to one of those so it'll have to do." And he leans toward me, his lips parting just enough for me to feel his breath and slow enough for a deep inhale of my own.

His lips are centimeters from me, millimeters.

"What doesn't make sense is the logo," I say against our almost-kiss.

His green eyes—that look almost blue under the disco lights—quiz me. Because I *am* different than I used to be. I'm playing with him instead of turning to putty.

"The Toilet Bowlers logo. The toilet is at the end of the bowling alley, but there's only one toilet instead of ten, like bowling pins. So it doesn't make sense." I taunt him. My palm rests on his chest and his heart beats like a kick-drum.

"I don't think it was supposed to make sense." He laughs, and the breath of it caresses my face. "But this does." He puts both of his hands on the sides of my face, pulls me in without any hesitation, so that I can no longer resist.

This kiss is completely different from our first kiss. Maybe because I am different. I am stronger now. More me. But mostly because we are different together. He sees me, and I recognize myself in his eyes.

His lips are hard against mine. My hair tangles in his fingers, untamed and wild after the motorcycle ride. His teeth bump against mine and a giggle bubbles out of me. He is a 17-year-old, somewhat inexperienced kisser, and I am in my 17-year-old body and—

I am suddenly aware that I am doing something horribly wrong.

He must feel me pull away because he steps closer to me, so close that his right foot steps on my left one. He searches my face, so I attempt to get back to when things were lighthearted.

"Wait, is this what you brought me here for?" I nervously tease. I step back from him. "Because I really wanted to bowl."

At first when he peers at me, I think he'll argue, but instead he says, "Alright, alright," all *Dazed and Confused* like.

I slide my hand down his arm—muscles and pulsing veins under my palm. I wrap both of my hands around his because I don't want this to end just yet. But I am letting go a little more every moment.

The demo restarts over the loudspeakers. There is only one song on it.

"So, this is what you want to do? Be a musician?" I ask.

"No," he answers quickly like it's not the first time he's been posed this question. "I want to do something less...stereotypical."

"Oh, right, because being a famous rock star drummer is such a stereotype."

He chuckles. "When you're a drummer, it is."

"So what do you want to do?"

"Travel," he answers more serious than he's been all night. "I want to see everything."

Under his gaze, I can't breathe. Or remember how.

He sits down on the bench and unties his shoes. I follow suit. "The best rock climbing place I've been to is in Grand Rapids because I haven't made it further than Michigan. I haven't seen anything, and I'm afraid I never will."

The adventurous, adrenaline-junky Levi has never left the state. And if I don't accomplish what I hope for tonight, then he won't get the chance.

"Everybody thinks I'm a daredevil or something. But I'm not.

I'm just restless." He removes his motorcycle boots while he talks, almost as though he's talking to himself. "When it comes to the things that count, I always play it safe. Dating Danielle was safe. Working for my dad is safe."

I want to say something, but I'm not sure what, so I take my time slipping off my shoes. It seems easier for him to talk openly when our hands are busy with something.

"I mean, what if I end up here in Stone River working for my dad fixing up cars for the rest of my life?" He shrugs, setting his boots aside and leaning his elbows on his knees. "There's nothing wrong with it. I love my dad. He works harder than anybody I know. But it's not what I want. And I think Dad knows. I mean, I'm not going to college. So what's left? How am I supposed make money roaming around the world like a nomad?"

I've never heard him talk like this. "Is that what you want? To be a nomad?"

"For now, yeah. Maybe someday it'll change but I want to pack up my stuff in the saddle bags of my bike and just drive. I've heard about youth hostels. I don't know how many there are but I'd figure something out. I just want to see all the things I've only ever heard about."

I smile, sleepily. His plan suits him, way more than being a rock star. I can picture him living it out. "I hope you do."

He scratches his forehead, as though the seriousness is now awkward, and returns his attention to the row of bowling balls. "I just haven't figured out how to make it happen yet." He stands abruptly and picks a black ball off the rack.

"You could go into photography and document your travels." I pick up a red ball but it's too heavy for me.

"That's more Juju's field, but she wants a more typical adventure."

"She was talking about moving to Texas." I laugh. "Don't know how adventurous that is."

"When you grow up in Stone River, going anywhere's an adventure."

"I guess so." I finally select a blue and green marble ball.

"You could come with me."

My head pops up and I give him a face says, "That's ridiculous." Traveling might sound romantic, but I have no interest in being a nomad, sleeping in youth hostels or in a sleeping bag under the stars. Sounds perfect for him, torture to me.

He laughs. "You'd have endless material for those books you want to write."

I give him the face again, to which he shakes his head.

He places his two middle fingers and thumb in the shocked face of the bowling ball. Wearing only socks, he crosses the glazed wood floor and sets up his first approach on the lane. "You've got books in you. I know you do."

As he releases the ball, I ask. "You do?"

He faces me, after his ball goes in the gutter. "I do."

I squint, lifting my ball up to my chest as I slide across the glossy floor. "Don't we need bowling shoes?"

"Ah, there's the rule-following Maggie we know and love." His ball returns from the pit with mechanical gusto and rolls into the rack. "When you break in to a bowling alley in the middle of the night, you can break the bowling shoes rule."

His next release is another gutter ball.

"I thought you worked here." I giggle at him.

"Worked is the key word. I hardly play, but I can spray some shoes."

I scrunch my nose at the thought of smelly, worn bowling shoes. He edges into my space on the runway, like he's going to teach me bowling form.

"Are you trying to show me how to get a gutter ball?" I gibe, but my skin prickles when his hand brush against my shoulder, every nerve reaching for him. This night is growing dangerous.

"If you'd like."

"I got it, thanks."

He raises his hands in surrender and steps back. I make a strike.

I wait a beat after my celebratory dance, then I crack myself open to reveal a deeper layer too. "I have the opposite problem as you." My hands hover over the fan, waiting for the ball to return. "I have this life already laid out for me that's beautiful and everything I've hoped for, but what if it's not enough? Although, if I throw it all away and the alternative is terrible too, then I could lose everything." Saying this out loud, I feel better and worse simultaneously. "What I have is great, but some days, I feel like I need more. Like I'm hiding myself away for everyone else's stuff to come first."

"Stop hiding," he says it as though it's obvious. "You don't have to throw everything away; you just have to speak up. Say what you want instead of guarding yourself so much."

I know he's right.

A quiet chuckle. "So you don't want to travel?" With the delivery of his question, he lets the ball roll down the alley with improved form. Seven pins fall.

"Sure, sometime. But that's why I like books. When I read, I can be two places at once."

"Why not be wholly, fully in one place?"

"Why do you give reading such a bad rap?" I ask, sitting in the cushioned chair awaiting my turn. "It's just a hobby."

"Because you don't treat it like a hobby." With the sound of metal grinding and air blowing, the bowling ball returns to its que and Levi picks it up.

"What do you mean?"

"You treat it like life. Like you only live through the characters you read. You aren't living life here and now."

"That's crazy."

"I know," he nods like I made his point. "You've missed a lot of living hiding behind those books."

The 17-year-old Maggie would pop back at him. But I understand, now, what he has always seen in me. His words ring true, having years to look back on, knowing what I have run from, what I found comfort in, what I longed for but hadn't the courage to dive toward.

Young Maggie wanted him to be wrong. I wanted life to happen to me without me having to make it happen. But that isn't the way it works. My feet were too hesitant to take the steps I needed or wanted, and it held me back. Safely, yes. But too safe.

"But I can learn a lot from books."

"At some point, you have to put the book down and live what you've learned."

"I guess we've both played it safe." It's nice to finally discover something Levi and I have in common.

His heavy eyes blink slowly.

"Should we call it a night? I don't want my grandparents to worry if they wake up and I'm gone."

"Okay."

I slide forward on my socks, like I'm skating toward him. When I am in front of him, I lift up on my tiptoes and kiss him on the cheek.

I leave it at that because I know who I am. I know who is waiting for me. And I don't want another regret when I return home.

Under the glittery ambiance of the disco ball, he gives a gentle nod that surprises and saddens me. Because that kiss on his cheek gave off no electricity. The heat between us is gone, and Levi seems to know it too.

My fingers search for his, wrapping them together like ten pinky-promises that I will learn from him, from his words.

I'm not holding hands with Levi my childhood crush any more but Levi my friend.

Twenty-Two

This night has been everything my 17-year-old self wanted. But it's no longer what my 27-year-old self wants. I want to be home, to tell Everett all the things I've been too afraid to say.

Levi's motorcycle stops in my grandparent's driveway, with only the waning moon watching us through the pine trees. He pops the kickstand, swings his leg over, then offers me his hand. Tonight is coming to an end—this dream world is coming to a close—but I'm afraid that I'll wake up 27 again, and Everett won't be there but neither will Levi.

I have one last chance.

"Levi," I swallow, imagining myself telling the full truth about this day, whatever that truth is. "Crazy things can happen in a year, but I need you to think about the future, about me. Don't do anything too dangerous. Nothing that could be permanent."

He hums out a tired laugh. "I'm adventurous, not reckless."

I don't know that I believe him.

"But I like that you are worried about me."

With Levi, I would always be worrying, wondering if his need to keep moving, to see the world, to chase the adrenaline spike would eventually be more important to him than me.

I know where I belong.

"Promise me," but I don't pause for an answer before saying, "When I come back next August, I want it to be just like this."

"Just like this," he promises but concern dances over his brows.

He accompanies me to the porch, a world away from our last goodbye. He opens the creaky screen door for me. This is the goodbye I always wanted, the goodbye that leaves no regrets and no questions in my mind.

I lean back against the siding of the porch, stealing a few more seconds with him. Now that I have the perfect good-bye, I don't want to say it. "We could hop back on the bike and drive away right now."

We both know I'm musing, but he goes with it.

"Your grandmother would accuse me of kidnapping you."

"I'd tell her it was my idea."

A truck ambles by, reminding me that we are not the only two humans alive or awake.

"We would barely make it out of Michigan before dawn." His voice creaks as he leans on the siding next to me, our shoulders touch. "We could stop and see the St. Louis Arch."

A breeze sweeps through our hair, bringing his scent to my nostrils and chilling my bones even in August. "There's this city we sometimes drive through on our way up here, Effingham. It's a horrible name, I know."

Vibrations from his chuckle pass through our touching shoulders.

"Right on the side of the highway is the largest cross in the country. It's huge, just standing there on the side of the road for everyone to see. My dad always makes us stop and stare at it. But not too far from the cross is a beautiful park and walking trails. I think you would like it there."

"I would."

Maybe it's not enough, but I have to believe I've done all I can to save him and my time here is done.

"Are you okay to drive home?"

He bumps his elbow against mine. "Yeah. I'm good on no sleep."

My tongue is thick as I swallow. "You aren't immortal. Remember that, okay." Tears threaten my eyes and throat, a mixture of sleep deprivation and good-byes.

He winks at me. "Not immortal. Noted."

I face him. Even in the dark I can see him staring at my mouth. In another lifetime, I would kiss him full on the lips. But I'm not that girl anymore. How differently this night could have gone if I'd jumped on his motorcycle and done all of this ten years ago. I bury my face in his chest, hugging tight, letting myself feel his muscle and bones one last time. "Thank you for tonight."

The same longing I remember from our first goodbye on this porch returns to his face, but this is all I can give him.

"Until next August," he says.

I nod, and my stomach knots. "Good night." I step inside the house and close the door behind me. For one last glimpse, I inch over to the window and push aside the sheer curtain to see him under the porch light. Even with no lights on inside the house, he looks right at me, like he knew I would return to this spot. He raises one hand in the air, but this time, he adds a smirk. I wave back, whether he can see me or not. Because this is how we should say goodbye, waving through the window clear of regrets.

When he has gone, I tiptoe down to the bedroom and climb over Drew, who has taken his rightful place on the air mattress. This is the only time in our lives I have snuck into the house after Drew is home and asleep. I don't bother to put on pajamas, only slip off my boots and climb in bed. Before I pull the covers over my body, I pat Drew on the shoulder, shaking him. He groans, not really conscious, but I say anyway, "Good night, Drew."

He responds with another groan, but the fact that he responds at all makes me smile.

I lay down on my right side, facing the side of the bed Everett always sleeps on. Because when I wake up, I want to be looking at Everett's face.

When I close my eyes, I imagine him exactly how he will be when I open them—his scruffy chin before he shaves it clean for work, his disheveled hair against the white pillow, his adoring eyes opening to meet mine.

Everett is my dream and my hopes. He is my future. And Levi, well, Levi is my first love, my childhood dream, my past. And dreams change.

It seems like no time from the moment I close my eyes, imaging my home, my husband, my life, to the moment I wake, opening my eyes to the sun blaring against my eyelids. I smile before I open them, hoping that I wake to the same life I left in this bed 24 hours ago.

My vision blurs around the sun beaming at me. But the space next to me is empty. My eyes close again, hoping Everett is getting ready for work as usual. Then I feel a hand shake my shoulders.

"Maggie," a male voice says.

Something isn't right.

"Maggie, we're late. We overslept."

I roll to my back, and a bed spring jabs me in the ribs.

"Hey, at least you're still dressed." Drew's face is above me.

Twenty-Three

"Why am I still here?" I bolt out of bed.

"I know. We were supposed to leave for the airport ten minutes ago." Drew's breath smells of minty toothpaste. "Grandma's freaking out."

I scan the room. It's exactly how I left it last night when I drove off on Levi's motorcycle. My suitcase is at the end of the bed, with today's clothes laid out over the brass footboard. Drew grabs the shirt and pants, throws them in the suitcase and zips it up.

"Here." He hands me my toothbrush and his toothpaste. "I'm going to go load this in the car."

I don't understand. Questions swirl around my head.

"Magdalene," Grandma hollers.

I close my eyes one more time, willing the room to change. But when I open them, I'm still here.

I jump out of bed and fumble my Docs on, squeeze toothpaste on my toothbrush and put it in my mouth on the go.

"Must have been a crazy night," Drew murmurs to me once we are in the backseat and well on our way to the airport. He wiggles his eyebrows at me.

I rub my temples at the headache setting in.

"Maybe you can sleep on the flight."

God, please don't let Drew be chatty.

Then I remember I never saw him at the field party with Graham but I'm assuming he was there.

"How'd you get home last night?" I whisper. There's a benefit to grandparents not hearing so well.

Drew looks at me like I'm crazy. "After Levi beat the living shit out of Graham, he paid somebody to take us home."

"How do you remember any of that? Weren't you plastered?"

"It's hard to forget your cousin getting his face busted by somebody you thought was your friend."

I roll my eyes at him. "There's more to it than that."

"Oh yeah? Is that why you ran off with Levi?"

I jab him in the ribs. "Shhh." I don't want to do this right now. I can't take any more teenage drama. "I just want to be home."

"Soon enough," Drew says, as he puts his Walkman headphones on and pushes play.

Nope, I want to retort, *definitely not soon enough.*

***

My grandparents walk us to the gate, because 9/11 hasn't happened yet. I try to be present as we say good-bye, but last night felt like all the good-byes I could take. The airplane hums. The flight attendant brings me water and peanuts. Her sympathetic expression tells me she sees the tear rolling down my face, but I ignore it, staring vacantly out the window.

By the time the plane lands, the tears are merely dried streaks on my face because I don't have the energy to wipe them away.

My parents come into view while Drew and I are still on the jetway, and as soon as I recognize the Asian couple in front of us, the same wave of emotion roils through my body as the first time. When we step out, I throw myself into Mom's arms, feeling both at home and so far away.

They look so young. My dad's hair is brown with no trace of gray, and my mom has a few laugh lines around her eyes but otherwise, her face is perfect. I can barely look at Robbie, who hugs my waist with voracity. I didn't think of him at all today, and I can't meet his eyes. Our family has become too distant over these ten years.

Breathing becomes ragged when I imagine living those ten years again. Or were they the dream and this is real? Did I only dream Everett up? And our house with the porch swing and the perfect buttery yellow walls?

My insides ache. The life I knew is an internal organ ripped from me, and I might bleed out.

When Mom hugs me, I wrap my arms around her and sob, right there in the middle of the gate, with strangers and businessmen hurrying by. I hear my dad make an exclamation, but I can't make the words out as my mother pets my hair with her hands.

"Oh my love," she says. Not once does she try to pull away. I know now that's one of my mother's parenting mottos: Never be the first to pull away from a hug.

I feel delusional, more and more as the day goes on. Walking through a life I've already lived through. Entering my bedroom, mixed emotions fight for my attention. Cry or vomit? My body can't decide. The room is brighter than in my memory. My fingers graze the bedpost I used to get in trouble for hanging my dirty clothes on. I scan the bookshelf which hold my favorite books. Hidden in the back are the *Babysitter's Club*. My dresser is covered in framed pictures of moments I barely remember. I pull out the Polaroid of me and Levi from my suitcase and set it in front. A memory I actually have.

When I go to sleep that night, I lay on my side, hoping once again, that I will wake up to Everett's face.

But I don't.

I live the life of a 17-year-old, more confused than I was the first time around.

After lunch, I lock myself in my bedroom to call Juju.

"'Sup chica. How was your flight?" she asks nonchalantly. "Levi didn't get home until the wee hours of the morn. You know something about that?" She giggles.

"Listen, I had this dream about you," I say. I want her ears perked as I talk. I can no longer afford to be subtle.

"Oh yeah. Give me the 411."

"It just freaked me out." I'm not lying. "Just don't go anywhere with Graham."

She exaggerates a sigh. "Are you still on this Graham thing? Levi's the one who went postal."

"Juju, I'm serious. I know it was just a dream, but I think you and Levi need to talk."

"About?"

"Levi told me why he let loose on Graham. He knows about some things Graham did—"

"Wait, do you mean Levi told you about it your dream?"

This is so confusing that I consider telling her all of it, but I know she'll think I'm crazy and paranoid, but if life started unfolding the way I tell her, would she pay attention then?

"No. Well, I guess so. In my dream, Graham invited you to a party at the Industrial, but when you got there, no one else was there except Graham. And he—"

"Were you there?"

"I guess, I don't know."

"You know I read this magazine article in *Seventeen* about dreams. It said if you aren't part of the dream, then it's because you want to see something change or you don't want to be part of it because you don't think it's right."

"Yes, exactly."

"Aren't dreams so interesting?"

"Juju, you're missing the point. Let me finish."

"Okay," she quiets.

"If Graham invites you to a party, just don't go alone, okay? Or at all."

Her response is stilted. "Okay."

"Pinky promise over the phone?" I ask, curling my finger into the phone cord.

"Pinky promise over the phone."

I don't know if I believe her. I never used to question her, but now I question everything.

***

After dinner while I help clear the table and rinse the dishes, Mom corners me. Her eyes bounce between me and my dad standing behind me. When she nods, his footsteps evacuate the kitchen, then she and I are alone.

"Is everything alright?" She takes a rinsed bowl from me and arranges it in the dishwasher.

I shrug, passing her another bowl. "Sure."

"It's just that you've been quiet all day—more than usual—and when we picked you up at the airport, you were so emotional, I thought maybe—" she tiptoes around the question, "Did something happen while you were in Michigan? Something traumatic?"

I lay my hand on top of hers and squeeze. It's not a 17-year-old's response, and she looks at our hands together with another question looming. I want to tell her yes, but instead I say, "No. Everything's great."

***

Each morning I wake up here, I come to grips with the fact that I might actually stay 17. All those little changes I made became cracks in the past, and I might be living out some alternate reality or a sideways life.

Gah, I should have read more sci-fi.

Except nothing has changed. Drew still doesn't want to have anything to do with me, and when he does, he rambles incessantly. Robbie still wants to play in my room. Dad is over enthusiastic, and Mom is self-deprecating. Ally is still my best friend here, which makes me really sad that I have stayed close with yet another friend.

The first day of school makes me want to throw up even more. This is what it's all led to. The first day of school. I dreaded it the first time; I am terrified of it now.

Still, I wake and dress myself in the clothes Mom and I picked out. I wait at the front door for the honk of Ally's car, but really, I'm waiting for Geometry. If I make it through Mr. Gonzalez' class without interruption, then I'll know.

I'm quiet in Ally's car. I don't have a snarky remark when Stephanie Willwright and her ridiculous license plate parks by us. I'm holding my breath until fourth period. Under any other circumstances, it might be fun to walk through the halls of my old school, remembering every corner's significance. But these halls get smaller the further in I go. I want to turn and run back to the parking lot, to my house, to the airport, back to Michigan. I want to camp out at the Industrial and make sure no one enters, but by then, I'd be too late.

I'm so stuck in my head I don't notice what Ally is talking about. I scan the halls like it's my first day and like it's my class reunion all in one. These people were my judge and jury. My self-esteem rose and fell on their glances or their whispers. How does anyone get through high school unscathed? Maybe no one does.

Third period ends with the slamming of books and the scuffing of chairs against the floors. I'm living that recurring dream, where I'm back in school and am expected to know a bunch of things I don't remember, ready to take a test I haven't studied for. I wish I knew how to wake myself up.

Mr. Gonzalez is just as scattered and kind as I remember, but I still hate seeing him walk through the door. I'm still holding my breath. I want to hide in the bathroom, lock the doors and pretend I'm lighting up in the handicap stall. But running would only prolong the truth.

It doesn't take long. The door clicks open; my head goes dizzy. The admin aide walks in just like I remember, but the room is spinning.

Oh god, I've lived through this once, I don't know if I can live through it again.

"Ms. Maggie Thayer?" Mr. Gonzalez calls my name, and I want to yell, *That isn't my name. My name is Maggie Lange. I'm 27 years old. I'm married to a wonderful man named Everett. I shouldn't be here.*

Instead I stand and walk with the aide out of the room. Yes, I leave all of my stuff even though I know what's coming. I walk the halls like a dead man. Except I'm not the one headed to my death, just my breaking.

I see my mother in the office, but I can't play along. When the doors open, I give her a flat look. "Who's dead?"

"Oh Maggie," she says, her eyes bloodshot and chin quivering.

"Just tell me," I manage.

"He's not dead."

"Who?"

I'm not walking with her outside. I'm not going anywhere or waiting any longer. I want her to say the name. What if it's Graham? I chide myself as soon as I think it.

"Levi James."

I'm crashing with him, thrown from the moving vehicle. The world spins upside down. I'm dizzy and I can't make out any sounds, but they are already locked away in my memory.

I stagger to the bathroom. My timeline is off yet again. I didn't stay to talk with my mom. I didn't make it back to class. But I'll hide in the bathroom until I can wake up. On the cold linoleum floor, my knees against my chest, I bang the back of my head against the wall. What did I do wrong? Why the hell am I living through this again?

Mom doesn't follow me. I guess she's waiting for Drew. Or she knows I need time.

But time folds into itself until I have no idea what hour it is or how many people have come in and out of the bathroom, stepping around me, giggling and talking to each other until they see me. I stare at one gray fleck in the tile. It's bigger than the others around it. Larger than life. As Levi was. He hasn't died yet. Machines keep him alive, but I know he's gone. Nothing I've done or can do will bring him back. So why am I still here?

The door opens and closes. There is a voice I recognize. Vanessa. I forget her last name, but I know what happens next. Something I actually want to relive. I want to hit her, to feel strong again, even if only for a second.

"We heard about your friend."

My hand is already balled into a fist, veins pulsing. I envision how Levi punched Graham, his arm whirling around. Anger and sadness swarm me like flies. Vanessa's smug expression reflects from the mirror.

"Drew told us," Stephanie says, standing next to Vanessa.

My fingernails press into my palm. I don't trust my response, so I stay quiet.

"Can I tell you something?" Vanessa starts with her piercing voice. I know her statement word for word. "I know this is really hard for you, but everything happens for a reason."

With each word, I can feel the anger rise like bile from my gut. The betrayal of whatever sent me here and whatever started this whole mess. Like a monster growing inside me, I feel it reach my hands. But when I blink, I see Levi staring at his own bleeding hands.

Levi's anger cost him his life. He let it take control for just a few minutes, and it ruined him. I can't let it ruin me. I promised to learn from him.

A ragged breath escapes. "I don't believe that," I say, too loudly.

Vanessa bristles.

"I don't believe everything happens for a reason. I believe we write our own story." Isn't that what Levi did? He knew better than to chase after Graham. He was so smart; he had to know it wasn't a good idea. I even warned him. But he lost himself to it anyway. He wrote his own story.

And I have to write mine too.

***

Every minute of waiting until Mom sets foot in my room to tell me Levi's gone is painstaking. The first time I hoped that he would wake up in the hospital. That was the danger. This time my hope was lost as soon as the accident happened.

I listen to Mom deliver the news with the same cadence. She moves with slow deliberation, her limbs heavy. I never considered what pain my mother must be in. Her best friend's son, the same age as her own son, dying so young. I can't imagine her worry. Had she even slept? I picture her pacing the floors, checking on us once we've cried ourselves to sleep, sobbing into my dad's arms. I never recognized my parent's brave faces.

"How are you, though?" I ask.

Tension drains from her face and her shoulders. "Oh honey," she grips my hand tight, "I could never imagine anything like this happening."

"Me either," I choke out. Again, I rest my head in her lap, and I avoid pivoting away from the pain. I choose to feel every moment of it.

After Mom leaves, I pick up the phone to call Juju, but I just can't. How the accident happened does matter anymore. Only that it happened. He's dead. I'm still here. And I don't know why either has happened.

Levi was our glue. Maybe the unraveling of our friendships would have been a natural progression of growing into adulthood. But now we can never know. With his death, spider web cracks split across the windshield of our friendships and lives. We would always see the split happening alongside the death, two events that changed everything, intertwined forever.

Unless…

Levi may be gone, but the four of us are still here. The weight of our friendship and our future presses on my chest until I can hardly breathe. Maybe this is why I was sent here all along. Not Levi. For those of us he left behind.

Twenty-Four

The first time I see Graham after Levi's death, I want to slap him, punch him in the gut, bruise the parts of him Levi left untouched.

Drew and I take our loquacious walk to the James' home, and there Graham stands in their home as if he didn't ruin their family. As if he didn't cause Levi's accident. Drew pats Graham on the back. I catch Drew's eyes, but he shrugs. *What?* he mouths. I roll my eyes. I want to tell him. Maybe I should, but the secret isn't mine to share.

Graham turns. One eye and sections of both sides of his jaw are shaded with blue and green bruises. "Hey guys," he says. The same regret I felt for ten years hangs in his expression. His disheveled hair says he just rolled out of bed, but everything else about his appearance screams that he hasn't slept in days. Without warning, he hugs me. His grip is tight, but not in the way he grabbed Juju at the Industrial. This is the unyielding hold of grief. For a moment, I expect him to cry as he buries his face in my shoulder, but he inhales and let's go, repeating the same behavior with Drew.

All of the anger and hatred leaks out of me. I think of the years to come and how he will deal with this pain: the drinking, the drugs, the rehab stints. None of us knew why except Juju.

Judging someone from the outside is so easy. As though we sit on a throne of perfection, pointing down when people are at their lowest, sentencing them to delinquency. But haven't we all tried to numb ourselves from the pain in different ways? Juju turned down scholarships and never pursued her bigger dreams, because Levi couldn't. I should know. I played it safe, since the one person I knew who took the big risks died.

In the end, we all allowed Levi to hold us back. And he would never have wanted that.

Now I have the chance to glue us back together and heal.

I extend my arm to Graham, grip his hand. His eyes connect with mine, and I'll never forget the brokenness in his face. "Come with me." I deliver those haunting words to Graham, let them hold new meaning.

Somehow he senses the need for privacy and steers us toward the basement. Neither of us want to continue all the way down this hall leading to Juju's room and then Levi's.

"I know," I tell him once we are alone. A question hangs in his expression. I don't want to say the words, but we all have to do things we don't want to now. "I know what happened with you and Juju. How Levi died."

Panic wrecks him. His entire body trembles. "It's all my fault." His voice cracks the way it did when he hit puberty, when he was still innocent.

"It's not," I say, in disbelief at my own statement. "Levi made his own choices." I place a hand on his shoulder, because I don't know if I can bear another of his fierce hugs.

He covers his face with his hands. They are crisscrossed with scratches that I can only assume happened at the field party. "I'm so scared. What if they find out?"

I don't ask which *they* he means—the police, Greg and Rose James, his parents. All of the above.

"It was an accident, Graham. It was just an accident."

He nods, gasping into his hands.

I ask the dark question that haunts me, that haunts Juju. "Why did you invite Juju there alone?"

His Adam's apple bobs, swallowing his pride to respond. He runs his hand over his close cut hair as he slowly answers, "I just wanted to talk to her. I've been stupid. With girls. But the way Juju looked at me about that damn picture—I didn't want to be stupid with Juju. I wanted to tell her it was different with her."

The pieces begin to shift, showing a clearer picture.

"But I was drinking. If I'd gotten drunk...." he finishes the thought with a choked gasp. "Maybe Levi was right." I have never seen Graham cry, but tears streak down his face. "I don't even know."

"Oh Graham," "Levi said he saw the way you looked at her."

He nods.

"You care about her."

He crosses his arms, protecting his heart. "It doesn't matter now. I ruined it all." His head hangs low, and I grab him into a hug. He buries his face into my shoulder, shifting his weight onto me. I hold him up, sharing the weight of what he has carried. Because I know something about regret, but my regrets compare little to his. "Oh god, I need help. I need help."

"It's okay," I whisper.

"No, it's never going to be okay again," he whimpers.

This boy who has always been my brother's friend, the one who gave ridiculous nicknames and laughed everything off, the one I was never close to, the one I had wished dead now bares his soul to me. I see him more clearly than I ever have. And even though he's always been my cousin, now he's my family. We've always had the same blood in our veins, but now we have the same pain running through them as well.

Shared regret is a powerful drug. Shared understanding, though, is a healing balm.

I reach out and tug his arm to release him from his own prison. "It will be okay. We'll get through this, but I need you to do something."

He drops his hands by his side waiting.

"I need you to tell Drew too."

There's a new fear in his eyes.

"It's the four of us now. You don't need to hold this all alone."

When we find Drew outside, Graham gestures to him. They sidle up against the fence.

Juju's lying on the trampoline, staring up into the sky, exactly as I remember. Drew and I lay down next to her. I whisper in her ear, "I talked to Graham."

Her head jerks my way, deciphering what I mean.

"He told me." I say this, even though in another life she is the one who told me, voice cracking over the phone, drowning in a secret she'd held for too long. Now, she can be free.

"Please don't tell anyone."

I stare at the sky and tell them both, "It'll be our secret. All four of us."

"I'm glad you're here." Juju glances past me to Graham. "All of you." She wraps her arms around the crooks of mine. It doesn't take long before the guys climb onto the trampoline too, Drew on the other side of Juju and Graham next to me. We link arms with theirs the same way.

We create a new friendship bracelet, sewn together by tragedy, the way the best of friends usually are.

"We should make a slideshow," Drew says. "With pictures and videos of Levi. To celebrate his life the way Ms. Rose wants."

"But no stuffy pictures," I add. "Only ones that show the Levi we knew."

Juju smiles against my shoulder where she has laid her head. "He would like that." Then she's up in the air, jumping, bouncing us like when we were little and used to play "Crack the Egg." Our laughter echoes through the backyard, through the sky, and rises through the clouds.

It surprises me how easy it is to laugh with us all together.

We follow Juju to her bedroom, squeezing down the halls, past the visitors, the mourners, the gawkers. By the time Drew and I turn the corner to Juju's room, she's already in the closet, up on her toes, reaching for the photo box on a high shelf. Her crop top lifts a few inches, revealing a pattern of freckles that I usually only see when she wears a bikini.

Graham's eyes are on Juju until he meets my stare. "I'm going to need a drink if we're going to do this."

Drew grunts. "I said the same thing. But I think we owe it to Levi to stay sober."

We all grow quiet again.

"You need help?" I ask, but Juju's already hauling a box down.

"She's a mile taller than you. How could you help?" Drew says. If I rolled my eyes at Drew every time I wanted to, they really would get stuck that way.

Juju pulls out her stash of Polaroids. They are carefully organized in bundles. A few photos have the date written her loopy handwriting on the back. She pulls out a few stacks, some wrapped in ribbons, others in twine.

"These are mine. Then we can go through the family photos in the basement."

We stare at the photos on her bed, unmoving. Then together we take the plunge, each grabbing a stack and unwrapping them carefully like they are shards of glass.

In every photo, Levi's face is either hidden or blurry.

Juju rifles through them, an unsatisfied line between her eyebrows. "I don't—" She fans the photographs across her purple bedspread.

I spot a corner of the photo of Levi, Graham, and Drew on the motorcycles, on the main street across from the bookstore. I grab the white edge of the photograph and pull it from beneath the others. Drew and Graham are facing the camera, laughing. Levi looks over his shoulder away from the lens, only the corner of his smiling mouth showing.

"I don't understand," Juju slumps. "I took photos of him all the time." Her eyes stop scanning. "How do I not have a single picture of his whole face?"

Drew picks one up. "This one shows his face."

Levi's overexposed face fills the photograph. It's blurry and the top of his head is cut off. Only his nostrils and eyes are really visible.

Drew gives Juju a weak smile.

"We'll just get the family photo albums. There'll be tons in there," I say with a shrug, but the weight of sadness presses on my shoulders.

Juju barely acknowledges what I said.

"Hey," Drew taps her forearm. "These are pictures of a happy life. That's what I see here. I see the blur of Levi on the go. And he was always on the go. All of this is just how he moved. It's how he lived." Drew lets her arm go and lifts up a stack of photos. "This is how Levi should be remembered."

He's right. Of course I am as sad as Juju to not have a picture of Levi's face, but this was Levi—a blur of rust hair and ocean eyes, chasing his next adventure.

Twenty-Five

Driving from my grandparent's home to the high school auditorium feeds the anxiety in my stomach. Grandpa always drives leisurely, but today seems exaggeratedly slow. My shoulder rubs against Drew's as we are squeezed into the backseat with Mom. The roads are as quiet as we are, as though the entire town has paused for Levi's memorial.

A field that I hadn't noticed before stretches out next to the road. Sunflowers upon sunflowers reach high toward the sky, their faces toward the sun.

"Wait," I holler at Grandpa, then lean forward and pat him on the shoulder.

Grandma jolts, but Grandpa isn't fazed.

"Pull over here," I reach between their seats and point at the sunflower fields bordering the road.

Without question, Grandpa obliges. Grandma and Mom, on the other hand, throw questions at me as I climb over Drew and bound out of the car just as it stops.

I pull at the thick sunflower stalks, but they don't budge. They are stronger than I expected, but I keep trying. In not too long, these flowers will wilt and shrivel until they are just another part of the earth. A flash of summer, then gone. Just like Levi.

Drew is suddenly next to me with Grandpa's pocket knife. He cuts the stalks for me until we have a full bouquet.

When we return to the backseat, Mom rubs my knee. "They're beautiful," is all she can manage.

I don't have a vase or an obnoxious bow like the other bouquets surrounding his casket. But those bouquets aren't for him; they're for Rose and Greg. These sunflowers are for Levi. I exchange the bouquet for the camera Juju hands me to capture moments of the ceremony that I vividly remember. She places my messy bouquet in a pile underneath a full-size flower arrangement. I'm happy with it there.

Our PowerPoint slideshow plays after the eulogy. I sit with Mom and Drew to take it all in. Photographs of Levi fade into one another to the perfect songs selected by Graham from a mixtape he found—one that I recognize intimately. Music whirls around me. I close my eyes. I've stared at these photos long enough making the slideshow. I don't know that I can take another time.

Mom wraps her arm around my shoulder and Drew squeezes my hand. I peek at his hand resting over mine, protecting it, guarding it. I've waited years for my brother to stand up for me, and here he is.

He gives me courage to study the screen, the treasures uncovered—even more that we found in the James family albums—and the tribute we created. Levi as a baby. Levi playing drums. Levi working on his motorcycle. Levi on a school field trip. Levi in the snow barely visible underneath his snow clothes.

A celebration of his life, as short-lived as a sunflower.

Not all of the pictures we found are in the slideshow. Some we held back just for us.

Twenty-Six

Mom says Drew and I can spend the night at Juju's. It's not Levi and Juju's any more. Just Juju's.

Graham comes too. We all camp out in the common room of the basement. The James house isn't as big as Graham's, but the closeness feels right. There is no comfy gray couch, but there are bean bags and an air mattress—bigger than the one at my grandparent's. We watch home movies on VHS tapes. They are worn and discolored, and tracking lines run through the picture every now and then. But they make us smile, when otherwise we feel like breaking.

One of the videos starts in the snow. The camera person, I think it's Rose, is in the bed of a truck. She points the camera at the trailer attached to the back, where all of us—a gaggle of kids—sit ready to be slid around on the ice.

There I am in my big puffy, hot pink and black snow jacket. Based on my haircut, I was probably nine. That was the one year of my entire life I had short hair. Rose says loud enough for the kids to hear that we're about to take off. I, for one, had no idea what I was headed for. My hands are bright red with cold, and

Levi is two kids over from me. His cheeks are as red as his hair, but he's prepared with winter gloves that make his hands look the size of an adult's. I glance at Drew and he winks at me. We both know Levi is about to give me those gloves. *That's when I knew Levi had a crush on you.*

***

Juju and I lay on the air mattress. She falls asleep before I do, holding my hand. I stare at her for a long time. Without any makeup, she looks so much like Levi. Her translucent eyelashes flutter and I wonder if she dreams about Levi like I do. I wonder if she dreams that she could go back and change it all. What happens when she wakes up?

***

I wake before I open my eyes. I didn't even realize I'd fallen asleep. I don't feel Juju's hand in mine anymore, so I wonder if she is already up. I take a deep breath, wondering what today will hold, the day after the funeral of one of my best friends.

I open my eyes. And the only face in front of me is Everett's.

Twenty-Seven

Everett. I watch him as he sleeps, the lines splaying out from his eyes, the crooked smile hiding beneath his sleeping face, all the things I'd missed. All the things I was uncertain I would get back. All the things I love.

Last night was the first night I hadn't fallen asleep wishing I was here. And yet, here I am.

I don't want to wake him, because I don't know what to say. When I last laid in this bed, I thought I was being crushed under the ordinary monotony of life. But what I thought was ordinary is the very essence of an extraordinary life. A life I had too long taken for granted.

I feel like I've been away for ages, like my heart has run away and returned without Everett even knowing. But I'm here. I can hardly keep my body still with my heart sprinting so.

His eyes flutter open, and I stare into his hazel eyes like it's the first time. His sandy blonde hair a mess, our breaths smell, and our eyes have crust in the corners. But there is no place I would rather be.

"Hi," his mouth moves crookedly but hardly a sound comes out.

"Hi," I say back, taking him all in. "I have something to tell you," I whisper, one last secret to share. I'm through letting my fears and uncertainty dictate my story.

"Okay," he says, adjusting his head on the pillow expectantly.

"Well, a few somethings."

"Okay," he repeats with a smirk. I think he's enjoying this.

"I'm going to write a book," I let out.

"It's time," he nods. "It'll be wonderful." His words are husky with sleep. "What will you write about?"

"Hmm," I purse my lips together. "Maybe about a girl who goes back in time for a day then wakes up at home and realizes she's right where she wants to be."

A comical expression lights his face. "That is very specific. Is it autobiographical?"

"Maybe." I inhale a deep sense of home. "There are so many possibilities." And I don't want to miss a single one of them.

"Yes."

"And I want to take a trip."

"Where to?"

"Michigan."

His brows and lips raise this time.

"To see my grandparents." Then I think of Juju. And Ms. Rose and Greg. Graham. "And the rest of my family." I will not cry. I will only smile.

He leans in and kisses me. Morning breath and all. "I'm sure they'll love to see us again."

Again?

He starts to get up, "I'll make breakfast and get the laptop so we can plan it."

"No," I grab his arm and pull him back down to the bed. "No, let's stay here a bit longer."

He sucks in his bottom lips in his crooked smile, and he pulls me on top of him. I shriek.

"Was this the something else you wanted to tell me? If so, I like it," he says against my lips.

I nod, kissing him again. Then I put my index finger up between us, gesturing for him to wait a second. I slide out from the covers. My legs are bare, and I recognize my 27-year-old body from one glance. I dash into the office and grab the purple box, then return to the bed and jump under the covers, setting the box between Everett's legs and mine.

He sits up with me, fluffing a pillow and propping it behind his back.

"There was this boy." I draw off the lid and on top rests the Polaroid photograph of Levi and me standing on the scaffolding of the Industrial. That's how I know it was real.

"Is that you?" Everett asks, snagging the photograph and peering at it. "Who are you with? Is that Juju's brother?"

I gape at him. "Levi," I say, my heart ramming against my rib cage. "You know about Levi?"

"Just from what you and Juju have said. I guess I've never seen a picture though." Everett studies it closer. "He looks like Juju."

I prop myself up on one elbow facing him. "You said my grandparents would love to see us again." Pause, catching my breath. "When were we last in Michigan?"

"In March." He surveys my face. "You okay?"

"I had a weird dream,"

"About your grandparents?"

I nod, "And Levi." As I say his name, new memories pass over my mind. Taking Everett to Michigan, visiting Rose and Greg, the four of us plus Everett going rock climbing in Grand Rapids.

279

The images are instantly familiar, like something almost forgotten but with a token reminder, everything comes back.

"How about I get us some coffee and you tell me the whole dream." He leans in for a kiss.

But first, I wrap my arms around his neck, not missing the chance to say what I really want to say. I've learned too much. If I am too shy now, I may never be brave enough to change. But Everett's alive. I'm awake, in this bed, in this time, as it should have been all along. I'm not going to miss it.

"I love your smile. It's sexy as hell." I draw myself up to him, my mouth against his. This is the kiss I want, the life I want.

Epilogue
AUGUST 2019

I know you're still wondering what really happened. Was it a dream? Was it an *It's a Wonderful Life* experience? Was it all in my imagination? I honestly don't know. I wish I did.

My best guess is that when I was holed up in my office the night of the ten year anniversary, and I cried out, wanting to know if I could have changed things, then someone answered. I hope that can be enough for you. I've had to learn to let it be enough for me, because whatever it was, this unexplainable journey changed my life.

Yes, I wrote my book. And a few others since. Everett and I visit Michigan every year.

My grandfather died two years later. It was difficult going to another funeral in Michigan, but Everett was at my side, and on the other were Juju, Drew, and Graham. Grandpa died in January, so the gravesites were covered in sparkling white snow, and it reminded me how beautiful new beginnings can be. That's all "the end" means anyway. The end is just another new beginning.

You want to know what changed from my time reliving that

August? I wish I could say I spared Graham from the drinking or rehab stints, but I didn't. Juju didn't magically turn into a soccer star when I woke up in 2009 either. For the most part, life was the same. But we lived it together, wounded but no longer splintered apart.

Some of the memories have melded together. I often wonder if I had the memories wrong the first time around, but my original memories are still there though somewhat faded, like a movie that I dozed off during and only recall bits and pieces.

Juju made us all copies of the funeral slideshow, so I have proof it happened. And we play *Sorry!* when we are together, remembering that night at my grandparent's house after the field party. She always says, "I miss your grandpa," while we play.

"I do too."

I guess that's the thing with memories, you remember what's most important to you. And I supposed there are memories in both of my realities that were important to me.

***

Everett drives a rental car that is roomier than our car back home. We don't have any kids yet. That's a long story for another day. He takes his hand off of the gear stick in between us—it's an automatic, so I don't know why he keeps his hand on it—and squeezes mine. "You ready?"

"I don't know that you're ever ready for something like this," I say to him.

He lifts my hand to his lips and kisses my knuckles.

We drive down the main street of Stone River that isn't called Main Street. We pass the park where this year's Homegrown

Festival took place a few days before. We pass the lot that used to be the Industrial. It was torn down last year. After being vacant for so long, it became part of the new mayor's campaign to turn it into something new for the town. I haven't heard what they're building in its place.

Everett pulls into a parking place in front of a familiar building. There's a banner over the front door with my name on it.

Welcome, Magdalene Lange

Today is a book signing for my fifth book. And inside this bookstore—yes, *the* bookstore—the owner waits for me to sit in front of a small group to read a portion of my book, answer questions about how I became an author—which I sometimes wonder myself—and what inspired this book. Readers will sit in a semicircle in front of me, looking to me for answers and inspiration, or something like it.

All the while, I'm wondering the same thing. How did I get here? I guess, in some way, it all goes back to Levi. If nothing else, he taught me to live in the moment.

Everett opens the door to a slew of people cheering for me. I laugh, truly surprised.

Next to the bookstore owner is Juju front and center. Greg and Rose. Uncle Frank and Aunt Tammy. I see my parents. Dad's hair is a white halo around his head, and Mom wears mom jeans all over again. I don't know how those have come back in style, but as always she's trendier than she gives herself credit for. Drew is next to her, with a pot belly that matches his wife, Amy's pregnant belly. And Robbie, all grown up and in his residency program at a hospital in California. I couldn't be more proud of him—even if he is in plastics. Grandma stands to the side, wearing a demure smile, her skin pleated with wrinkles. Seeing her creates an ache for Grandpa.

I've barely had a chance to take them all in before they rush toward me and hug me. I'm almost in tears—happy, euphoric tears—but I hold them back knowing I'm about to speak in front of strangers. In fact, I see those strangers over everyone's shoulders chatting. Somehow they must be in on all of this, since none of them look confused.

"What is everyone doing here?" I ask no one in particular. I almost correct myself. Everyone is not here. Of course Levi isn't, but there is someone else missing.

A few people start to answer, but they stop when Mom says, "We thought we'd make it a party."

"I can't believe everyone was able to come at the same time."

Juju shrugs. "It's the twentieth anniversary. We all wanted to be together."

Today is August 26th. The twentieth anniversary of a day that feels like a lifetime ago. If I hadn't told Everett the entire story, I would feel like that was a different Maggie. Which is why I'm glad I stopped hiding it away in the purple box. I'm glad I brought it out to the light of day, so that he could share in the laughter and sadness. Telling Everett freed me as much as it freed Graham to hear he wasn't alone in his secret.

The bell rings behind me as the front door opens. Before I can turn, a hand touches my arm, rough and calloused.

"Hey there, Mincemeat," Graham says.

I can no longer hold the tears at bay. I bring him in for a hug. He has aged more than the rest of us, had a harder twenty years than us, but there is still hope. Last month, he posted a picture on Facebook when he received his three-year sobriety chip. I commented, "I'm so proud of you."

Everett pats him on the back, and Juju bounds toward him with her typical exuberance. "It's about time," she says.

Graham kisses her on the cheek, his hand on her waist. Neither of them are married, and the glance they exchange says there is more between them.

Juju blushes, "Now we can take our photo."

She is the original selfie queen. I suspect it is because of her long arms. We all squeeze together as she raises her camera phone and squats down in front so that everyone's faces can be seen.

Around me are all the people I love, and I wonder if I'm the glue now. Levi kept us together for so long. He was the bridge that crossed between the boys and the girls, the family and the friends. When he was gone, we needed something to I pieced us back together. A crack in a windshield never goes back together perfectly, but you can mend it and keep from it shattering to tiny separate pieces. That's what I've done. Brought us back together, and together we are stronger.

Lynn, the bookshop owner, ushers everyone to the back of the store. I can see the two high back chairs that she and I will sit in.

I touch her arm gently. "Can I have a moment to gather my thoughts?"

She returns a smile. "Of course."

"I won't be long."

She nods and scurries off.

I walk toward the back wall of books. The shelves haven't changed much, only the collection of books on them. I can almost feel him again, but this time I know it's only in my memory. My feet are grounded beneath me. My fingertips tingle, remembering. I touch the wooden shelf, between Grafton and Grisham. The blue-spined book is gone, and I suddenly wish I knew which book it was. But the book itself doesn't matter, really. What matters is that every time I stand in this spot, I remember it was all real.

I spent years waiting for August, when I should have been living big every month of every year. I may not know exactly what happened, but with a little change in my perspective, I've learned to love every August. And all the months and days in between. Even the hard ones. For they are the days that carry me to the good ones.

Breathing in the scent of books and memories, I step around the corner to the crowd awaiting me. I sit in the maroon chair opposite Lynn, and I take questions. Some answers I can give, and some I'm okay with not knowing.

Enjoy *Waiting For August*? You can make a big difference.

Honest reviews not only helpful for me as an author, but it also spreads the word and gets this book in front of other readers. If you've enjoyed this book, I would be grateful for you to take a few minutes leaving a review (it doesn't have to be long, just spoiler-free!) on Amazon and other online book retailers.

Don't forget to share your review and even a photo on social media with the hashtag #WaitingForAugust to encourage others to read the story too.

Thank you so much!

ACKNOWLEDGMENTS

Book ideas come from a million different places. A dream, a song, a question, a moment in the author's life. This idea developed slowly, much like Juju's Polaroid photographs.

See, there was once a boy who wrote me letters. As a kid, I traveled a lot with my parents, so I had a few pen pals. (Back in the old days!) But I kept all of this boy's letters. He was just a friend—okay, I had a little crush on him at 15—and I wish we'd had a different good-bye. Some pieces of him are reflected in Levi, but not all of them. He wasn't reckless and never hurt anyone, but I came to realize I didn't know him as well as I would have liked. Thus the idea of Maggie and Levi was formed. What if?

So, Tim Freeman, thanks for the letters. Maybe we'll get that motorcycle ride on streets of gold.

Sally Hall, for loving this idea in the parking lot of Barnes & Nobles, and for loving it all the way to print. I am a better writer with you.

Brittany McWhorter, for every Marco Polo, every laugh, and every push.

Angelica Plata, thank you for getting me passed all the past grammar mistakes. (Was that right?!)

Dani Abernathy, for every valuable and hilarious comment.

Mom and Dad, because of you, writing is in my blood. I'm forever grateful.

Thank you to my launch team: Angela, Crista, Lisa, Sandra, Kristal, Baj, Lauryn, João, Reagan, Beth, Liz, Eddie, Louetta, Rebecca, Olivia, Jenna, Ashley, Crystal. For every comment, like, share and word of encouragement. Y'all are the best around.

To my Lord and Savior. I am a creator because I am made in Your image. May my gifts and my life reflect You.

Jude, Rhema, Lucas, and Canaan, I dream big because of you. I follow my dreams so that you know that you can too. Never stop dreaming.

Isaiah, you have dissolved any *what if* question I could have asked. Our life is the only life I want. Thank you for reminding me of who I am when I question myself, for reading my words and supporting these wild dreams. Plus, this cover...all the heart eyes. And thank you for countless dinners you cooked while I sat at the computer screen. You are my dream, my future, my love.

To you, my dear readers. You kept me going even when I thought I had nothing to say. When I questioned if I should even write another book, you brought me back to why I write in the first place. I am honored to be on your bookshelves (digital or physical!).

ALSO BY JESSICA SHOOK

Shrapnel

Jade Can't Be Blue

ABOUT THE AUTHOR

Jessica Shook writes and has for as long as she can remember. Her first book about a teenage rock band was complete when she was 15 but corrupted on a floppy disk. Regardless, the addiction to writing never subsided, but years later the environment where the inspiration happens certainly changed. Jessica now writes while being a short order cook, taxi driver, homeschool mom, cheerleader, and anything else her family of six needs. Her love of books and coffee runs deep.

Jessica lives in Texas with her husband and four children. More information on her writing can be found at jessicashook.com.

38519900R00183

Made in the USA
San Bernardino, CA
11 June 2019